Praise for
CHARLAINE HARRIS
and her Sookie Stackhouse novels

"It's the kind of book you look forward to reading before you go to bed, thinking you're only going to read one chapter, and then you end up reading seven."
—Alan Ball on *Dead Until Dark*

"Vivid, subtle, and funny in her portrayal of southern life." —*Entertainment Weekly*

"Charlaine Harris has vividly imagined telepathic barmaid Sookie Stackhouse and her small-town Louisiana milieu, where humans, vampires, shapeshifters, and other sentient critters live . . . Her mash-up of genres is delightful, taking elements from mysteries, horror stories, and romances." —*Milwaukee Journal Sentinel*

"[A] light, fun series." —*Los Angeles Times*

"It's a bit hard to imagine having vampires and werewolves lurking around every corner, but Harris has a way of making the reader buy it hook, line, and sinker."
—*The Monroe (LA) News-Star*

"I love the imaginative, creative world of Charlaine Harris!" —Christine Feehan, #1 *New York Times* bestselling author

continued . . .

LIVING DEAD IN DALLAS

CHARLAINE HARRIS

ACE BOOKS, NEW YORK

THE BERKLEY PUBLISHING GROUP
Published by the Penguin Group
Penguin Group (USA) Inc.
375 Hudson Street, New York, New York 10014, USA
Penguin Group (Canada), 90 Eglinton Avenue East, Suite 700, Toronto, Ontario M4P 2Y3, Canada
(a division of Pearson Penguin Canada Inc.)
Penguin Books Ltd., 80 Strand, London WC2R 0RL, England
Penguin Group Ireland, 25 St. Stephen's Green, Dublin 2, Ireland (a division of Penguin Books Ltd.)
Penguin Group (Australia), 250 Camberwell Road, Camberwell, Victoria 3124, Australia
(a division of Pearson Australia Group Pty. Ltd.)
Penguin Books India Pvt. Ltd., 11 Community Centre, Panchsheel Park, New Delhi—110 017, India
Penguin Group (NZ), 67 Apollo Drive, Rosedale, North Shore 0632, New Zealand
(a division of Pearson New Zealand Ltd.)
Penguin Books (South Africa) (Pty.) Ltd., 24 Sturdee Avenue, Rosebank, Johannesburg 2196,
South Africa

Penguin Books Ltd., Registered Offices: 80 Strand, London WC2R 0RL, England

LIVING DEAD IN DALLAS

PRINTING HISTORY
Ace mass-market edition / April 2002
Ace hardcover edition / January 2009
Ace trade paperback edition / August 2009

Ace trade paperback ISBN: 978-0-441-01826-0

PRINTED IN THE UNITED STATES OF AMERICA

10   9   8   7   6   5   4   3   2   1

ACKNOWLEDGMENTS

My thanks go to Patsy Asher of Remember the Alibi in San Antonio, Texas; Chloe Green of Dallas; and the helpful cyberfriends I've made on DorothyL, who answered all my questions promptly and enthusiastically. I have the greatest job in the world.

1

ANDY BELLEFLEUR WAS AS DRUNK AS A SKUNK. THIS wasn't normal for Andy—believe me, I know all the drunks in Bon Temps. Working at Sam Merlotte's bar for several years has pretty much introduced me to all of them. But Andy Bellefleur, native son and detective on Bon Temps's small police force, had never been drunk in Merlotte's before. I was mighty curious as to why tonight was an exception.

Andy and I aren't friends by any stretch of the imagination, so I couldn't ask him outright. But other means were open to me, and I decided to use them. Though I try to limit employing my disability, or gift, or whatever you want to call it, to find out things that might have an effect on me or mine, sometimes sheer curiosity wins out.

I let down my mental guard and read Andy's mind. I was sorry.

Andy had had to arrest a man that morning for kidnapping. The man had taken his ten-year-old neighbor to a place in the woods and raped her. The girl was in the hospital, and the man was in jail, but the damage that had been dealt was irreparable. I felt weepy and sad. It was a crime that touched too closely on my own past. I liked Andy a little better for his depression.

"Andy Bellefleur, give me your keys," I said. His broad face turned up to me, showing very little comprehension. After a long pause while my meaning filtered through to his addled brain, Andy fumbled in the pocket of his khakis and handed me his heavy key ring. I put another bourbon and Coke on the bar in front of him. "My treat," I said, and went to the phone at the end of the bar to call Portia, Andy's sister. The Bellefleur siblings lived in a decaying, large white two-story antebellum, formerly quite a showplace, on the prettiest street in the nicest area of Bon Temps. On Magnolia Creek Road, all the homes faced the strip of park through which ran the stream, crossed here and there by decorative bridges for foot traffic only; a road ran on both sides. There were a few other old homes on Magnolia Creek Road, but they were all in better repair than the Bellefleur place, Belle Rive. Belle Rive was just too much for Portia, a lawyer, and Andy, a cop, to maintain, since the money to support such a home and its grounds was long since gone. But their grandmother, Caroline, stubbornly refused to sell.

Portia answered on the second ring.

"Portia, this is Sookie Stackhouse," I said, having to raise my voice over the background noise in the bar.

"You must be at work."

"Yes. Andy's here, and he's three sheets to the wind. I took his keys. Can you come get him?"

"Andy had too much to drink? That's rare. Sure, I'll be there in ten minutes," she promised, and hung up.

"You're a sweet girl, Sookie," Andy volunteered unexpectedly.

He'd finished the drink I'd poured for him. I swept the glass out of sight and hoped he wouldn't ask for more. "Thanks, Andy," I said. "You're okay yourself."

"Where's . . . boyfriend?"

"Right here," said a cool voice, and Bill Compton appeared just behind Andy. I smiled at him over Andy's drooping head. Bill was about five foot ten, with dark brown hair and eyes. He had the broad shoulders and hard, muscular arms of a man who's done manual labor for years. Bill had worked a farm with his father, and then for himself, before he'd gone to be a soldier in the war. That would be the Civil War.

"Hey, V. B.!" called Charlsie Tooten's husband, Ralph. Bill raised a casual hand to return the greeting, and my brother, Jason, said, "Evening, Vampire Bill," in a perfectly polite way. Jason, who had not exactly welcomed Bill into our little family circle, had turned over a whole new leaf. I was sort of mentally holding my breath, waiting to see if his improved attitude was permanent.

"Bill, you're okay for a bloodsucker," Andy said judiciously, rotating on his bar stool so he could face Bill. I upgraded my opinion of Andy's drunkenness, since he had never otherwise been enthusiastic about the acceptance of vampires into America's mainstream society.

"Thanks," Bill said dryly. "You're not too bad for a

Bellefleur." He leaned across the bar to give me a kiss. His lips were as cool as his voice. You had to get used to it. Like when you laid your head on his chest, and you didn't hear a heartbeat inside. "Evening, sweetheart," he said in his low voice. I slid a glass of the Japanese-developed synthetic B negative across the bar, and he knocked it back and licked his lips. He looked pinker almost immediately.

"How'd your meeting go, honey?" I asked. Bill had been in Shreveport the better part of the night.

"I'll tell you later."

I hoped his work-related story was less distressing than Andy's. "Okay. I'd appreciate it if you'd help Portia get Andy to her car. Here she comes now," I said, nodding toward the door.

For once, Portia was not wearing the skirt, blouse, jacket, hose, and low-heeled pumps that constituted her professional uniform. She'd changed into blue jeans and a ragged Sophie Newcomb sweatshirt. Portia was built as squarely as her brother, but she had long, thick chestnut hair. Keeping it beautifully tended was Portia's one signal that she hadn't given up yet. She plowed single-mindedly through the rowdy crowd.

"Well, he's soused, all right," she said, evaluating her brother. Portia was trying to ignore Bill, who made her very uneasy. "It doesn't happen often, but if he decides to tie one on, he does a good job."

"Portia, Bill can carry him to your car," I said. Andy was taller than Portia and thick in body, clearly too much of a burden for his sister.

"I think I can handle him," she told me firmly, still not looking toward Bill, who raised his eyebrows at me.

So I let her get one arm around her brother and try to hoist him off the stool. Andy stayed perched. Portia glanced around for Sam Merlotte, the bar owner, who was small and wiry in appearance but very strong. "Sam's bartending at an anniversary party at the country club," I said. "Better let Bill help."

"All right," the lawyer said stiffly, her eyes on the polished wood of the bar. "Thanks very much."

Bill had Andy up and moving toward the door in seconds, in spite of Andy's legs tending to turn to jelly. Ralph Tooten jumped up to open the door, so Bill was able to sweep Andy right out into the parking lot.

"Thanks, Sookie," Portia said. "Is his bar tab settled up?"

I nodded.

"Okay," she said, slapping her hand on the bar to signal she was out of there. She had to listen to a chorus of well-meant advice as she followed Bill out the front door of Merlotte's.

That was how Detective Andy Bellefleur's old Buick came to sit in the parking lot at Merlotte's all night and into the next day. The Buick had certainly been empty when Andy had gotten out to enter the bar, he would later swear. He'd also testify that he'd been so preoccupied by his internal turmoil that he'd forgotten to lock the car.

At some point between eight o'clock, when Andy had arrived at Merlotte's, and ten the next morning, when I arrived to help open the bar, Andy's car acquired a new passenger.

This one would cause considerable embarrassment for the policeman.

This one was dead.

* * *

I shouldn't have been there at all. I'd worked the late shift the night before, and I should've worked the late shift again that night. But Bill had asked me if I could switch with one of my coworkers, because he needed me to accompany him to Shreveport, and Sam hadn't objected. I'd asked my friend Arlene if she'd work my shift. She was due a day off, but she always wanted to earn the better tips we got at night, and she agreed to come in at five that afternoon.

By all rights, Andy should've collected his car that morning, but he'd been too hungover to fool with getting Portia to run him over to Merlotte's, which was out of the way to the police station. She'd told him she would pick him up at work at noon, and they'd eat lunch at the bar. Then he could retrieve his car.

So the Buick, with its silent passenger, waited for discovery far longer than it should have.

I'd gotten about six hours' sleep the night before, so I was feeling pretty good. Dating a vampire can be hard on your equilibrium if you're truly a daytime person, like me. I'd helped close the bar, and left for home with Bill by one o'clock. We'd gotten in Bill's hot tub together, then done other things, but I'd gotten to bed by a little after two, and I didn't get up until almost nine. Bill had long been in the ground by then.

I drank lots of water and orange juice and took a multivitamin and iron supplement for breakfast, which was my regimen since Bill had come into my life and brought (along with love, adventure, and excitement) the constant threat of anemia. The weather was getting cooler, thank

God, and I sat on Bill's front porch wearing a cardigan and the black slacks we wore to work at Merlotte's when it was too cool for shorts. My white golf shirt had MER-LOTTE'S BAR embroidered on the left breast.

As I skimmed the morning paper, with one part of my mind I was recording the fact that the grass was definitely not growing as fast. Some of the leaves appeared to be beginning to turn. The high school football stadium might be just about tolerable this coming Friday night.

The summer just hates to let go in Louisiana, even northern Louisiana. Fall begins in a very halfhearted way, as though it might quit at any minute and revert to the stifling heat of July. But I was on the alert, and I could spot traces of fall this morning. Fall and winter meant longer nights, more time with Bill, more hours of sleep.

So I was cheerful when I went to work. When I saw the Buick sitting all by its lonesome in front of the bar, I remembered Andy's surprising binge the night before. I have to confess, I smiled when I thought of how he'd be feeling today. Just as I was about to drive around in back and park with the other employees, I noticed that Andy's rear passenger door was open just a little bit. That would make his dome light stay on, surely? And his battery would run down. And he'd be angry and have to come in the bar to call the tow truck or ask someone to jump him . . . so I put my car in park and slid out, leaving it running. That turned out to be an optimistic error.

I shoved the door to, but it would only give an inch. So I pressed my body to it, thinking it would latch and I could be on my way. Again, the door would not click shut. Impatiently, I yanked it all the way open to find out what was in the way. A wave of smell gusted out into the parking lot, a dreadful smell. Dismay clutched at my throat, because the odor was not unknown to me. I peered into the backseat of the car, my hand covering my mouth, though that hardly helped with the smell.

"Oh, man," I whispered. "Oh, shit." Lafayette, the cook for one shift at Merlotte's, had been shoved into the backseat. He was naked. It was Lafayette's thin brown foot, its toenails painted a deep crimson, that had kept the door from shutting, and it was Lafayette's corpse that smelled to high heaven.

I backed away hastily, then scrambled into my car and drove around back behind the bar, blowing my horn. Sam came running out of the employee door, an apron tied around his waist. I turned off my car and was out of it so quick I hardly realized I'd done it, and I wrapped myself around Sam like a static-filled sock.

"What is it?" Sam's voice said in my ear. I leaned back to look at him, not having to gaze up too much since Sam is a smallish man. His reddish gold hair was gleaming in the morning sun. He has true-blue eyes, and they were wide with apprehension.

"It's Lafayette," I said, and began crying. That was ridiculous and silly and no help at all, but I couldn't help it. "He's dead, in Andy Bellefleur's car."

Sam's arms tightened behind my back and drew me into his body once more. "Sookie, I'm sorry you saw it," he said. "We'll call the police. Poor Lafayette."

Being a cook at Merlotte's does not exactly call for any extraordinary culinary skill, since Sam just offers a few sandwiches and fries, so there's a high turnover. But Lafayette had lasted longer than most, to my surprise.

Lafayette had been gay, flamboyantly gay, makeup-and-long-fingernails gay. People in northern Louisiana are less tolerant of that than New Orleans people, and I expect Lafayette, a man of color, had had a doubly hard time of it. Despite—or because of—his difficulties, he was cheerful, entertainingly mischievous, clever, and actually a good cook. He had a special sauce he steeped hamburgers in, and people asked for Burgers Lafayette pretty regular.

"Did he have family here?" I asked Sam. We eased apart self-consciously and went into the building, to Sam's office.

"He had a cousin," Sam said, as his fingers punched 9-1-1. "Please come to Merlotte's on Hummingbird Road," he told the dispatcher. "There's a dead man in a car here. Yes, in the parking lot, in the front of the place. Oh, and you might want to alert Andy Bellefleur. It's his car."

I could hear the squawk on the other end of the line from where I stood.

Danielle Gray and Holly Cleary, the two waitresses on the morning shift, came through the back door laughing. Both divorced women in their midtwenties, Danielle and Holly were lifelong friends who seemed to be quite happy working their jobs as long as they were together. Holly had a five-year-old son who was at kindergarten, and Danielle had a seven-year-old daughter and a boy too young for school who stayed with Danielle's mother while Danielle was at Merlotte's. I would never be any closer to the two women—who, after all, were around my age—because they were careful to be sufficient unto themselves.

"What's the matter?" Danielle asked when she saw my face. Her own, narrow and freckled, became instantly worried.

"Why's Andy's car out front?" Holly asked. She'd dated Andy Bellefleur for a while, I recalled. Holly had short blond hair that hung around her face like wilted daisy petals, and the prettiest skin I'd ever seen. "He spend the night in it?"

"No," I said, "but someone else did."

"Who?"

"Lafayette's in it."

"Andy let a black queer sleep in his car?" This was Holly, who was the blunt, straightforward one.

"What happened to him?" This was Danielle, who was the smarter of the two.

"We don't know," Sam said. "The police are on the way."

"You mean," Danielle said, slowly and carefully, "that he's dead."

"Yes," I told her. "That's exactly what we mean."

"Well, we're set to open in an hour." Holly's hands settled on her round hips. "What are we gonna do about that? If the police let us open, who's gonna cook for us? People come in, they'll want lunch."

"We better get ready, just in case," Sam said. "Though I'm thinking we won't get to open until sometime this afternoon." He went into his office to begin calling substitute cooks.

It felt strange to be going about the opening routine, just as if Lafayette were going to mince in any minute with a story about some party he'd been to, the way he had a few days before. The sirens came shrieking down the county road that ran in front of Merlotte's. Cars crunched across Sam's gravel parking lot. By the time we had the chairs down, the tables set, and extra silverware rolled in napkins and ready to replace used settings, the police came in.

Merlotte's is out of the city limits, so the parish sheriff, Bud Dearborn, would be in charge. Bud Dearborn, who'd been a good friend of my father's, was gray-haired now. He had a mashed-in face, like a human Pekinese, and opaque brown eyes. As he came in the front door of the bar, I noticed Bud was wearing heavy boots and his Saints cap. He must have been called in from working on his farm. With Bud was Alcee Beck, the only African American detective on the parish force. Alcee was so black that his white shirt gleamed in contrast. His tie was knotted precisely, and his suit was absolutely correct. His shoes were polished and shining.

Bud and Alcee, between them, ran the parish . . . at least some of the more important elements that kept it functional. Mike Spencer, funeral home director and parish coroner, had a heavy hand in local affairs, too, and he was a good friend of Bud's. I was willing to bet Mike was already out in the parking lot, pronouncing poor Lafayette dead.

Bud Dearborn said, "Who found the body?"

"I did." Bud and Alcee changed course slightly and headed toward me.

"Sam, can we borrow your office?" Bud asked. Without waiting for Sam's response, he jerked his head to indicate I should go in.

"Sure, go right ahead," my boss said dryly. "Sookie, you okay?"

"Fine, Sam." I wasn't sure that was true, but there wasn't anything Sam could do about it without getting into trouble, and all to no avail. Though Bud gestured to me to sit down, I shook my head as he and Alcee settled themselves in the office chairs. Bud, of course, took Sam's big chair, while Alcee made do with the better extra chair, the one with a little padding left.

"Tell us about the last time you saw Lafayette alive," Bud suggested.

I thought about it.

"He wasn't working last night," I said. "Anthony was working, Anthony Bolivar."

"Who is that?" Alcee's broad forehead wrinkled. "Don't recognize the name."

"He's a friend of Bill's. He was passing through, and he needed a job. He had the experience." He'd worked in a diner during the Great Depression.

"You mean the short-order cook at Merlotte's is a *vampire*?"

"So?" I asked. I could feel my mouth setting stubborn, and my brows drawing in, and I knew my face was getting mad. I was trying hard not to read their minds, trying hard to stay completely out of this, but it wasn't easy. Bud Dearborn was average, but Alcee projected his thoughts like a lighthouse sends a signal. Right now he was beaming disgust and fear.

In the months before I'd met Bill, and found that he treasured that disability of mine—my gift, as he saw it—I'd done my best to pretend to myself and everyone else that I couldn't really "read" minds. But since Bill had liberated me from the little prison I'd built for myself, I'd been practicing and experimenting, with Bill's encouragement. For him, I had put into words the things I'd been feeling for years. Some people sent a clear, strong message, like Alcee. Most people were more off and on, like Bud Dearborn. It depended a lot on how strong their emotions were, how clearheaded they were, what the weather was, for all I knew. Some people were murky as hell, and it was almost impossible to tell what they were thinking. I could get a reading of their moods, maybe, but that was all.

I had admitted that if I was touching people while I tried to read their thoughts, it made the picture clearer— like getting cable, after having only an antenna. And I'd found that if I "sent" a person relaxing images, I could flow through his brain like water.

There was nothing I wanted less than to flow through Alcee Beck's mind. But absolutely involuntarily I was getting a full picture of Alcee's deeply superstitious reaction to finding out there was a vampire working at Merlotte's, his revulsion on discovering I was the woman he'd heard about who was dating a vampire, his deep conviction that the openly gay Lafayette had been a disgrace to the black community. Alcee figured someone must have it in for Andy Bellefleur, to have parked a gay black man's carcass in Andy's car. Alcee was wondering if Lafayette had had AIDS, if the virus could have seeped into Andy's car seat somehow and survived there. He'd sell the car, if it were his.

If I'd touched Alcee, I would have known his phone number and his wife's bra size.

Bud Dearborn was looking at me funny. "Did you say something?" I asked.

"Yeah. I was wondering if you had seen Lafayette in here during the evening. Did he come in to have a drink?"

"I never saw him here." Come to think of it, I'd never seen Lafayette have a drink. For the first time, I realized that though the lunch crowd was mixed, the night bar patrons were almost exclusively white.

"Where did he spend his social time?"

"I have no idea." All Lafayette's stories were told with the names changed to protect the innocent. Well, actually, the guilty.

"When did you see him last?"

"Dead, in the car."

Bud shook his head in exasperation. "Alive, Sookie."

"Hmmm. I guess . . . three days ago. He was still here when I got here to work my shift, and we said hello to each other. Oh, he told me about a party he'd been to." I tried to recall his exact words. "He said he'd been to a house where there were all kinds of sex hijinks going on."

The two men gaped at me.

"Well, that's what he said! I don't know how much truth was in it." I could just see Lafayette's face as he'd told me about it, the coy way he kept putting his finger across his lips to indicate he wasn't telling me any names or places.

"Didn't you think someone should know about that?" Bud Dearborn looked stunned.

"It was a private party. Why should I tell anyone about it?"

But that kind of party shouldn't happen in their parish. Both men were glaring at me. Through compressed lips, Bud said, "Did Lafayette tell you anything about drugs being used at this get-together?"

"No, I don't remember anything like that."

"Was this party at the home of someone white, or someone black?"

"White," I said, and then wished I'd pled ignorance.

But Lafayette had been really impressed by the home—though not because it was large or fancy. Why had he been so impressed? I wasn't too sure what would constitute impressive for Lafayette, who had grown up poor and stayed that way, but I was sure he'd been talking about the home of someone white, because he'd said, "All the pictures on the walls, they all white as lilies and smiling like alligators." I didn't offer that comment to the police, and they didn't ask further.

When I'd left Sam's office, after explaining why Andy's car had been in the parking lot in the first place, I went back to stand behind the bar. I didn't want to watch the activity out in the parking lot, and there weren't any customers to wait on because the police had the entrances to the lot blocked off.

Sam was rearranging the bottles behind the bar, dusting as he went, and Holly and Danielle had plunked themselves down at a table in the smoking section so Danielle could have a cigarette.

"How was it?" Sam asked.

"Not much to it. They didn't like hearing about Anthony working here, and they didn't like what I told them about the party Lafayette was bragging about the other day. Did you hear him telling me? The orgy thing?"

"Yeah, he said something to me about that, too. Must have been a big evening for him. If it really happened."

"You think Lafayette made it up?"

"I don't think there are too many biracial, bisexual parties in Bon Temps," he said.

"But that's just because no one invited you to one," I said pointedly. I wondered if I really knew at all what went on in our little town. Of all the people in Bon

Temps, I should be the one to know the ins and the outs, since all that information was more or less readily available to me, if I chose to dig for it. "At least, I assume that's the case?"

"That's the case," Sam said, smiling at me a little as he dusted a bottle of whiskey.

"I guess my invitation got lost in the mail, too."

"You think Lafayette came back here last night to talk more to you or me about this party?"

I shrugged. "He may have just arranged to meet someone in the parking lot. After all, everyone knows where Merlotte's is. Had he gotten his paycheck?" It was the end of the week, when Sam normally paid us.

"No. Maybe he'd come in for that, but I'd have given it to him at work the next day. Today."

"I wonder who invited Lafayette to that party."

"Good question."

"You don't reckon he'd have been dumb enough to try to blackmail anyone, do you?"

Sam rubbed the fake wood of the bar with a clean rag. The bar was already shining, but he liked to keep his hands busy, I'd noticed. "I don't think so," he said, after he'd thought it over. "No, they sure asked the wrong person. You know how indiscreet Lafayette was. Not only did he tell us that he went to such a party—and I'm betting he wasn't supposed to—he might have wanted to build more on it than the other, ah, participants would feel comfortable with."

"Like keep in contact with the people at the party? Give them a sly wink in public?"

"Something like that."

"I guess if you have sex with someone, or watch them

having sex, you feel pretty much like you're their equal."
I said this doubtfully, having limited experience in that
area, but Sam was nodding.

"Lafayette wanted to be accepted for what he was
more than anything else," he said, and I had to agree.

$2 \sim$

W<small>E</small> <small>REOPENED AT FOUR THIRTY, BY WHICH TIME WE</small> were all as bored as we could possibly be. I was ashamed of that, since after all, we were there because a man we knew had died, but it was undeniable that after straightening up the storeroom, cleaning out Sam's office, and playing several hands of bourre (Sam won five dollars and change) we were all ready to see someone new. When Terry Bellefleur, Andy's cousin and a frequent substitute barman or cook at Merlotte's, came through the back door, he was a welcome sight.

I guess Terry was in his late fifties. A Vietnam vet, he'd been a prisoner of war for a year and a half. Terry had some obvious facial scarring, and my friend Arlene told me that the scars on his body were even more drastic. Terry was redheaded, though he was graying a little more each month, it seemed like.

I'd always been fond of Terry, who bent over backward to be kind to me—except when he was in one of his black moods. Everyone knew not to cross Terry Bellefleur when he was in one of his moods. Terry's dark days were inevitably preceded by nightmares of the worst kind, as his neighbors testified. They could hear Terry hollering on the nightmare nights.

I never, never read Terry's mind.

Terry looked okay today. His shoulders were relaxed, and his eyes didn't dart from side to side. "You okay, sweet thing?" he asked, patting my arm sympathetically.

"Thanks, Terry, I'm fine. Just sorry about Lafayette."

"Yeah, he wasn't too bad." From Terry, that was high praise. "Did his job, always showed up on time. Cleaned the kitchen good. Never a bad word." Functioning on that level was Terry's highest ambition. "And then he dies in Andy's Buick."

"I'm afraid Andy's car is kind of . . ." I groped for the blandest term.

"It's cleanable, he said." Terry was anxious to close that subject.

"Did he tell you what had happened to Lafayette?"

"Andy says it looks like his neck was broken. And there was some, ah, evidence that he'd been . . . messed with." Terry's brown eyes flickered away, revealing his discomfort. "Messed with" meant something violent and sexual to Terry.

"Oh. Gosh, how awful." Danielle and Holly had come

up behind me, and Sam, with another sack of garbage he'd cleaned out of his office, paused on his way to the Dumpster out back.

"He didn't look that . . . I mean, the car didn't look that . . ."

"Stained?"

"Right."

"Andy thinks he was killed somewhere else."

"Yuck," said Holly. "Don't talk about it. That's too much for me."

Terry looked over my shoulder at the two women. He had no great love for either Holly or Danielle, though I didn't know why and had made no effort to learn. I tried to leave people privacy, especially now that I had better control over my own ability. I heard the two moving away, after Terry had kept his gaze trained on them for a few seconds.

"Portia came and got Andy last night?" he asked.

"Yes, I called her. He couldn't drive. Though I'm betting he wishes I'd let him, now." I was just never going to be number one on Andy Bellefleur's popularity list.

"She have trouble getting him to her car?"

"Bill helped her."

"Vampire Bill? Your boyfriend?"

"Uh-huh."

"I hope he didn't scare her," Terry said, as if he didn't remember I was still there.

I could feel my face squinching up. "There's no reason on earth why Bill would ever scare Portia Bellefleur," I said, and something about the way I said it penetrated Terry's fog of private thought.

"Portia ain't as tough as everyone thinks she is," Terry

told me. "You, on the other hand, are a sweet little éclair on the outside and a pit bull on the inside."

"I don't know whether I should feel flattered, or whether I should sock you in the nose."

"There you go. How many women—or men, for that matter—would say such a thing to a crazy man like me?" And Terry smiled, as a ghost would smile. I hadn't known how conscious of his reputation Terry was, until now.

I stood on tiptoe to give him a kiss on the scarred cheek, to show him I wasn't scared of him. As I sank back to my heels, I realized that wasn't exactly true. Under some circumstances, not only would I be quite wary of this damaged man, but I might become very frightened indeed.

Terry tied the strings of one of the white cook's aprons and began to open up the kitchen. The rest of us got back into the work mode. I wouldn't have long to wait tables, since I was getting off at six tonight to get ready to drive to Shreveport with Bill. I hated for Sam to pay me for the time I'd spent lollygagging around Merlotte's today, waiting to work; but straightening the storeroom and cleaning out Sam's office had to count for something.

As soon as the police opened up the parking lot, people began streaming in, in as heavy a flow as a small town like Bon Temps ever gets. Andy and Portia were among the first in, and I saw Terry look out the hatch from the kitchen at his cousins. They waved at him, and he raised a spatula to acknowledge their greeting. I wondered how close a cousin Terry actually was. He wasn't a first cousin, I was sure. Of course, here you could call someone your cousin or your aunt or your uncle with little or no blood relation at all. After my mother and father had died in a flash flood that swept their car off a bridge, my mother's best friend tried to come by my Gran's every week or two with a little present for me; and I'd called her Aunt Patty my whole life.

I answered all the customers' questions if I had time, and served hamburgers and salads and chicken breast strips—and beer—until I felt dazed. When I glanced at the clock, it was time for me to go. In the ladies' room I found my replacement, my friend Arlene. Arlene's flaming red hair (two shades redder this month) was arranged in an elaborate cluster of curls on the back of her head, and her tight pants let the world know she'd lost seven pounds. Arlene had been married four times, and she was on the lookout for number five.

We talked about the murder for a couple of minutes, and I briefed her on the status of my tables, before I grabbed my purse from Sam's office and scooted out the back door. It wasn't quite dark when I pulled up to my house, which is a quarter mile back in the woods off a seldom-traveled parish road. It's an old house, parts of it dating back a hundred-and-forty-plus years, but it's been altered and added onto so often we don't count it as an antebellum house. It's just an old farmhouse, anyway. My grandmother, Adele Hale Stackhouse, left me this house, and I treasured it. Bill had spoken of me moving into his place, which sat on a hill just across the cemetery from my home, but I was reluctant to leave my own turf.

I yanked off my waitress outfit and opened my closet. If we were going over to Shreveport on vampire business, Bill would want me to dress up a little. I couldn't quite figure that out, since he didn't want anyone else making a pass at me, but he always wanted me to look extra pretty when we were going to Fangtasia, a vampire-owned bar catering mainly to tourists.

Men.

I couldn't make up my mind, so I hopped in the shower. Thinking about Fangtasia always made me tense. The vampires who owned it were part of the vampire power structure, and once they'd discovered my unique talent, I'd become a desirable acquisition to them. Only Bill's determined entry into the vampire self-governing system had kept me safe; that is, living where I wanted to live, working at my chosen job. But in return for that safety, I was still obliged to show up when I was summoned, and to put my telepathy to use for them. Milder measures than their former choices (torture and terror) were what "mainstreaming" vampires needed. The hot water immediately made me feel better, and I relaxed as it beat on my back.

"Shall I join you?"

"Shit, Bill!" My heart pounding a mile a minute, I leaned against the shower wall for support.

"Sorry, sweetheart. Didn't you hear the bathroom door opening?"

"No, dammit. Why can't you just call, 'Honey, I'm home,' or something?"

"Sorry," he said again, not sounding very sincere. "Do you need someone to scrub your back?"

"No, thank you," I hissed. "I'm not in the back-scrubbing kind of mood."

Bill grinned (so I could see his fangs were retracted) and pulled the shower curtain closed.

When I came out of the bathroom, towel wrapped around me more or less modestly, he was stretched out on my bed, his shoes neatly lined up on the little rug by the night table. Bill was wearing a dark blue long-sleeved shirt and khakis, with socks that matched the shirt, and polished loafers. His dark brown hair was brushed straight back, and his long sideburns looked retro.

Well, they were, but more retro than most people could ever have imagined.

He has high arched brows and a high-bridged nose. His mouth is the kind you see on Greek statues, at least the ones I've seen in pictures. He died five years after the end of the Civil War (or the War of Northern Aggression, as my grandmother always called it).

"What's the agenda for tonight?" I asked. "Business, or pleasure?"

"Being with you is always pleasure," Bill said.

"We're going to Shreveport for what reason?" I asked, since I know a dodgy answer when I hear one.

"We were summoned."

"By?"

"Eric, of course."

Now that Bill had run for, and accepted, a position as Area 5 investigator, he was at Eric's beck and call—and under Eric's protection. That meant, Bill had explained, that anyone attacking Bill would also have to deal with Eric, and it meant that Bill's possessions were sacred to Eric. Which included me. I wasn't thrilled to be numbered among Bill's possessions, but it was better than some of the alternatives.

I made a face in the mirror.

"Sookie, you made a deal with Eric."

"Yeah," I admitted, "I did."

"So you must stick by it."

"I plan on it."

"Wear those tight blue jeans that lace up the sides," Bill suggested.

They weren't denim at all, but some kind of stretchy stuff. Bill just loved me in those jeans, which came down low. More than once, I had wondered if Bill had some kind of Britney Spears–fantasy thing going on. Since I was fully aware that I looked good in the jeans, I pulled them on, with a dark-blue-and-white-checked short-sleeved shirt that buttoned up the front and stopped about two inches below my bra. Just to exhibit a little independence (after all, he'd better remember I was my own woman), I brushed my hair into a ponytail high up on my head. I pinned a blue bow over the elastic band and slapped on a little makeup. Bill glanced at his watch once or twice, but I took my time. If he was so all-fired concerned about how I was going to impress his vampire friends, he could just wait for me.

Once we were in the car and on our way west to Shreveport, Bill said, "I started a new business venture today."

Frankly, I'd been wondering where Bill's money came from. He never seemed rich: he never seemed poor. But he never worked, either; unless it was on the nights we weren't together.

I was uneasily aware that any vampire worth his salt could become wealthy; after all, when you can control the minds of humans to some extent, it's not that difficult to persuade them to part with money or stock tips or investment opportunities. And until vampires gained the legal right to exist, they hadn't had to pay taxes, see. Even the U.S. government had to admit it couldn't tax the dead. But if you gave them rights, Congress had figured, and gave them the vote, then you could obligate them into paying taxes.

When the Japanese had perfected the synthetic blood that actually enabled vampires to "live" without drinking human blood, it had been possible for vampires to come out of the coffin. "See, we don't have to victimize mankind to exist," they could say. "We are not a threat."

But I knew Bill's big thrill was when he drank from me. He might have a pretty steady diet of TrueBlood (the most popular marketing name for the synthetic blood), but nipping my neck was incomparably better. He could drink some bottled A positive in front of a whole bar full of people, but if he planned on a mouthful of Sookie Stackhouse, we had better by golly be in private—the effect was that different. Bill didn't get any kind of erotic thrill from a wineglass of TrueBlood.

"So what's this new business?" I asked.

"I bought the strip mall by the highway, the one where LaLaurie's is."

"Who owned that?"

"The Bellefleurs originally owned the land. They let Sid Matt Lancaster do a development deal for them."

Sid Matt Lancaster had acted as my brother's lawyer before. He'd been around for donkey's years and had way more clout than Portia.

"That's good for the Bellefleurs. They've been trying to sell that for a couple of years. They need the cash, bad. You bought the land and the strip mall? How big a parcel of land is that?"

"Just an acre, but it's in a good location," Bill said, in a businesslike voice that I'd never heard before.

"That same strip's got LaLaurie's, and a hair salon, and Tara's Togs?" Aside from the country club, LaLaurie's was the only restaurant with any pretensions in the Bon Temps area. It was where you took your wife for your twenty-fifth wedding anniversary, or your boss when you wanted a promotion, or a date you really, really wanted to impress. But it didn't make a lot of money, I'd heard.

I have no inkling of how to run a business, or manage business dealings, having been just a step or two ahead of poor all my life. If my parents hadn't had the good fortune to find a little oil on their land and save all the money from it before the oil ran out, Jason and Gran and I would've had a hand-to-mouth time of it. At least twice, we had been close to selling my parents' place, just to keep up Gran's house and taxes, while she raised the two of us.

"So, how does that work? You own the building that houses those three businesses, and they pay you rent?"

Bill nodded. "So now, if you want to get something done to your hair, go to Clip and Curl."

I'd only been to a hairdresser once in my life. If the ends got ragged, I usually went over to Arlene's trailer and she trimmed them evenly. "Do you think my hair needs something done to it?" I asked uncertainly.

"No, it's beautiful." Bill was reassuringly positive. "But if you should want to go, they have, ah, manicures, and hair-care products." He said "hair-care products" as if it were in a foreign language. I stifled a smile.

"And," he continued, "take anyone you want to LaLaurie's, and you won't have to pay."

I turned in my seat to stare at him.

"And Tara knows that if you come in, she will put any clothes you buy on my account."

I could feel my temper creak and give way. Bill, unfortunately, could not. "So, in other words," I said, proud of the evenness of my voice, "they know to indulge the boss's fancy woman."

Bill seemed to realize he'd made a mistake. "Oh, Sookie," he began, but I wasn't having any of it. My pride had risen up and whopped me in the face. I don't lose my temper a lot, but when I do, I make a good job of it.

"Why can't you just send me some damn flowers, like anyone else's boyfriend? Or some candy. I like candy. Just buy me a Hallmark card, why don't you? Or a kitten or a scarf!"

"I meant to give you something," he said cautiously.

"You've made me feel like a kept woman. And you've certainly given the people who work at those businesses the impression I am."

As far as I could tell in the dim dashboard light, Bill looked like he was trying to figure out the difference. We were just past the turnoff to Mimosa Lake, and I could see the deep woods on the lake side of the road in Bill's headlights.

To my complete surprise, the car coughed and stopped dead. I took it as a sign.

Bill would've locked the doors if he'd known what I was going to do, because he certainly looked startled when I scrambled out of the car and marched over to the woods by the road.

"Sookie, get back in here right now!" Bill was mad now, by God. Well, it had taken him long enough.

I shot him the bird as I stepped into the woods.

I knew if Bill wanted me in the car, I'd be in the car, since Bill's about twenty times stronger and faster than me. After a few seconds in the darkness, I almost wished he'd catch up with me. But then my pride gave a twitch, and I knew I'd done the right thing. Bill seemed to be a little confused about the nature of our relationship, and I wanted him to get it straight in his head. He could just take his sorry ass to Shreveport and explain my absence to his superior, Eric. By golly, that'd show him.

"Sookie," Bill called from the road, "I'm going to go to the nearest service station to get a mechanic."

"Good luck," I muttered under my breath. A service station with a full-time mechanic, open at night? Bill was thinking of the fifties, or some other era.

"You're acting like a child, Sookie," Bill said. "I could come to get you, but I'm not going to waste the time. When you're calm, come get in the car and lock it. I'm going now." Bill had his pride, too.

To my mingled relief and concern, I heard the faint footfalls along the road that meant Bill was running at vampire speed. He'd really left.

He probably thought *he* was teaching *me* a lesson. When it was just the opposite. I told myself that several times. After all, he'd be back in a few minutes. I was sure. All I had to do was be sure I didn't stumble far enough through the woods to fall into the lake.

It was *really dark* in the pines. Though the moon was not full, it was a cloudless night, and the shadows in the trees were pitch-black in contrast with the cool, remote glow of the open spaces.

I made my way back to the road, then took a deep breath and began marching back toward Bon Temps, the opposite direction from Bill. I wondered how many miles we'd put between us and Bon Temps before Bill had begun our conversation. Not so very many, I reassured myself, and patted myself on the back that I was wearing sneakers, not high-heeled sandals. I hadn't brought a sweater, and the exposed skin between my cropped top and my low-cut blue jeans felt goose pimply. I began to run down the shoulder in an easy jog. There weren't any streetlights, so I would have been in bad shape if it weren't for the moonlight.

Just about the time I recalled that there was someone out there who'd murdered Lafayette, I heard footsteps in the woods parallel to my own path.

When I stopped, the movement in the trees did also.

I'd rather know now. "Okay, who's there?" I called. "If you're going to eat me, let's just get it over with."

A woman stepped out of the woods. With her was a razorback, a feral hog. Its tusks gleamed from the shadows. In her left hand she carried a sort of stick or wand, with a tuft of something on its end.

"Great," I whispered to myself. "Just great." The woman was as scary as the razorback. I was sure she wasn't a vampire, because I could feel the activity in her mind; but she was sure some supernatural being, so she didn't send a clear signal. I could snatch the tenor of her thoughts anyway. She was amused.

That couldn't be good.

I hoped the razorback was feeling friendly. They were very rarely seen around Bon Temps, though every now and then a hunter would spot one, even more rarely bring one down. That was a picture-in-the-paper occasion. This hog smelled, an awful and distinctive odor.

I wasn't sure which to address. After all, the razorback might not be a true animal at all, but a shapeshifter. That was one thing I'd learned in the past few months. If vampires, so long thought of as thrilling fiction, actually did exist, so did other things that we'd regarded as equally exciting fiction.

I was really nervous, so I smiled.

She had long snarled hair, an indeterminate dark in the uncertain light, and she was wearing almost nothing. She had a kind of shift on, but it was short and ragged and stained. She was barefoot. She smiled back at me. Rather than scream, I grinned even more brightly.

"I have no intention of eating you," she said.

"Glad to hear it. What about your friend?"

"Oh, the hog." As if she'd just noticed it, the woman reached over and scratched the razorback's neck, like I would a friendly dog's. The ferocious tusks bobbed up and down. "She'll do what I tell her," the woman said casually. I didn't need a translator to understand the threat. I tried to look equally casual as I glanced around the open space where I stood, hoping to locate a tree that I could climb if I had to. But all the trunks close enough for me to reach in time were bare of branches; they were the loblolly pines grown by the millions in our neck of the woods, for their lumber. The branches start about fifteen feet up.

I realized what I should've thought of sooner; Bill's car stopping there was no accident, and maybe even the fight we'd had was no coincidence.

"You wanted to talk to me about something?" I asked her, and in turning to her I found she'd come several feet closer. I could see her face a little better now, and I was in no wise reassured. There was a stain around her mouth, and when it opened as she spoke, I could see the teeth had dark margins; Miss Mysterious had been eating a raw mammal. "I see you've already had supper," I said nervously, and then could've slapped myself.

"Mmmm," she said. "You are Bill's pet?"

"Yes," I said. I objected to the terminology, but I wasn't in much position to take a stand. "He would be really awfully upset if anything happened to me."

"As if a vampire's anger is anything to me," she said offhandedly.

"Excuse me, ma'am, but what are you? If you don't mind me asking."

She smiled again, and I shuddered. "Not at all. I'm a maenad."

That was something Greek. I didn't know exactly what, but it was wild, female, and lived in nature, if my impressions were correct.

"That's very interesting," I said, grinning for all I was worth. "And you are out here tonight because . . . ?"

"I need a message taken to Eric Northman," she said, moving closer. This time I could see her do it. The hog snuffled along at her side as if she were tied to the woman. The smell was indescribable. I could see the little brushy tail of the razorback—it was switching back and forth in a brisk, impatient sort of way.

"What's the message?" I glanced up at her—and whirled to run as quickly as I could. If I hadn't ingested some vampire blood at the beginning of the summer, I couldn't have turned in time, and I would've taken the blow on my face and chest instead of my back. It felt exactly as though someone very strong had swung a heavy rake and the points had caught in my skin, gone deeper, and torn their way across my back.

I couldn't keep to my feet, but pitched forward and landed on my stomach. I heard her laughing behind me, and the hog snuffling, and then I registered the fact that she had gone. I lay there crying for a minute or two. I was trying not to shriek, and I found myself panting like a woman in labor, attempting to master the pain. My back hurt like hell.

I was mad, too, with the little energy I could spare. I was just a living bulletin board to that bitch, that maenad, whatever the hell she was. As I crawled, over twigs and rough ground, pine needles and dust, I grew angrier and angrier. I was shaking all over from the pain and the rage, dragging myself along, until I didn't feel I was worth killing, I was such a mess. I'd begun the crawl back to the car, trying to head back to the likeliest spot for Bill to find me, but when I was almost there I had second thoughts about staying out in the open.

I'd been assuming the road meant help—but of course, it didn't. I'd found out a few minutes before that not everyone met by chance was in a helping kind of mood. What if I met up with something else, something hungry? The smell of my blood might be attracting a predator at this very moment; a shark is said to be able to detect the tiniest particles of blood in the water, and a vampire is surely the shark's land equivalent.

So I crawled inside the tree line, instead of staying out beside the road where I'd be visible. This didn't seem like a very dignified or meaningful place to die. This was no Alamo, or Thermopylae. This was just a spot in the vegetation by a road in northern Louisiana. I was probably lying in poison ivy. I would probably not live long enough to break out, though.

I expected every second that the pain would begin to abate, but it only increased. I couldn't prevent the tears from coursing down my cheeks. I managed not to sob out loud, so I wouldn't attract any more attention, but it was impossible to keep completely still.

I was concentrating so desperately on maintaining my silence that I almost missed Bill. He was pacing along the road looking into the woods, and I could tell by the way he was walking that he was alert to danger. Bill knew something was wrong.

"Bill," I whispered, but with his vampire hearing, it was like a shout.

He was instantly still, his eyes scanning the shadows. "I'm here," I said, and swallowed back a sob. "Watch out." I might be a living booby trap.

In the moonlight, I could see that his face was clean of emotion, but I knew he was weighing the odds, just as I was. One of us had to move, and I realized if I came out into the moon glow, at least Bill could see more clearly if anything attacked.

I stuck my hands out, gripped the grass, and pulled. I couldn't even get up to my knees, so this progress was my best speed. I pushed a little with my feet, though even that use of my back muscles was excruciating. I didn't want to look at Bill while I moved toward him, because I didn't want to soften at the sight of his rage. It was an almost palpable thing.

"What did this to you, Sookie?" he asked softly.

"Get me in the car. Please, get me out of here," I said, doing my best to hold myself together. "If I make a lot of noise, she might come back." I shivered all over at the thought. "Take me to Eric," I said, trying to keep my voice even. "She said this was a message for Eric Northman."

Bill squatted beside me. "I have to lift you," he told me.

Oh, no. I started to say, "There must be some other way," but I knew there wasn't. Bill knew better than to hesitate. Before I could anticipate the pain to its full extent, he scooted an arm under me and applied his other hand to my crotch, and in an instant he had me dangling across his shoulder.

I screamed out loud. I tried not to sob after that, so Bill could listen for an attack, but I didn't manage that very well. Bill began to run along the road, back to the car. It was running already, its engine idling smoothly. Bill flung open the back door and tried to feed me gently but quickly onto the backseat of the Cadillac. It was impossible not to cause me more pain by doing this, but he made the attempt.

"It was her," I said, when I could say anything coherent. "It was her who made the car stop and made me get out." I was keeping an open mind about whether she'd caused the fight to begin with.

"We'll talk about it in a little while," he said. He sped toward Shreveport, at the highest speed he could, while I clawed at the upholstery in an attempt to keep control over myself.

All I remember about that ride was that it was at least two years long.

Bill got me to the back door of Fangtasia somehow, and kicked it to get attention.

"What?" Pam sounded hostile. She was a pretty blond vampire I'd met a couple of times before, a sensible sort of individual with considerable business acumen. "Oh, Bill. What's happened? Oh, yum, she's bleeding."

"Get Eric," Bill said.

"He's been waiting in here," she began, but Bill strode right by her with me bouncing on his shoulder like a bag of bloody game. I was so out of it by that time that I wouldn't have cared if he'd carried me onto the dance floor of the bar out front, but instead, Bill blew into Eric's office laden with me and rage.

"This is on your account," Bill snarled, and I moaned as he shook me as though he were drawing Eric's attention to me. I hardly see how Eric could have been looking anywhere else, since I was a full-grown female and probably the only bleeding woman in his office.

I would have loved to faint, to pass right out. But I didn't. I just sagged over Bill's shoulder and hurt. "Go to hell," I mumbled.

"What, my darling?"

"Go to *hell*."

"We must lay her on her stomach on the couch," Eric said. "Here, let me . . ." I felt another pair of hands grip my legs, Bill sort of turned underneath me, and together they deposited me carefully on the broad couch that Eric had just bought for his office. It had that new smell, and it was leather. I was glad, staring at it from the distance of half an inch, that he hadn't gotten cloth upholstery. "Pam, call the doctor." I heard footsteps leave the room, and Eric crouched down to look into my face. It was quite a crouch, because Eric, tall and broad, looks exactly like what he is, a former Viking.

"What has happened to you?" he asked.

I glared at him, so incensed I could hardly speak. "I

am a message to you," I said, almost in a whisper. "This woman in the woods made Bill's car stop, and maybe even made us argue, and then she came up to me with this hog."

"A *pig?*" Eric could not have been more astonished if I'd said she had a canary up her nose.

"Oink, oink. Razorback. Wild pig. And she said she wanted to send you a message, and I turned in time to keep her from getting my face, but she got my back, and then she left."

"Your face. She would have gotten your face," Bill said. I saw his hands clenching by his thighs, and the back of him as he began pacing around the office. "Eric, her cuts are not so deep. What's wrong with her?"

"Sookie," Eric said gently, "what did this woman look like?"

His face was right by mine, his thick golden hair almost touching my face.

"She looked nuts, I'll tell you how she looked. And she called you Eric Northman."

"That's the last name I use for human dealings," he said. "By looking nuts, you mean she looked . . . how?"

"Her clothes were all ragged and she had blood around her mouth and in her teeth, like she'd just eaten something raw. She was carrying this kind of wand thing, with something on the end of it. Her hair was long and tangled . . . look, speaking of hair, my hair is getting stuck to my back." I gasped.

"Yes, I see." Eric began trying to separate my long hair from my wounds, where blood was acting as an adherent as it thickened.

Pam came in then, with the doctor. If I had hoped Eric

meant a regular doctor, like a stethoscope and tongue depressor kind of person, I was once again doomed to disappointment. This doctor was a dwarf, who hardly had to bend over to look me in the eyes. Bill hovered, vibrating with tension, while the small woman examined my wounds. She was wearing a pair of white pants and a tunic, just like doctors at the hospital; well, just like doctors used to, before they started wearing that green color, or blue, or whatever crazy print came their way. Her face was full of her nose, and her skin was olive. Her hair was golden brown and coarse, incredibly thick and wavy. She wore it clipped fairly short. She put me in mind of a hobbit. Maybe she *was* a hobbit. My understanding of reality had taken several raps to the head in the past few months.

"What kind of doctor are you?" I asked, though it took some time for me to collect myself enough.

"The healing kind," she said in a surprisingly deep voice. "You have been poisoned."

"So that's why I keeping thinking I'm gonna die," I muttered.

"You will, quite soon," she said.

"Thanks a lot, Doc. What can you do about that?"

"We don't have a lot of choices. You've been poisoned. Have you ever heard of Komodo dragons? Their mouths are teeming with bacteria. Well, maenad wounds have the same toxic level. After a dragon has bitten you, the creature tracks you for hours, waiting for the bacteria to kill you. For maenads, the delayed death adds to the fun. For Komodo dragons, who knows?"

Thanks for the *National Geographic* side trip, Doc. "What can you do?" I asked, through gritted teeth.

"I can dose the exterior wounds. But your bloodstream

has been compromised, and your blood must be removed and replaced. That is a job for the vampires." The good doctor seemed positively jolly at the prospect of everyone working together. On me.

She turned to the gathered vamps. "If only one of you takes the poisoned blood, that one will be pretty miserable. It's the element of magic that the maenad imparts. The Komodo dragon bite would be no problem for you guys." She laughed heartily.

I hated her. Tears streamed down my face from the pain.

"So," she continued, "when I'm finished, each of you take a turn, removing just a little. Then we'll give her a transfusion."

"Of human blood," I said, wanting to make that perfectly clear. I'd had to have Bill's blood once to survive massive injuries and once to survive an examination of sorts, and I'd had another vampire's blood by accident, unlikely as that sounds. I'd been able to see changes in me after that blood ingestion, changes I didn't want to amplify by taking another dose. Vampire blood was the drug of choice among the wealthy now, and as far as I was concerned, they could have it.

"If Eric can pull some strings and get the human blood," the dwarf said. "At least half the transfusion can be synthetic. I'm Dr. Ludwig, by the way."

"I can get the blood, and we owe her the healing," I heard Eric say, to my relief. I would have given a lot to see Bill's face, at that moment. "What is your type, Sookie?" Eric asked.

"O positive," I said, glad my blood was so common.

"That shouldn't be a problem," Eric said. "Can you take care of that, Pam?"

Again, a sense of movement in the room. Dr. Ludwig bent forward and began licking my back. I shrieked.

"She's the doctor, Sookie," Bill said. "She will heal you this way."

"But she'll get poisoned," I said, trying to think of an objection that wouldn't sound homophobic and sizist. Truly, I didn't want anyone licking my back, female dwarf or large male vampire.

"She is the healer," Eric said, in a rebuking kind of way. "You must accept her treatment."

"Oh, all right," I said, not even caring how sullen I sounded. "By the way, I haven't heard an 'I'm sorry' from you yet." My sense of grievance had overwhelmed my sense of self-preservation.

"I am sorry that the maenad picked on you."

I glared at him. "Not enough," I said. I was trying hard to hang on to this conversation.

"Angelic Sookie, vision of love and beauty, I am prostrate that the wicked, evil maenad violated your smooth and voluptuous body, in an attempt to deliver a message to me."

"That's more like it." I would have taken more satisfaction in Eric's words if I hadn't been jabbed with pain just then. (The doctor's treatment was not exactly comfortable.) Apologies had better be either heartfelt or elaborate, and since Eric didn't have a heart to feel (or at least I hadn't noticed it so far) he might as well distract me with words.

"I take it the message means that she's going to war with you?" I asked, trying to ignore the activities of Dr. Ludwig. I was sweating all over. The pain in my back was excruciating. I could feel tears trickling down my face.

The room seemed to have acquired a yellow haze; everything looked sickly.

Eric looked surprised. "Not exactly," he said cautiously. "Pam?"

"It's on the way," she said. "This is bad."

"Start," Bill said urgently. "She's changing color."

I wondered, almost idly, what color I'd become. I couldn't hold my head off the couch anymore, as I'd been trying to do to look a little more alert. I laid my cheek on the leather, and immediately my sweat bound me to the surface. The burning sensation that radiated through my body from the claw marks on my back grew more intense, and I shrieked because I just couldn't help it. The dwarf leaped from the couch and bent to examine my eyes.

She shook her head. "Yes, if there's to be any hope," she said, but she sounded very far away to me. She had a syringe in her hand. The last thing I registered was Eric's face moving closer, and it seemed to me he winked.

I OPENED MY EYES WITH GREAT RELUCTANCE. I FELT LIKE I'd been sleeping in a car, or like I'd taken a nap in a straight-back chair; I'd definitely dozed off somewhere inappropriate and uncomfortable. I felt groggy, and I ached all over. Pam was sitting on the floor a yard away, her wide blue eyes fixed on me.

"It worked," she commented. "Dr. Ludwig was right."

"Great."

"Yes, it would have been a pity to lose you before we'd gotten a chance to get some good out of you," she said with shocking practicality. "There are many other humans associated with us the maenad could have picked, and those humans are far more expendable."

"Thanks for the warm fuzzies, Pam," I muttered. I felt

the last degree of nasty, as if I'd been dipped in a vat of sweat and then rolled in the dust. Even my teeth felt scummy.

"You're welcome," she said, and she almost smiled. So Pam had a sense of humor, not something vampires were noted for. You never saw vampire stand-up comedians, and human jokes just left vampires cold, ha-ha. (Some of *their* humor could give you nightmares for a week.)

"What happened?"

Pam relaced her fingers around her knee. "We did as Dr. Ludwig said. Bill, Eric, Chow, and I all took a turn, and when you were almost dry, we began the transfusion."

I thought about that for a minute, glad I'd checked out of consciousness before I could experience the procedure. Bill always took blood when we were making love, so I associated it with the height of erotic activity. To have "donated" to so many people would have been extremely embarrassing to me if I'd been there for it, so to speak. "Who's Chow?" I asked.

"See if you can sit up," Pam advised. "Chow is our new bartender. He is quite a draw."

"Oh?"

"Tattoos," Pam said, sounding almost human for a moment. "He's tall for an Asian, and he has a wonderful set of . . . tattoos."

I tried to look like I cared. I pushed up, feeling a certain tenderness that made me very cautious. It was like my back was covered with wounds that had just healed, wounds that might break open again if I weren't careful. And that, Pam told me, was exactly the case.

Also, I had no shirt on. Or anything else. Above the

waist. Below, my jeans were still intact, though remarkably nasty.

"Your shirt was so ragged we had to tear it off," Pam said, smiling openly. "We took turns holding you on our laps. You were much admired. Bill was furious."

"Go to hell" was all I could think of to say.

"Well, as to that, who knows?" Pam shrugged. "I meant to pay you a compliment. You must be a modest woman." She got up and opened a closet door. There were shirts hanging inside; an extra store for Eric, I assumed. Pam pulled one off a hanger and tossed it to me. I reached up to catch it and had to admit that movement was comparatively easy.

"Pam, is there a shower here?" I hated to pull the pristine white shirt over my grimy self.

"Yes, in the storeroom. By the employees' bathroom."

It was extremely basic, but it was a shower with soap and a towel. You had to step right out into the storeroom, which was probably just fine with the vampires, since modesty is not a big issue with them. When Pam agreed to guard the door, I enlisted her help in pulling off the jeans and shucking my shoes and socks. She enjoyed the process a little too much.

It was the best shower I'd ever had.

I had to move slowly and carefully. I found I was as shaky as though I'd passed through a grave illness, like pneumonia or a virulent strain of the flu. And I guess I had. Pam opened the door enough to pass me some underwear, which was a pleasant surprise, at least until I dried myself and prepared to struggle into it. The underpants were so tiny and lacy they hardly deserved to be called panties. At least they were white. I knew I was better when I caught myself wishing I could see how I looked in a mirror. The underpants and the white shirt were the only garments I could bear to put on. I came out barefoot, to find that Pam had rolled up the jeans and everything else and stuffed them in a plastic bag so I could get them home to the wash. My tan looked extremely brown against the white of the snowy shirt. I walked very slowly back to Eric's office and fished in my purse for my brush. As I began to try to work through the tangles, Bill came in and took the brush from my hand.

"Let me do that, darling," he said tenderly. "How are you? Slide off the shirt, so I can check your back." I did anxiously hoping there weren't cameras in the office—though from Pam's account, I might as well relax.

"How does it look?" I asked him over my shoulder.

Bill said briefly, "There will be marks."

"I figured." Better on my back than on my front. And being scarred was better than being dead.

I slipped the shirt back on, and Bill began working on my hair, a favorite thing for him. I grew tired very quickly and sat in Eric's chair while Bill stood behind me.

"So why did the maenad pick me?"

"She would have been waiting for the first vampire to come through. That I had you with me—so much easier to hurt—that was a bonus."

"Did she cause our fight?"

"No, I think that was just chance. I still don't understand why you got so angry."

"I'm too tired to explain, Bill. We'll talk about it tomorrow, okay?"

Eric came in, along with a vampire I knew must be Chow. Right away I could see why Chow would bring in customers. He was the first Asian vampire I'd seen, and he was extremely handsome. He was also covered—at least the parts I could see—with that intricate tattooing that I'd heard members of the Yakuza favored. Whether Chow had been a gangster when he was human or not, he was certainly sinister now. Pam slid through the door after another minute had passed, saying, "All locked up. Dr. Ludwig left, too."

So Fangtasia had closed its doors for the night. It must be two in the morning, then. Bill continued to brush my hair, and I sat in the office chair with my hands on my thighs, acutely conscious of my inadequate clothing. Though, come to think of it, Eric was so tall his shirt covered as much of me as some of my short sets. I guess it was the French-cut bikini panties underneath that made me so embarrassed. Also, no bra. Since God was generous with me in the bosom department, there's no mistaking when I leave off a bra.

But no matter if my clothes showed more of me than I wanted, no matter if all of these people had seen even more of my boobs than they could discern now, I had to mind my manners.

"Thank you all for saving my life," I said. I didn't succeed in sounding warm, but I hope they could tell I was sincere.

"It was truly my pleasure," said Chow, with an unmistakable leer in his voice. He had a trace of an accent, but I don't have enough experience with the different characteristics of the many strains of Asians to tell you where he came from originally. I am sure "Chow" was not his complete name, either, but it was all the other vampires called him. "It would have been perfect, without the poison."

I could feel Bill tense behind me. He laid his hands on my shoulders, and I reached up to put my fingers over his.

Eric said, "It was worth ingesting the poison." He held his fingers to his lips and kissed them, as if praising the bouquet of my blood. Ick.

Pam smiled. "Any time, Sookie."

Oh, just fantastic. "You, too, Bill," I said, leaning my head back against him.

"It was my privilege," he said, controlling his temper with an effort.

"You two had a fight before Sookie's encounter with the maenad?" Eric asked. "Is that what I heard Sookie say?"

"That's our business," I snapped, and the three vampires smiled at each other. I didn't like that one bit. "By the way, why did you want us to come over here tonight, anyway?" I asked, hoping to get off of the topic of Bill and me.

"You remember your promise to me, Sookie? That you would use your mental ability to help me out, as long as I let the humans involved live?"

"Of course I remember." I am not one to forget a promise, especially one made to a vampire.

"Since Bill has been appointed investigator of Area 5, we have not had a lot of mysteries. But Area 6, in Texas, has need of your special asset. So we have loaned you out."

I realized I'd been rented, like a chainsaw or backhoe. I wondered if the vampires of Dallas had had to put down a deposit against damage.

"I won't go without Bill." I looked Eric steadily in the eye. Bill's fingers gave me a little squeeze, so I knew I'd said the right thing.

"He'll be there. We drove a hard bargain," Eric said, smiling broadly. The effect was really disconcerting, because he was happy about something, and his fangs were out. "We were afraid they might keep you, or kill you, so an escort was part of our deal all along. And who better than Bill? If anything should render Bill incapable of guarding you, we will send another escort right out. And the vampires of Dallas have agreed to provide a car and chauffeur, lodgings and meals, and of course, a nice fee. Bill will get a percentage of that."

When I'd be doing the work? "You must work out your financial arrangement with Bill," Eric said smoothly. "I am sure he will at least recompense you for your time away from your bar job."

Had Ann Landers ever covered "When Your Date Becomes Your Manager"?

"Why a maenad?" I asked, startling all of them. I hoped I was pronouncing the word correctly. "Naiads are water and dryads are trees, right? So why a maenad, out there in the woods? Weren't maenads just women driven mad by the god Bacchus?"

"Sookie, you have unexpected depths," Eric said, after an appreciable pause. I didn't tell him I'd learned that from reading a mystery. Let him think I read ancient Greek literature in the original language. It couldn't hurt.

Chow said, "The god entered some women so completely that they became immortal, or very close to it. Bacchus was the god of the grape, of course, so bars are very interesting to maenads. In fact, so interesting that they don't like other creatures of the darkness becoming involved. Maenads consider that the violence sparked by the consumption of alcohol belongs to them; that's what they feed off, now that no one formally worships their god. And they are attracted to pride."

That rang a chime. Hadn't Bill and I both been feeling our pride, tonight?

"We had only heard rumors one was in the area," Eric said. "Until Bill brought you in."

"So what was she warning you of? What does she want?"

"Tribute," Pam said. "We think."

"What kind?"

Pam shrugged. It seemed that was the only answer I was going to get.

"Or what?" I asked. Again with the stares. I gave a deep sigh of exasperation. "What's she gonna do if you don't pay her tribute?"

"Send her madness." Bill sounded worried.

"Into the bar? Merlotte's?" Though there were plenty of bars in the area.

The vampires eyed each other.

"Or into one of us," Chow said. "It has happened. The Halloween massacre of 1876, in St. Petersburg."

They all nodded solemnly. "I was there," Eric said. "It took twenty of us to clean up. And we had to stake Gregory; it took all of us to do that. The maenad Phryne received tribute after that, you can be sure."

For the vampires to stake one of their own, things had to be pretty serious. Eric had staked a vampire who had stolen from him, and Bill had told me Eric had had to pay a severe penalty. Who to, Bill hadn't said, and I hadn't asked. There were some things I could live quite well without knowing.

"So you'll give a tribute to this maenad?"

They were exchanging thoughts on this, I could tell. "Yes," Eric said. "It is better if we do."

"I guess maenads are pretty hard to kill," Bill said, a question in his voice.

Eric shuddered. "Oh, yes," he said. "Oh, yes."

During our ride back to Bon Temps, Bill and I were silent. I had a lot of questions about the evening, but I was tired from my bones out to my skin.

"Sam should know about this," I said, as we stopped at my house.

Bill came around to open my door. "Why, Sookie?" He took my hand to pull me from the car, knowing that I could barely walk.

"Because . . ." and then I stopped dead. Bill knew Sam was supernatural, but I didn't want to remind him. Sam owned a bar, and we had been closer to Bon Temps than Shreveport when the maenad had interfered.

"He owns a bar, but he should be all right," Bill said reasonably. "Besides, the maenad said the message was for Eric."

That was true.

"You think too much about Sam to suit me," Bill said, and I gaped up at him.

"You're jealous?" Bill was very wary when other vampires seemed to be admiring me, but I'd assumed that was just territorial. I didn't know how to feel about this new development. I'd never had anyone feel jealous of my attentions before.

Bill didn't answer, in a very snitty way.

"Hmmm," I said thoughtfully. "Well, well, well." I was smiling to myself as Bill helped me up the steps and through the old house, into my room; the room my grandmother had slept in for so many years. Now the walls were painted pale yellow, the woodwork was off-white, the curtains were off-white with bright flowers scattered over them. The bed had a matching cover.

I went into the bathroom for a moment to brush my teeth and take care of necessities, and came out still in Eric's shirt.

"Take it off," Bill said.

"Look, Bill, normally I'd be hot to trot, but tonight—"

"I just hate to see you in his shirt."

Well, well, *well.* I could get used to this. On the other hand, if he carried it to extremes, it could be a nuisance.

"Oh, all right," I said, making a sigh he could hear from yards away. "I guess I'll just have to take this ole shirt off." I unbuttoned it slowly, knowing Bill's eyes were watching my hands move down the buttons, pulling the shirt apart a little more each time. Finally, I doffed it and stood there in Pam's white underwear.

"Oh," Bill breathed, and that was tribute enough for me. Maenads be damned, just seeing Bill's face made me feel like a goddess.

Maybe I'd go to Foxy Femme Lingerie in Ruston my next day off. Or maybe Bill's newly acquired clothing store carried lingerie?

Explaining to Sam that I needed to go to Dallas wasn't easy. Sam had been wonderful to me when I'd lost my grandmother, and I counted him as a good friend, a great boss, and (every now and then) a sexual fantasy. I just told Sam that I was taking a little vacation; God knows, I'd never asked for one before. But he pretty much had figured out what the deal was. Sam didn't like it. His brilliant blue eyes looked hot and his face stony, and even his red-blond hair seemed to sizzle. Though he practically muzzled himself to keep from saying so, Sam obviously thought Bill should not have agreed to my going. But Sam didn't know all the circumstances of my dealings with the vampires, just as only Bill, of the vampires I knew, realized that Sam was a shapeshifter. And I tried not to remind Bill. I didn't want Bill thinking about Sam any more than he already did. Bill might decide Sam was an enemy, and I definitely didn't want Bill to do that. Bill is a really bad enemy to have.

I am good at keeping secrets and keeping my face blank, after years of reading unwanted items out of people's minds. But I have to confess that compartmentalizing Bill and Sam took a lot of energy.

Sam had leaned back in his chair after he'd agreed to give me the time off, his wiry build hidden by a big kingfisher-blue Merlotte's Bar tee shirt. His jeans were old but clean, and his boots were heavy-soled and ancient. I was sitting on the edge of the visitor's chair in front of Sam's desk, the office door shut behind me. I knew no one could be standing outside the door listening; after all, the bar was as noisy as usual, with the jukebox wailing a zydeco tune and the bellowing of people who'd had a few drinks. But still, when you talked about something like the maenad, you wanted to lower your voice, and I leaned across the desk.

Sam automatically mimicked my posture, and I put my hand on his arm and said in a whisper, "Sam, there's a maenad out by the Shreveport road." Sam's face went blank for a long second before he whooped with laughter.

Sam didn't get over his convulsions for at least three minutes, during which time I got pretty mad. "I'm sorry," he kept saying, and off he'd go again. You know how irritating that can be when you're the one who triggered it? He came around the desk, still trying to smother his chuckles. I stood because he was standing, but I was fuming. He grasped my shoulders. "I'm sorry, Sookie," he repeated. "I've never seen one, but I've heard they're nasty. Why does this concern you? The maenad, that is."

"Because she's not happy, as you would know if you could see the scars on my back," I snapped, and his face changed then, by golly.

"You were hurt? How did this happen?"

So I told him, trying to leave some of the drama out of it, and toning down the healing process employed by the vampires of Shreveport. He still wanted to see the scars. I turned around, and he pulled up my tee shirt, not past bra strap level. He didn't make a sound, but I felt a touch on my back, and after a second I realized Sam had kissed my skin. I shivered. He pulled the tee shirt over my scars and turned me around.

"I'm very sorry," he said, with complete sincerity. He wasn't laughing now, wasn't even close to it. He was awful close to me. I could practically feel the heat radiating from his skin, electricity crackling through the fine hairs on his arms.

I took a deep breath. "I'm worried she'll turn her attention to you," I explained. "What do maenads want as tribute, Sam?"

"My mother used to tell my father that they love a proud man," he said, and for a moment I thought he was still teasing me. But I looked at his face, and he was not. "Maenads love nothing more than to tear a proud man down to size. Literally."

"Yuck," I said. "Anything else satisfy them?"

"Large game. Bears, tigers, so on."

"Hard to find a tiger in Louisiana. Maybe you could find a bear, but how'd you get it to the maenad's territory?" I pondered this for a while, but didn't come to any answer. "I assume she'd want it alive," I said, a question in my voice.

Sam, who seemed to have been watching me instead of thinking over the problem, nodded, and then he leaned forward and kissed me.

I should have seen it coming.

He was so warm after Bill, whose body never got up to warm. Tepid, maybe. Sam's lips actually felt hot, and his tongue, too. The kiss was deep, intense, unexpected; like the excitement you feel when someone gives you a present you didn't know you wanted. His arms were around me, mine were around him, and we were giving it everything we had, until I came back to earth.

I pulled away a little, and he slowly raised his head from mine.

"I do need to get out of town for a little while," I said.

"Sorry, Sookie, but I've been wanting to do that for years."

There were a lot of ways I could go from that statement, but I ratcheted up my determination and took the high road. "Sam, you know I am . . ."

"In love with Bill," he finished my sentence.

I wasn't completely sure I was in love with Bill, but I loved him, and I had committed myself to him. So to simplify the matter, I nodded in agreement.

I couldn't read Sam's thoughts clearly, because he was a supernatural being. But I would have been a dunce, a telepathic null, not to feel the waves of frustration and longing that rolled off of him.

"The point I was trying to make," I said, after a minute, during which time we disentangled and stepped away from each other, "is that if this maenad takes a special interest in bars, this is a bar run by someone who is not exactly a run-of-the-mill human, like Eric's bar in Shreveport. So you better watch out."

Sam seemed to take heart that I was warning him, seemed to get some hope from it. "Thanks for telling me, Sookie. The next time I change, I'll be careful in the woods."

I hadn't even thought of Sam encountering the maenad in his shapeshifting adventures, and I had to sit down abruptly as I pictured that.

"Oh, no," I told him emphatically. "Don't change at all."

"It's full moon in four days," Sam said, after a glance at the calendar. "I'll have to. I've already got Terry scheduled to work for me that night."

"What do you tell him?"

"I tell him I have a date. He hasn't looked at the calendar to figure out that every time I ask him to work, it's a full moon."

"That's something. Did the police come back any more about Lafayette?"

"No." Sam shook his head. "And I hired a friend of Lafayette's, Khan."

"As in Sher Khan?"

"As in Chaka Khan."

"Okay, but can he cook?"

"He's been fired from the Shrimp Boat."

"What for?"

"Artistic temperament, I gather." Sam's voice was dry.

"Won't need much of that around here," I observed, my hand on the doorknob. I was glad Sam and I had had a conversation, just to ease down from our tense and unprecedented situation. We had never embraced each other at work. In fact, we'd only kissed once, when Sam brought me home after our single date months before. Sam was my boss, and starting something with your boss is always a bad idea. Starting something with your boss when your boyfriend is a vampire is another bad idea, possibly a fatal idea. Sam needed to find a woman. Quickly.

When I'm nervous, I smile. I was beaming when I said, "Back to work," and stepped through the door, shutting it behind me. I had a muddle of feelings about everything that had happened in Sam's office, but I pushed it all away, and prepared to hustle some drinks.

There was nothing unusual about the crowd that night in Merlotte's. My brother's friend Hoyt Fortenberry was drinking with some of his cronies. Kevin Prior, whom I was more accustomed to seeing in uniform, was sitting with Hoyt, but Kevin was not having a happy evening. He looked as though he'd rather be in his patrol car with his partner, Kenya. My brother, Jason, came in with his more and more frequent arm decoration, Liz Barrett. Liz al-

ways acted glad to see me, but she never tried to ingrati-
ate herself, which earned her high points in my book. My
grandmother would have been glad to know Jason was
dating Liz so often. Jason had played the scene for years,
until the scene was pretty darned tired of Jason. After all,
there is a finite pool of women in Bon Temps and its surrounding area, and Jason had fished that pool for years.
He needed to restock.

Besides, Liz seemed willing to ignore Jason's little
brushes with the law.

"Baby sis!" he said in greeting. "Bring me and Liz a
Seven-and-Seven apiece, would you?"

"Glad to," I said, smiling. Carried away on a wave of
optimism, I listened in to Liz for a moment; she was hoping that very soon Jason would pop the question. The
sooner the better, she thought, because she was pretty
sure she was pregnant.

Good thing I've had years of concealing what I was
thinking. I brought them each a drink, carefully shielding
myself from any other stray thoughts I might catch, and
tried to think what I should do. That's one of the worst
things about being telepathic; things people are thinking
but not talking about are things other people (like me) really don't want to know. Or shouldn't want to know. I've
heard enough secrets to choke a camel, and believe me,
not a one of them was to my advantage in any way.

If Liz was pregnant, the last thing she needed was a
drink, no matter who the baby's daddy was.

I watched her carefully, and she took a tiny sip from
her glass. She wrapped her hand around it to partially
hide it from public view. She and Jason chatted for a
minute, then Hoyt called out to him, and Jason swung

around on the bar stool to face his high school buddy. Liz stared down at her drink, as if she'd really like to gulp it in one swallow. I handed her a similar glass of plain 7UP and whisked the mixed drink away.

Liz's big round brown eyes gazed up at me in astonishment. "Not for you," I said very quietly. Liz's olive complexion turned as white as it could. "You have good sense," I said. I was struggling to explain why I'd intervened, when it was against my personal policy to act on what I learned in such a surreptitious way. "You have good sense; you can do this right."

Jason turned back around then, and I got a call for another pitcher from one of my tables. As I moved out from behind the bar to answer the summons, I noticed Portia Bellefleur in the doorway. Portia peered around the dark bar as though she were searching for someone. To my astonishment, that someone turned out to be me.

"Sookie, do you have a minute?" she asked.

I could count the personal conversations I'd had with Portia on one hand, almost on one finger, and I couldn't imagine what was on her mind.

"Sit over there," I said, nodding at an empty table in my area. "I'll be with you in a minute."

"Oh, all right. And I'd better order a glass of wine, I guess. Merlot."

"I'll have it right there." I poured her glass carefully, and put it on a tray. After checking visually to make sure all my customers looked content, I carried the tray over to Portia's table and sat opposite her. I perched on the edge of the chair, so anyone who ran out of a drink could see I was fixing to hop up in just a second.

"What can I do for you?" I reached up to check that my ponytail was secure and smiled at Portia.

She seemed intent on her wineglass. She turned it with her fingers, took a sip, positioned it on the exact center of the coaster. "I have a favor to ask you," she said.

No shit, Sherlock. Since I'd never had a casual conversation with Portia longer than two sentences, it was obvious she needed something from me.

"Let me guess. You were sent here by your brother to ask me to listen in on people's thoughts when they're in the bar, so I can find out about this orgy thing Lafayette went to." Like I hadn't seen that coming.

Portia looked embarrassed, but determined. "He would never have asked you if he wasn't in serious trouble, Sookie."

"He would never have asked me because he doesn't like me. Though I've never been anything but nice to him his whole life! But now, it's okay to ask me for help, because he really needs me."

Portia's fair complexion was turning a deep unbecoming red. I knew it wasn't very pleasant of me to take out her brother's problems on her, but she had, after all, agreed to be the messenger. You know what happens to messengers. That made me think of my own messenger role the night before, and I wondered if I should be feeling lucky today.

"I wasn't for this," she muttered. It hurt her pride, to ask a favor of a barmaid; a Stackhouse, to boot.

Nobody liked me having a "gift." No one wanted me to use it on her. But everyone wanted me to find out something to her advantage, no matter how I felt about sifting through the thoughts (mostly unpleasant and irrelevant) of bar patrons to glean pertinent information.

"You'd probably forgotten that just recently Andy arrested my brother for murder?" Of course he'd had to let Jason go, but still.

If Portia had turned any redder, she'd have lit a fire. "Just forget it, then," she said, scraping together all her dignity. "We don't need help from a freak like you, anyway."

I had touched her at the quick, because Portia had always been courteous, if not warm.

"Listen to me, Portia Bellefleur. I'll listen a little. Not for you or your brother, but because I liked Lafayette. He was a friend of mine, and he was always sweeter to me than you or Andy."

"I don't like you."

"I don't care."

"Darling, is there a problem?" asked a cool voice from behind me.

Bill. I reached with my mind, and felt the relaxing empty space right behind me. Other minds just buzzed like bees in a jar, but Bill's was like a globe filled with air. It was wonderful. Portia stood up so abruptly that her chair almost went over backwards. She was frightened of even being close to Bill, like he was a venomous snake or something.

"Portia was just asking me for a favor," I said slowly, aware for the first time that our little trio was attracting a certain amount of attention from the crowd.

"In return for the many kind things the Bellefleurs have done for you?" Bill asked. Portia snapped. She whirled around to stalk out of the bar. Bill watched her leave with the oddest expression of satisfaction.

"Now I have to find out what that was about," I said, and leaned back against him. His arms circled me and drew me back closer to him. It was like being cuddled by a tree.

"The vampires in Dallas have made their arrangements," Bill said. "Can you leave tomorrow evening?"

"What about you?"

"I can travel in my coffin, if you're willing to make sure I'm unloaded at the airport. Then we'll have all night to find out what it is the Dallas vampires want us to do."

"So I'll have to take you to the airport in a hearse?"

"No, sweetheart. Just get yourself there. There's a transportation service that does that kind of thing."

"Just takes vampires places in daytime?"

"Yes, they're licensed and bonded."

I'd have to think about that for a while. "Want a bottle? Sam has some on the heater."

"Yes, please, I'd like some O positive."

My blood type. How sweet. I smiled at Bill, not my strained normal grin, but a true smile from my heart. I was so lucky to have him, no matter how many problems we had as a couple. I couldn't believe I'd kissed someone else, and I blotted out that idea as soon as it skittered across my mind.

Bill smiled back, maybe not the most reassuring sight, since he was happy to see me. "How soon can you get off?" he asked, leaning closer.

I glanced down at my watch. "Thirty minutes," I promised.

"I'll be waiting for you." He sat at the table Portia had vacated, and I brought him the blood, tout de suite.

Kevin drifted over to talk to him, ended up sitting

down at the table. I was near enough only twice to catch fragments of the conversation; they were talking about the types of crimes we had in our small town, and the price of gas, and who would win the next sheriff's election. It was so normal! I beamed with pride. When Bill had first started coming into Merlotte's, the atmosphere had been on the strained side. Now, people came and went casually, speaking to Bill or only nodding, but not making a big issue of it either way. There were enough legal issues facing vampires without the social issues involved, too.

As Bill drove me home that night, he seemed to be in an excited mood. I couldn't account for that until I figured out that he was pleased about his visit to Dallas.

"Got itchy feet?" I asked, curious and not too pleased about his sudden case of travel lust.

"I have traveled for years. Staying in Bon Temps these months has been wonderful," he said as he reached over to pat my hand, "but naturally I like to visit with others of my own kind, and the vampires of Shreveport have too much power over me. I can't relax when I'm with them."

"Were vampires this organized before you went public?" I tried not to ask questions about vampire society, because I was never sure how Bill would react, but I was really curious.

"Not in the same way," he said evasively. I knew that was the best answer I'd get from him, but I sighed a little anyway. Mr. Mystery. Vampires still kept limits clearly drawn. No doctor could examine them, no vampires could be required to join the armed forces. In return for these legal concessions, Americans had demanded that vampires who were doctors and nurses—and there were more than a few—had to hang up their stethoscopes, because humans were too leery of a blood-drinking health care professional. Even though, as far as humans knew, vampirism was an extreme allergic reaction to a combination of various things, including garlic and sunlight.

Though I was a human—albeit a weird one—I knew better. I'd been a lot happier when I believed Bill had some classifiable illness. Now, I knew that creatures we'd shoved off into the realm of myth and legend had a nasty habit of proving themselves real. Take the maenad. Who'd have believed an ancient Greek legend would be strolling through the woods of northern Louisiana?

Maybe there really *were* fairies at the bottom of the garden, a phrase I remembered from a song my grandmother had sung when she hung out the clothes on the line.

"Sookie?" Bill's voice was gently persistent.

"What?"

"You were thinking mighty hard about something."

"Yes, just wondering about the future," I said vaguely. "And the flight. You'll have to fill me in on all the arrangements, and when I have to be at the airport. And what clothes should I take?"

Bill began to turn that over in his head as we pulled up in the driveway in front of my old house, and I knew he would take my request seriously. It was one of the many good things about him.

"Before you pack, though," he said, his dark eyes solemn under the arch of his brows, "there is something else we have to discuss."

"What?" I was standing in the middle of my bedroom floor, staring in the open closet door, when his words registered.

"Relaxation techniques."

I swung around to face him, my hands on my hips. "What on earth are you talking about?"

"This." He scooped me up in the classic Rhett Butler carrying stance, and though I was wearing slacks rather than a long red—negligee? gown?—Bill managed to make me feel like I was as beautiful, as unforgettable, as Scarlett O'Hara. He didn't have to traipse up any stairs, either; the bed was very close. Most evenings, Bill took things very slow, so slow I thought I would start screaming before we came to the point, so to speak. But tonight, excited by the trip, by the imminent excursion, Bill's speed had greatly accelerated. We reached the end of the tunnel together, and as we lay together during the little aftershocks following successful love, I wondered what the vampires of Dallas would make of our association.

I'd only been to Dallas once, on a senior trip to Six Flags, and it hadn't been a wonderful time for me. I'd been clumsy at protecting my mind from the thoughts eternally broadcasting from other brains, I'd been unprepared for the unexpected pairing of my best friend, Marianne, and a classmate named Dennis Engelbright, and I'd never been away from home before.

This would be different, I told myself sternly. I was going at the request of the vampires of Dallas; was that glamorous, or what? I was needed because of my unique skills. I should focus on not calling my quirks a disability. I had learned how to control my telepathy, at least to have much more precision and predictability. I had my own man. No one would abandon me.

Still, I have to admit that before I went to sleep, I cried a few tears for the misery that had been my lot.

4 ~

It was as hot as the six shades of hell in Dallas, especially on the pavement at the airport. Our brief few days of fall had relapsed back into summer. Torch-hot gusts of air bearing all the sounds and smells of the Dallas–Fort Worth airport—the workings of small vehicles and airplanes, their fuel and their cargo—seemed to accumulate around the foot of the ramp from the cargo bay of the plane I'd been waiting for. I'd flown a regular commercial flight, but Bill had had to be shipped specially.

I was flapping my suit jacket, trying to keep my underarms dry, when the Catholic priest approached me.

Initially, I was so respectful of his collar that I didn't object to his approach, even though I didn't really want to talk to anyone. I had just emerged from one totally new experience, and I had several more such hurdles ahead of me.

"Can I be of some service to you? I couldn't help but notice your situation," the small man said. He was soberly clothed in clerical black, and he sounded chock-full of sympathy. Furthermore, he had the confidence of someone used to approaching strangers and being received politely. He had what I thought was sort of an unusual haircut for a priest, though; his brown hair was longish, and tangled, and he had a mustache, too. But I only noticed this vaguely.

"My situation?" I asked, not really paying attention to his words. I'd just glimpsed the polished wood coffin at the edge of the cargo hold. Bill was such a traditionalist; metal would have been more practical for travel. The uniformed attendants were rolling it to the head of the ramp, so they must have put wheels under it somehow. They'd promised Bill it would get to its destination without a scratch. And the armed guards behind me were insurance that no fanatic would rush over and tear the lid off. That was one of the extras Anubis Air had plugged in its ad. Per Bill's instructions, I'd also specified that he be first off the plane.

So far, so good.

I cast a look at the dusky sky. The lights around the field had come on minutes ago. The black jackal's head on the airplane's tail looked savage in the harsh light, which created deep shadows where none had been. I checked my watch again.

"Yes. I'm very sorry."

I glanced sideways at my unwanted companion. Had

he gotten on the plane in Baton Rouge? I couldn't remember his face, but then, I'd been pretty nervous the
whole flight. "Sorry," I said. "For what? Is there some
kind of problem?"

He looked elaborately astonished. "Well," he said, nodding his head toward the coffin, which was now descending the ramp on a roller system. "Your bereavement. Was
this a loved one?" He edged a little closer to me.

"Well, sure," I said, poised between puzzlement and
aggravation. Why was he out here? Surely the airline
didn't pay a priest to meet every person traveling with a
coffin? Especially one being unloaded from Anubis Air.
"Why else would I be standing here?"

I began to worry.

Slowly, carefully, I slid down my mental shields and
began to examine the man beside me. I know, I know: an
invasion of his privacy. But I was responsible for not only
my own safety, but Bill's.

The priest, who happened to be a strong broadcaster,
was thinking about approaching nightfall as intently as
I was, and with a lot more fear. He was hoping his friends
were where they were supposed to be.

Trying not to show my increasing anxiety, I looked upward again. Deep into dusk, there was only the faintest
trace of light remaining in the Texas sky.

"Your husband, maybe?" He curved his fingers
around my arm.

Was this guy creepy, or what? I glanced over at him.
His eyes were fixed on the baggage handlers who were
clearly visible in the hold of the plane. They were wearing black and silver jumpsuits with the Anubis logo on
the left chest. Then his gaze flickered down to the airline

employee on the ground, who was preparing to guide the coffin onto the padded, flat-bedded baggage cart. The priest wanted . . . what did he want? He was trying to catch the men all looking away, preoccupied. He didn't want them to see. While he . . . what?

"Nah, it's my boyfriend," I said, just to keep our pretence up. My grandmother had raised me to be polite, but she hadn't raised me to be stupid. Surreptitiously, I opened my shoulder bag with one hand and extracted the pepper spray Bill had given me for emergencies. I held the little cylinder down by my thigh. I was edging away from the false priest and his unclear intentions, and his hand was tightening on my arm, when the lid of the coffin swung open.

The two baggage handlers in the plane had swung down to the ground. Now they bowed deeply. The one who'd guided the coffin onto the cart said, "Shit!" before he bowed, too (new guy, I guess). This little piece of obsequious behavior was also an airline extra, but I considered it way over the top.

The priest said, "Help me, Jesus!" But instead of falling to his knees, he jumped to my right, seized me by the arm holding the spray, and began to yank at me.

At first, I thought he felt he was trying to remove me from the danger represented by the opening coffin, by pulling me to safety. And I guess that was what it looked like to the baggage handlers, who were wrapped up in their role-playing as Anubis Air attendants. The upshot was, they didn't help me, even though I yelled, "Let go!" at the top of my well-developed lungs. The "priest" kept yanking at my arm and trying to run, and I kept digging in my two-inch heels and pulling back. I flailed at him with my free hand. I'm not letting anyone haul me off somewhere I don't want to go, not without a good fight.

"Bill!" I was really frightened. The priest was not a big man, but he was taller and heavier than me, and almost as determined. Though I was making his struggle as hard as possible, inch by inch he was moving me toward a staff door into the terminal. A wind had sprung up from nowhere, a hot, dry wind, and if I sprayed the chemicals, they would blow right back in my face.

The man inside the coffin sat up slowly, his large dark eyes taking in the scene around him. I caught a glimpse of him running a hand over his smooth brown hair.

The staff door opened and I could tell there was someone right inside, reinforcements for the priest.

"Bill!"

There was a whoosh through the air around me, and all of a sudden the priest let go and zipped through the door like a rabbit at a greyhound track. I staggered and would have landed on my butt if Bill hadn't slowed to catch me.

"Hey, baby," I said, incredibly relieved. I yanked at the jacket of my new gray suit, and felt glad I'd put on some more lipstick when the plane landed. I looked in the direction the priest had taken. "*That* was pretty weird." I tucked the pepper spray back in my purse.

"Sookie," Bill said, "are you all right?" He leaned down to give me a kiss, ignoring the awed whispers of the baggage handlers at work on a charter plane next to the Anubis gate. Even though the world at large had learned two years ago that vampires were not only the stuff of legends and horror movies, but truly led a centuries-long existence among us, lots of people had never seen a vampire in the flesh.

Bill ignored them. Bill is good at ignoring things that he doesn't feel are worth his attention.

"Yes, I'm fine," I said, a little dazed. "I don't know why he was trying to grab me."

"He misunderstood our relationship?"

"I don't think so. I think he knew I was waiting for you and he was trying to get me away before you woke up."

"We'll have to think about this," said Bill, master of the understatement. "Other than this bizarre incident, how did the evening go?"

"The flight was all right," I said, trying not to stick my bottom lip out.

"Did anything else untoward happen?" Bill sounded just a wee bit dry. He was quite aware that I considered myself put-upon.

"I don't know what normal is for airplane trips, never having done it before," I said tartly, "but up until the time the priest appeared, I'd say things pretty much ran smooth." Bill raised one eyebrow in that superior way he has, so I'd elaborate. "I don't think that man was really a priest at all. What did he meet the plane for? Why'd he come over to talk to me? He was just waiting till everyone working on the plane was looking in another direction."

"We'll talk about it in a more private place," my vampire said, glancing at the men and women who'd begun to gather around the plane to check out the commotion. He stepped over to the uniformed Anubis employees, and in a quiet voice he chastised them for not coming to my help. At least, I assumed that was the burden of his conversation, from the way they turned white and began to babble. Bill slid an arm around my waist and we began to stroll to the terminal.

"Send the coffin to the address on the lid," Bill called back over his shoulder. "The Silent Shore Hotel." The Silent Shore was the only hotel in the Dallas area that had undergone the extensive renovation necessary to accommodate vampire patrons. It was one of the grand old downtown hotels, the brochure had said, not that I'd ever seen downtown Dallas or any of its grand old hotels before.

We stopped in the stairwell of a grubby little flight leading up to the main passenger concourse. "Now, tell me," he demanded. I glanced up at him while I related the odd little incident from start to finish. He was very white. I knew he must be hungry. His eyebrows looked black against the pallor of his skin, and his eyes looked an even darker brown than they really were.

He held open a door and I passed through into the bustle and confusion of one of the biggest airports in the world.

"You didn't listen to him?" I could tell Bill didn't mean with my ears.

"I was still pretty heavily shielded from the plane," I said. "And by the time I got concerned, began to try to read him, you came out of your coffin and he took off. I had the funniest feeling, before he ran . . ." I hesitated, knowing this was far-fetched.

Bill just waited. He's not one to waste words. He lets me finish what I'm saying. We stopped walking for a second, edged over to the wall.

"I felt like he was there to kidnap me," I said. "I know that sounds nuts. Who would know who I am, here in Dallas? Who would know to be meeting the plane? But that's definitely the impression I got." Bill took my warm hands in his cool ones.

I looked up into Bill's eyes. I'm not that short, and he's not that tall, but I still have to look up at him. And it's a little pride issue with me, that I can meet his eyes and not get glamoured. Sometimes I wish Bill *could* give me a different set of memories—for example, I wouldn't mind forgetting about the maenad—but he can't.

Bill was thinking over what I'd said, filing it away for future reference. "So the flight itself was boring?" he asked.

"Actually, it was pretty exciting," I admitted. "After I made sure the Anubis people had stowed you on their plane and I was boarded on mine, the woman showed us what to do when we crashed. I was sitting on the row with the emergency exit. She said to switch if we didn't think we could handle that. But I think I could, don't you? Handle an emergency? She brought me a drink and a magazine." I seldom got waited on myself, being a barmaid by profession, you might say, so I really enjoyed being served.

"I'm sure you can handle just about anything, Sookie. Were you frightened when the plane took off?"

"No. I was just a little worried about this evening. Aside from that, it went fine."

"Sorry I couldn't be with you," he murmured, his cool and liquid voice flowing around me. He pressed me against his chest.

"That's okay," I said into his shirt, mostly meaning it. "First time flying, you know, it's kind of nerve-wracking. But it went all right. Until we landed."

I might grouse and I might moan, but I was truly glad Bill had risen in time to steer me through the airport. I was feeling more and more like the poor country cousin.

We didn't talk any more about the priest, but I knew Bill hadn't forgotten. He walked me through collecting our luggage and finding transportation. He would've parked me somewhere and arranged it all, except, as he reminded me frequently, I'd have to do this on my own sometime, if our business demanded we land somewhere in full daylight.

Despite the fact that the airport seemed incredibly crowded, full of people who all appeared heavily burdened and unhappy, I managed to follow the signs with a little nudge from Bill, after reinforcing my mental shields. It was bad enough, getting washed with the weary misery of the travelers, without listening to their specific laments. I directed the porter with our luggage (which Bill could easily have carried under one arm) to the taxi stand, and Bill and I were on our way to the hotel within forty minutes of Bill's emergence. The Anubis people had sworn up and down that his coffin would be delivered within three hours.

We'd see. If they didn't make it, we got a free flight.

I'd forgotten the sprawl of Dallas, in the seven years since I'd graduated from high school. The lights of the city were amazing, and the busyness. I stared out of the windows at everything we passed, and Bill smiled at me with an irritating indulgence.

"You look very pretty, Sookie. Your clothes are just right."

"Thanks," I said, relieved and pleased. Bill had insisted that I needed to look "professional," and after I'd said, "Professional what?" he'd given me one of those looks. So I was wearing a gray suit over a white shell, with pearl earrings and a black purse and heels. I'd even smoothed my hair back into a twisted shape at the back of my head with one of those Hairagamis I'd ordered from

TV. My friend Arlene had helped me. To my mind, I looked like a professional, all right—a professional funeral home attendant—but Bill seemed to approve. And I'd charged the whole outfit to him at Tara's Togs, since it was a legitimate business expense. So I couldn't complain about the cost.

I'd have been more comfortable in my barmaid's outfit. Give me shorts and a T-shirt over a dress and hose any day. And I could've been wearing my Adidas with my barmaid uniform, not these damn heels. I sighed.

The taxi pulled up to the hotel, and the driver got out to extract our luggage. There was enough of it for three days. If the vampires of Dallas had followed my directions, I could wind this up and we could go back to Bon Temps tomorrow night, to live there unmolested and uninvolved in vampire politics—at least until the next time Bill got a phone call. But it was better to bring extra clothes than to count on that.

I scooted across the seat to emerge after Bill, who was paying the driver. A uniformed bellboy from the hotel was loading the luggage onto a rolling cart. He turned his thin face to Bill and said, "Welcome to Silent Shore Hotel, sir! My name is Barry, and I'll . . ." Then Bill stepped forward, the light from the lobby door spilling onto his face. "I'll be your porter," Barry finished weakly.

"Thank you," I said, to give the boy, who couldn't be more than eighteen, a second to compose himself. His hands were a little trembly. I cast a mental net out to check the source of his distress.

To my startled delight, I realized (after a quick rummage in Barry's head) that he was a telepath, like me! But he was at the level of organization and development I'd been when I was, maybe, twelve years old. He was a mess, that boy. He couldn't control himself at all, and his shields were a shambles. He was heavy into denial. I didn't know whether to grab him and hug him, or smack him upside the head. Then I realized his secret was not mine to give away. I glanced off in another direction, and shifted from one foot to another, as if I were bored.

"I'll just follow you with your luggage," Barry mumbled, and Bill smiled at him gently. Barry smiled tentatively back, and then got busy bringing in the cart. It had to be Bill's appearance that unnerved Barry, since he couldn't read Bill's mind, the great attraction of the undead for people like me. Barry was going to have to learn how to relax around vampires, since he'd agreed to work at a hotel that catered to them.

Some people think all vampires look terrifying. To me, it depends on the vampire. I remember thinking, when I first met Bill, that he looked incredibly different; but I hadn't been frightened.

The one that was waiting for us in the lobby of Silent Shores, now, *she* was scary. I bet she made ole Barry wet his pants. She approached after we'd checked in, as Bill was putting his credit card back in his wallet (you just try applying for a credit card when you're a hundred sixty years old; that process had been a *bear*) and I sidled a little closer to him as he tipped Barry, hoping she wouldn't notice me.

"Bill Compton? The detective from Louisiana?" Her voice was as calm and cool as Bill's, with considerably less inflection. She had been dead a long time. She was as white as paper and as flat as a board, and her thin, ankle-length blue and gold dress didn't do a thing for her except accentuate both whiteness and flatness. Light brown hair (braided and long enough to tap her butt) and glittery green eyes emphasized her otherness.

"Yes." Vampires don't shake hands, but the two made eye contact and gave each other a curt nod.

"This is the woman?" She had probably gestured toward me with one of those lightning quick movements, because I caught a blur from the corner of my eyes.

"This is my companion and coworker, Sookie Stackhouse," Bill said.

After a moment, she nodded to show she was picking up the hint. "I am Isabel Beaumont," she said, "and after you take your luggage to your room and take care of your needs, you are to come with me."

Bill said, "I have to feed."

Isabel swiveled an eye toward me thoughtfully, no doubt wondering why I wasn't supplying blood for my escort, but it was none of her business. She said, "Just punch the telephone button for room service."

Measly old mortal me would just have to order from the menu. But as I considered the time frame, I realized I'd feel much better if I waited to eat after this evening's business was finished.

After our bags had been put in the bedroom (big enough for the coffin and a bed), the silence in the little living room became uncomfortable. There was a little refrigerator well stocked with TrueBlood, but this evening Bill would want the real thing.

"I have to call, Sookie," Bill said. We'd gone over this before the trip.

"Of course." Without looking at him, I retreated into

the bedroom and shut the door. He might have to feed off someone else so I could keep my strength up for coming events, but I didn't have to watch it or like it. After a few minutes, I heard a knock on the corridor door and I heard Bill admit someone—his Meal on Wheels. There was a little murmur of voices and then a low moan.

Unfortunately for my tension level, I had too much common sense to do something like throw my hairbrush or one of the damn high heels across the room. Maybe retaining some dignity figured in there, too; and a healthy sense of how much temperament Bill would put up with. So I unpacked my suitcase and laid my makeup out in the bathroom, using the facility even though I didn't feel especially needy. Toilets were optional in the vampire world, I'd learned, and even if a functional facility was available in a house occupied by vampires, occasionally they forgot to stock toilet paper.

Soon I heard the outer door open and close again, and Bill knocked lightly before coming into the bedroom. He looked rosy and his face was fuller.

"Are you ready?" he asked. Suddenly, the fact that I was going out on my first real job for the vampires hit me, and I felt scared all over again. If I wasn't a success, my life would become out-and-out perilous, and Bill might become even deader than he was now. I nodded, my throat dry with fear.

"Don't bring your purse."

"Why not?" I stared down at it, astonished. Who could object?

"Things can be hidden in purses." Things like stakes, I assumed. "Just slip a room key into . . . does that skirt have a pocket?"

"No."

"Well, slip the key into your underthings."

I raised my hem so Bill could see exactly what underthings I had to tuck something into. I enjoyed the expression on his face more than I can say.

"Those are . . . would that be a . . . thong?" Bill seemed a little preoccupied all of a sudden.

"It would. I didn't see the need to be professional down to the skin."

"And what skin it is," Bill murmured. "So tan, so . . . smooth."

"Yep, I figured I didn't need to wear any hose." I tucked the plastic rectangle—the "key"—under one of the side straps.

"Oh, I don't think it'll stay there," he said, his eyes large and luminous. "We might get separated, so you definitely need to take it with you. Try another spot."

I moved it somewhere else.

"Oh, Sookie. You'll never get at it in a hurry there. We have . . . ah, we have to go." Bill seemed to shake himself out of his trance.

"All right, if you insist," I said, smoothing the skirt of the suit over my "underthings."

He gave me a dark look, patted his pockets like men do, just to make sure they have everything. It was an oddly human gesture, and it touched me in a way I couldn't even describe to myself. We gave each other a sharp nod and walked down the corridor to the elevator. Isabel Beaumont would be waiting, and I had a distinct feeling she wasn't used to that.

The ancient vampire, who looked no more than thirty-five, was standing exactly where we'd left her. Here at the

Silent Shore Hotel, Isabel felt free to be her vampire self, which included immobile downtime. People fidget. They are compelled to look engaged in an activity, or purposeful. Vampires can just occupy space without feeling obliged to justify it. As we came out of the elevator, Isabel looked exactly like a statue. You could have hung your hat on her, though you'd have been sorry.

Some early-warning system kicked in when we were within six feet of the vamp. Isabel's eyes flicked in our direction and her right hand moved, as though someone had thrown her "on" switch. "Come with me," she said, and glided out the main door. Barry could hardly open it for her fast enough. I noticed he had enough training to cast his eyes down as she passed. Everything you've heard about meeting vampires' eyes is true.

Predictably, Isabel's car was a black Lexus loaded with options. Vampires won't go around in any Geo. Isabel waited until I'd buckled my seat belt (she and Bill didn't bother to use them) before pulling away from the curb, which surprised me. Then we were driving through Dallas, down a main thoroughfare. Isabel seemed to be the strong silent type, but after we'd been in the car for maybe five minutes, she seemed to shake herself, as if she had been reminded she had orders.

We began a curve to the left. I could see some sort of grassy area, and a vague shape that would be some kind of historical marker, maybe. Isabel pointed to her right with a long bony finger. "The Texas School Book Depository," she said, and I understood she felt obliged to inform me. That meant she had been ordered to do so, which was very interesting. I followed her finger eagerly, taking in as much of the brick building as I could see. I was surprised it didn't look more notable.

"That's the grassy knoll?" I breathed, excited and impressed. It was like I'd happened upon the *Hindenburg* or some other fabled artifact.

Isabel nodded, a barely perceptible movement that I only caught because her braid jerked. "There is a museum in the old depository," she said.

Now, that was something I'd like to see in the daytime. If we were here long enough, I'd walk or maybe find out how to catch a cab while Bill was in his coffin.

Bill smiled over his shoulder at me. He could pick up on my slightest mood, which was wonderful about eighty percent of the time.

We drove for at least twenty more minutes, leaving business areas and entering residential. At first the structures were modest and boxy; but gradually, though the lots didn't seem that much larger, the houses began to grow as if they'd taken steroids. Our final destination was a huge house shoehorned onto a small lot. With its little ruffle of land around the cube of the house, it looked ridiculous, even in the dark.

I sure could have stood a longer ride and more delay.

We parked on the street in front of the mansion, for so it seemed to me. Bill opened my door for me. I stood for a moment, reluctant to start the—project. I knew there were vampires inside, lots of them. I knew it the same way I would be able to discern that humans were waiting. But instead of positive surges of thought, the kind I'd get to indicate people, I got mental pictures of . . . how can I put it? There were holes in the air inside the house. Each hole represented a vampire. I went a few feet down the short sidewalk to the front door, and there, finally, I caught a mental whiff of human.

The light over the door was on, so I could tell the house was of beige brick with white trim. The light, too, was for my benefit; any vampire could see far better than the sharpest-eyed human. Isabel led the way to the front door, which was framed in graduating arches of brick. There was a tasteful wreath of grapevines and dried flowers on the door, which almost disguised the peephole. This was clever mainstreaming. I realized there was nothing apparent in this house's appearance to indicate that it was any different from any of the other oversized houses we'd passed, no outward indication that within lived vampires.

But they were there, in force. As I followed Isabel inside, I counted four in the main room onto which the front door opened, and there were two in the hall and at least six in the vast kitchen, which looked designed to produce meals for twenty people at a time. I knew immediately that the house had been purchased, not built, by a vampire, because vampires always plan tiny kitchens, or leave the kitchen out entirely. All they need is a refrigerator, for the synthetic blood, and a microwave, to heat it up. What are they going to cook?

At the sink, a tall, lanky human was washing a few dishes, so perhaps some humans did live here. He half turned as we passed through, and nodded to me. He was wearing glasses and his shirtsleeves were rolled up. I didn't have a chance to speak, because Isabel was ushering us into what appeared to be the dining room.

Bill was tense. I might not be able to read his mind,

but I knew him well enough to interpret the set of his shoulders. No vampire is ever comfortable entering another vamp's territory. Vampires have as many rules and regulations as any other society; they just try to keep them secret. But I was figuring things out.

Among all the vampires in the house, I quickly spotted the leader. He was one of those sitting at the long table in the large dining room. He was a total geek. That was my first impression. Then I realized that he was carefully disguised as a geek: he was quite . . . other. His sandy hair was slicked back, his physique was narrow and unimpressive, his black-rimmed glasses were sheer camouflage, and his pinstriped oxford cloth shirt was tucked into cotton-polyester blend pants. He was pale— well, duh—and freckled, with invisible eyelashes and minimal eyebrows.

"Bill Compton," the geek said.

"Stan Davis," Bill said.

"Yeah, welcome to the city." There was a faint trace of foreign accent in the geek's voice. *He used to be Stanislaus Davidowitz,* I thought, and then wiped my mind clean like a slate. If any of them found out that every now and then I picked a stray thought out of the silence of their minds, I'd be bloodless before I hit the floor.

Even Bill didn't know that.

I packed the fear down in the cellar of my mind as the pale eyes fixed on me and scrutinized me feature by feature.

"She comes in an agreeable package," he said to Bill, and I supposed that was meant to be a compliment, a pat on the back, for Bill.

Bill inclined his head.

Vampires didn't waste time saying a lot of things humans would under similar circumstances. A human executive would ask Bill how Eric, his boss, was doing; would threaten Bill a little in case I didn't perform; would maybe introduce Bill and me to at least the more important people in the room. Not Stan Davis, head vampire. He lifted his hand, and a young Hispanic vampire with bristly black hair left the room and returned with a human girl in tow. When she saw me, she gave a screech and lunged, trying to break free of the grip the vampire had on her upper arm.

"Help me," she shrieked. "You have to help me!"

I knew right away that she was stupid. After all, what could I do against a roomful of vampires? Her appeal was ridiculous. I told myself that several times, very fast, so I could go through with what I had to do.

I caught her eyes, and held up my finger to tell her to be silent. Once she'd looked at me, locked on to me, she obeyed. I don't have the hypnotic eyes of a vamp, but I don't look the least bit threatening. I look exactly like the girl you'd see in a low-paying job any place in any town in the South: blond and bosomy and tan and young. Possibly, I don't look very bright. But I think it's more that people (and vampires) assume that if you're pretty and blond and have a low-paying job, you are ipso facto dumb.

I turned to Stan Davis, very grateful that Bill was right behind me. "Mr. Davis, you understand that I need more privacy when I question this girl. And I have to know what you need from her."

The girl began to sob. It was slow and heartrending, and almost unbelievably irritating under the circumstances.

Davis's pale eyes fastened on mine. He was not trying

to glamour me, or subdue me; he was just examining me. "I understood your escort knew the terms of my agreement with his leader," Stan Davis said. All right, I got the point. I was beneath contempt since I was a human. My talking to Stan was like a chicken talking to the buyer from KFC. But still, I had to know our goal. "I'm aware you met Area 5's conditions," I said, keeping my voice as steady as I could, "and I'm going to do my best. But without a goal, I can't get started."

"We need to know where our brother is," he said, after a pause.

I tried not to look as astonished as I felt.

As I've said, some vampires, like Bill, live by themselves. Others feel more secure in a cluster, called a nest. They call each other brother and sister when they've been in the same nest for a while, and some nests lasted decades. (One in New Orleans has lasted two centuries.) I knew from Bill's briefing before we left Louisiana that the Dallas vampires lived in an especially large nest.

I'm no brain surgeon, but even I realized that for a vampire as powerful as Stan to be missing one of his nest brothers was not only very unusual, it was humiliating.

Vampires like to be humiliated about as much as people do.

"Explain the circumstances, please," I said in my most neutral voice.

"My brother Farrell has not returned to his nest for five nights," Stan Davis said.

I knew they would have checked Farrell's favorite hunting grounds, have asked every other vampire in the Dallas nest to find out if Farrell had been seen. Nevertheless, I opened my mouth to ask, as humans are compelled to do. But Bill touched my shoulder, and I glanced behind me to see a tiny headshake. My questions would be taken as a serious insult.

"This girl?" I asked instead. She was still quiet, but she was shivering and shaking. The Hispanic vampire seemed to be the only thing holding her up.

"Works in the club where he was last seen. It's one we own, the Bat's Wing." Bars were favorite enterprises for vampires, naturally, because their heaviest traffic came at night. Somehow, fanged all-night dry cleaners didn't have the same allure that a vampire-studded bar did.

In the past two years, vampire bars had become the hottest form of nightlife a city could boast. The pathetic humans who became obsessed with vampires—fang-bangers—hung out in vampire bars, often in costumes, in the hopes of attracting the attention of the real thing. Tourists came in to gape at the undead and the fang-bangers. These bars weren't the safest place to work.

I caught the eyes of the Hispanic vampire, and indicated a chair on my side of the long table. He eased the girl into it. I looked down at her, preparing to slide into her thoughts. Her mind had no protection whatsoever. I closed my eyes.

Her name was Bethany. She was twenty-one, and she had thought of herself as a wild child, a real bad girl. She had had no idea what trouble that could get her into, until now. Getting a job at the Bat's Wing had been the rebellious gesture of her life, and it might just turn out to be fatal.

I turned my eyes back to Stan Davis. "You understand," I said, taking a great risk, "that if she yields the information you want, she goes free, unharmed." He'd said he understood the terms, but I had to be sure.

Bill heaved a sigh behind me. Not a happy camper. Stan Davis's eyes actually glowed for a second, so angry was he. "Yes," he said, biting out the words, his fangs half-out, "I agreed." We met each other's eyes for a second. We both knew that even two years ago, the vampires of Dallas would have kidnapped Bethany and tortured her until they had every scrap of information she had stored in her brain, and some she'd made up.

Mainstreaming, going public with the fact of their existence, had many benefits—but it also had its price. In this instance, the price was my service.

"What does Farrell look like?"

"Like a cowboy." Stan said this without a trace of humor. "He wears one of those string ties, jeans, and shirts with fake pearl snaps."

The Dallas vampires didn't seem to be into haute couture. Maybe I could have worn my barmaid outfit after all. "What color hair and eyes?"

"Brown hair going gray. Brown eyes. A big jaw. About . . . five feet eleven inches." Stan was translating from some other method of measurement. "He would look about thirty-eight, to you," Stan said. "He's clean-shaven, and thin."

"Would you like me to take Bethany somewhere else? You got a smaller room, less crowded?" I tried to look agreeable, because it seemed like such a good idea.

Stan made a movement with his hand, almost too fast for me to detect, and in a second—literally—every vampire, except Stan himself and Bill, had left the kitchen.

Without looking, I knew that Bill was standing against the wall, ready for anything. I took a deep breath. Time to start this venture.

"Bethany, how are you?" I said, making my voice gentle.

"How'd you know my name?" she asked, slumping down in her seat. It was a breakfast nook chair on wheels, and I rolled it out from the table and turned it to face the one I now settled in. Stan was still sitting at the head of the table, behind me, slightly to my left.

"I can tell lots of things about you," I said, trying to look warm and omniscient. I began picking thoughts out of the air, like apples from a laden tree. "You had a dog named Woof when you were little, and your mother makes the best coconut cake in the world. Your dad lost too much money at a card game one time, and you had to hock your VCR to help him pay up, so your mom wouldn't find out."

Her mouth was hanging open. As much as it was possible, she had forgotten the fact that she was in terrible danger. "That's amazing, you're as good as the psychic on TV, the one in the ads!"

"Well, Bethany, I'm not a psychic," I said, a little too sharply. "I'm a telepath, and what I do is read your thoughts, even some you maybe didn't know you had. I'm going to relax you, first, and then we're going to remember the evening you worked at the bar—not tonight, but five nights ago." I glanced back at Stan, who nodded.

"But I wasn't thinking about my mother's cake!" Bethany said, stuck on what had struck her.

I tried to suppress my sigh.

"You weren't aware of it, but you did. It slid across

your mind when you looked at the palest vampire—
Isabel—because her face was as white as the icing for
the cake. And you thought of how much you missed your
dog when you were thinking of how your parents would
miss you."

I knew that was a mistake as soon as the words went
out of my mouth, and sure enough, she began crying
again, recalled to her present circumstances.

"So what are you here for?" she asked between sobs.

"I'm here to help you remember."

"But you said you're not psychic."

"And I'm not." Or was I? Sometimes I thought I had a
streak mixed in with my other "gift," which was what the
vampires thought it was. I had always thought of it as
more of a curse myself, until I'd met Bill. "Psychics can
touch objects and get information about the wearers.
Some psychics see visions of past or future events. Some
psychics can communicate with the dead. I'm a telepath.
I can read some people's thoughts. Supposedly, I can
send thoughts, too, but I've never tried that." Now that I'd
met another telepath, the attempt was an exciting possibility, but I stowed that idea away to explore at my
leisure. I had to concentrate on the business at hand.

As I sat knee to knee with Bethany, I was making a series of decisions. I was new to the idea of using my "listening in" to some purpose. Most of my life had been
spent struggling *not* to hear. Now, hearing was my job,
and Bethany's life probably depended on it. Mine almost
certainly did.

"Listen, Bethany, here's what we're going to do.
You're going to remember that evening, and I'm going to
go through it with you. In your mind."

"Will it hurt?"

"No, not a bit."

"And after that?"

"Why, you'll go."

"Go home?"

"Sure." With an amended memory that wouldn't include me, or this evening, courtesy of a vampire.

"They won't kill me?"

"No way."

"You promise?"

"I do." I managed to smile at her.

"Okay," she said, hesitantly. I moved her a little, so she couldn't see Stan over my shoulder. I had no idea what he was doing. But she didn't need to see that white face while I was trying to get her to relax.

"You're pretty," she said suddenly.

"Thanks, and back at you." At least, she might be pretty under better circumstances. Bethany had a mouth that was too small for her face, but that was a feature some men found attractive, since it looked like she was always puckered up. She had a great quantity of brown hair, thick and bushy, and a thin body with small breasts. Now that another woman was looking at her, Bethany was worried about her wrinkled clothes and stale makeup.

"You look fine," I said quietly, taking her hands into mine. "Now, we're just gonna hold hands here for a minute—I swear I'm not making a pass." She giggled, and her fingers relaxed a little more. Then I began my spiel.

This was a new wrinkle for me. Instead of trying to avoid using my telepathy, I'd been trying to develop it, with Bill's encouragement. The human staff at Fangtasia had acted as guinea pigs. I'd found out, almost by accident, that I could hypnotize people in a jiffy. It didn't put them under my spell or anything, but it let me into their minds with a frightening ease. When you can tell what really relaxes someone, by reading his or her mind, it's relatively easy to relax that person right into a trancelike state.

"What do you enjoy the most, Bethany?" I asked. "Do you get a massage every now and then? Or maybe you like getting your nails done?" I looked in Bethany's mind delicately. I selected the best channel for my purpose.

"You're getting your hair fixed," I said, keeping my voice soft and even, "by your favorite hairdresser . . . Jerry. He's combed it and combed it, there's not a tangle left. He's sectioned it off, so carefully, because your hair is so thick. It's gonna take him a long time to cut it, but he's looking forward to it, because your hair is healthy and shiny. Jerry's lifting a lock, and trimming it . . . the scissors give a little snick. A little bit of hair falls on the plastic cape and slides off to the floor. You feel his fingers in your hair again. Over and over, his fingers move in your hair, lift a lock, snip it. Sometimes he combs it again, to see if he got it even. It feels so good, just sitting and having someone work on your hair. There's no one else . . ." No, wait. I'd raised a hint of unease. "There's only a few people in the shop, and they're just as busy as Jerry. Someone's got a blow-dryer going. You can barely hear voices murmuring in the next booth. His fingers run through, lift, snip, comb, over and over . . ."

I didn't know what a trained hypnotist would say

about my technique, but it worked for me this time, at least. Bethany's brain was in a restful, fallow state, just waiting to be given a task. In the same even voice I said, "While he's working on your hair, we're going to walk through that night at work. He won't stop cutting, okay? Start with getting ready to go to the bar. Don't mind me, I'm just a puff of air right behind your shoulder. You might hear my voice, but it's coming from another booth in that beauty salon. You won't even be able to hear what I'm saying unless I use your name." I was informing Stan as well as reassuring Bethany. Then I submerged deeper into the girl's memory.

Bethany was looking at her apartment. It was very small, fairly neat, and she shared it with another Bat's Wing employee, who went by the name Desiree Dumas. Desiree Dumas, as seen by Bethany, looked exactly like her made-up name: a self-designated siren, a little too plump, a little too blond, and convinced of her own eroticism.

Taking the waitress through this experience was like watching a film, a really dull one. Bethany's memory was almost too good. Skipping over the boring parts, like Bethany and Desiree's argument over the relative merits of two brands of mascara, what Bethany remembered was this: she had prepared for work as she always did, and she and Desiree had ridden together to their job. Desiree worked in the gift shop section of the Bat's Wing. Dressed in a red bustier and black boots, she hawked vampire souvenirs for big bucks. Wearing artificial fangs, she posed for pictures with tourists for a good tip. Bony and shy Bethany was a humble waitress; for a year she'd been waiting for an opening in the more congenial gift shop, where she wouldn't make the big tips but her base salary would be higher, and she could sit down when she wasn't busy. Bethany hadn't gotten there yet. Big grudge against Desiree, there, on Bethany's part; irrelevant, but I heard myself telling Stan about it as if it were crucial information.

I had never been this deep into someone else's mind. I was trying to weed as I went, but it wasn't working. Finally, I just let it all come. Bethany was completely relaxed, still getting that haircut. She had excellent visual recall, and she was as deeply engaged as I was in the evening she'd spent at work.

In her mind, Bethany served synthetic blood to only four vampires: a red-haired female; a short, stocky Hispanic female with eyes as black as pitch; a blond teenager with ancient tattoos; and a brown-haired man with a jutting jaw and a bolo tie. There! Farrell was embedded in Bethany's memory. I had to suppress my surprise and recognition, and try to steer Bethany with more authority.

"That's the one, Bethany," I whispered. "What do you remember about him?"

"Oh, him," Bethany said out loud, startling me so much I almost jumped out of my chair. In her mind, she turned to look at Farrell, thinking of him. He'd had two synthetic bloods, O positive, and he'd left her a tip.

There was a crease between Bethany's eyebrows as she became focused on my request. She was trying hard now, searching her memory. Bits of the evening began to compact, so she could reach the parts containing the memory of the brown-haired vampire. "He went back to the bathroom with the blond," she said, and I saw in her mind the image of the blond tattooed vampire, the very young-looking one. If I'd been an artist, I could have drawn him.

"Young vampire, maybe sixteen. Blond, tattoo," I murmured to Stan, and he looked surprised. I barely caught that, having so much to concentrate on—this was like trying to juggle—but I did think surprise was the flash of feeling on Stan's face. That was puzzling.

"Sure he was a vampire?" I asked Bethany.

"He drank the blood," she said flatly. "He had that pale skin. He gave me the creeps. Yes, I'm sure."

And he'd gone into the bathroom with Farrell. I was disturbed. The only reason a vampire would enter a bathroom was if there were a human inside he wanted to have sex with, or drink from, or (any vamp's favorite) do both simultaneously. Submerging myself again in Bethany's recollections, I watched her serve a few more customers, no one I recognized, though I got as good a look as I could at the other patrons. Most of them seemed like harmless tourist types. One of them, a dark-complexioned man with a bushy mustache, seemed familiar, so I tried to note his companions: a tall, thin man with shoulder-length blond hair and a squatty woman with one of the worst haircuts I'd ever seen.

I had some questions to ask Stan, but I wanted to finish up with Bethany first. "Did the cowboy-looking vampire come out again, Bethany?"

"No," she said after a perceptible pause. "I didn't see him again." I checked her carefully for blank spots in her mind; I could never replace what had been erased, but I might know if her memory had been tampered with. I found nothing. And she was trying to remember, I could tell. I could sense her straining to recall another glimpse of Farrell. I realized, from the sense of her straining, that I was losing control of Bethany's thoughts and memories.

"What about the young blond one? The one with the tattoos?"

Bethany pondered that. She was about half out of her trance now. "I didn't see him, neither," she said. A name slid through her head.

"What's that?" I asked, keeping my voice very quiet and calm.

"Nothing! Nothing!" Bethany's eyes were wide open now. Her haircut was over: I'd lost her. My control was far from perfect.

She wanted to protect someone; she wanted him not to go through the same thing she was going through. But she couldn't stop herself from thinking the name, and I caught it. I couldn't quite understand why she thought this man would know something else, but she did. I knew no purpose would be served by letting her know I'd picked up on her secret, so I smiled at her and told Stan, without turning to look at him, "She can go. I've gotten everything."

I absorbed the look of relief on Bethany's face before I turned to look at Stan. I was sure he realized I had something up my sleeve, and I didn't want him to say anything. Who can tell what a vampire is thinking when the vamp is being guarded? But I had the distinct feeling Stan understood me.

He didn't speak out loud, but another vampire came in, a girl who'd been about Bethany's age when she went over. Stan had made a good choice. The girl leaned over Bethany, took her hand, smiled with fangs fully retracted, and said, "We'll take you home now, okay?"

"Oh, great!" Bethany's relief was written in neon on her forehead. "Oh, great," she said again, less certainly. "Ah, you really are going to my house? You . . ."

But the vampire had looked directly into Bethany's eyes and now she said, "You won't remember anything about today or this evening except the party."

"Party?" Bethany's voice sounded sluggish. Only mildly curious.

"You went to a party," the vampire said as she led Bethany from the room. "You went to a great party, and you met a cute guy there. You've been with him." She was still murmuring to Bethany as they went out. I hoped she was giving her a good memory.

"What?" Stan asked, when the door shut behind the two.

"Bethany thought the club bouncer would know more. She watched him go into the men's room right on the heels of your friend Farrell and the vampire you didn't know." What *I* didn't know, and hardly liked to ask Stan, was whether vampires ever had sex with each other. Sex and food were so tied together in the vampire life system that I couldn't imagine a vampire having sex with someone nonhuman, that is, someone he couldn't get blood from. Did vampires ever take blood from each other in noncrisis situations? I knew if a vampire's life was at stake (har de har) another vampire would donate blood to revive the damaged one, but I had never heard of another situation involving blood exchange. I hardly liked to ask Stan. Maybe I'd broach the subject with Bill, when we got out of this house.

"What you uncovered in her mind was that Farrell was at the bar, and that he went into the toilet room with another vampire, a young male with long blond hair and many tattoos," Stan summarized. "The bouncer went into the toilet while the two were in there."

"Correct."

There was a sizeable pause while Stan made up his mind about what to do next. I waited, delighted not to hear one word of his inner debate. No flashes, no glimpses.

At least such momentary glimpses into a vampire mind were extremely rare. And I'd never had one from Bill; I hadn't known it was possible for some time after I'd been introduced to the vampiric world. So his company remained pure pleasure to me. It was possible, for the first time in my life, to have a normal relationship with a male. Of course, he wasn't a *live* male, but you couldn't have everything.

As if he knew I'd been thinking of him, I felt Bill's hand on my shoulder. I put my own over it, wishing I could get up and give him a full-length hug. Not a good idea in front of Stan. Might make him hungry.

"We don't know the vampire who went in with Farrell," Stan said, which seemed a little bit of an answer after all that thinking. Maybe he'd imagined giving me a longer explanation, but decided I wasn't smart enough to understand the answer. I would rather be underestimated than overrated any day. Besides, what real difference did it make? But I filed my question away under facts I needed to know.

"So, who's the bouncer at the Bat's Wing?"

"A man called Re-Bar," Stan said. There was a trace of distaste in the way he said it. "He is a fangbanger."

So Re-Bar had his dream job. Working with vampires, working for vampires, and being around them every night. For someone who had gotten fascinated by the undead, Re-Bar had hit a lucky streak. "What could he do if a vampire got rowdy?" I asked, out of sheer curiosity.

"He was only there for the human drunks. We found that a vampire bouncer tended to overuse his strength."

I didn't want to think about that too much. "Is Re-Bar here?"

"It will take a short time," Stan said, without consulting anyone in his entourage. He almost certainly had some kind of mind contact with them. I'd never seen that before, and I was sure Eric couldn't approach Bill mentally. It must be Stan's special gift.

While we waited, Bill sat down in the chair next to me. He reached over and took my hand. I found it very comforting, and loved Bill for it. I kept my mind relaxed, trying to maintain energy for the questioning ahead. But I was beginning to frame some worries, very serious worries, about the situation of the vampires of Dallas. And I was concerned about the glimpse I'd had of the bar patrons, especially the man I'd thought I recognized.

"Oh, no," I said sharply, suddenly recalling where I'd seen him.

The vampires shot to full alert. "What, Sookie?" Bill asked.

Stan looked like he'd been carved from ice. His eyes actually glowed green, I wasn't just imagining it.

I stumbled all over my words in my haste to explain what I was thinking. "The priest," I told Bill. "The man that ran away at the airport, the one who tried to grab me.

He was at the bar." The different clothes and setting had fooled me when I was deep into Bethany's memory, but now I was sure.

"I see," Bill said slowly. Bill seems to have almost total recall, and I could rely on him to have the man's face imprinted in his memory.

"I didn't think he was really a priest then, and now I know he was at the bar the night Farrell vanished," I said. "Dressed in regular clothes. Not, ah, the white collar and black shirt."

There was a pregnant pause.

Stan said, delicately, "But this man, this pretend priest, at the bar, even with two human companions, he could not have taken Farrell if Farrell didn't want to go."

I looked directly down at my hands and didn't say one word. I didn't want to be the one to say this out loud. Bill, wisely, didn't speak, either. At last, Stan Davis, head vampire of Dallas, said, "Someone went in the bathroom with Farrell, Bethany recalled. A vampire I didn't know."

I nodded, keeping my gaze directed elsewhere.

"Then this vampire must have helped to abduct Farrell."

"Is Farrell gay?" I asked, trying to sound as if my question had just oozed out of the walls.

"He prefers men, yes. You think—"

"I don't think a thing." I shook my head emphatically, to let him know how much I wasn't thinking. Bill squeezed my fingers. Ouch.

The silence was tense until the teenage-looking vamp returned with a burly human, one I'd seen in Bethany's memories. He didn't look like Bethany saw him, though; through her eyes, he was more robust, less fat; more glamorous, less unkempt. But he was recognizable as Re-Bar.

It was apparent to me immediately that something was wrong with the man. He followed after the girl vamp readily enough, and he smiled at everyone in the room; but that was off, wasn't it? Any human who sensed vampire trouble would be worried, no matter how clear his conscience. I got up and went over to him. He watched me approach with cheerful anticipation.

"Hi, buddy," I said gently, and shook his hand. I dropped it as soon as I decently could. I took a couple of steps back. I wanted to take some Advil and lie down.

"Well," I said to Stan, "he sure enough has a hole in his head."

Stan examined Re-Bar's skull with a skeptical eye. "Explain," he said.

"How ya doin', Mr. Stan?" Re-Bar asked. I was willing to bet no one had ever spoken to Stan Davis that way, at least not in the past five hundred years or so.

"I'm fine, Re-Bar. How are you?" I gave Stan credit for keeping it calm and level.

"You know, I just feel great," Re-Bar said, shaking his head in wonderment. "I'm the luckiest sumbitch on earth—'scuse me, lady."

"You're excused." I had to force the words out.

Bill said, "What has been done to him, Sookie?"

"He's had a hole burned in his head," I said. "I don't know how else to explain it, exactly. I can't tell how it was done, because I've never seen it before, but when I look in his thoughts, his memories, there's just a big old ragged hole. It's like Re-Bar needed a tiny tumor removed, but the surgeon took his spleen and maybe his appendix, too, just to be sure. You know when y'all take away someone's memory, you replace it with another one?" I waved a hand to show I meant all vampires. "Well, someone took a chunk out of Re-Bar's mind, and didn't replace it with anything. Like a lobotomy," I added, inspired. I read a lot. School was tough for me with my little problem, but reading by myself gave me a means of escape from my situation. I guess I'm self-educated.

"So whatever Re-Bar knew about Farrell's disappearance is lost," Stan said.

"Yep, along with a few components of Re-Bar's personality and a lot of other memories."

"Is he still functional?"

"Why, yeah, I guess so." I'd never encountered anything like this, never even realized it was possible. "But I don't know how effective a bouncer he'll be," I said, trying to be honest.

"He was hurt while he was working for us. We'll take care of him. Maybe he can clean the club after it closes," Stan said. I could tell from Stan's voice that he wanted to be sure I was marking this down mentally; that vampires could be compassionate, or at least fair.

"Gosh, that would be great!" Re-Bar beamed at his boss. "Thanks, Mr. Stan."

"Take him back home," Mr. Stan told his minion. She departed directly, with the lobotomized man in tow.

"Who could've done such a crude job on him?" Stan wondered. Bill did not reply, since he wasn't there to stick his neck out, but to guard me and do his own detecting when it was required. A tall red-haired female vampire came in, the one who'd been at the bar the night Farrell was taken.

"What did you notice the evening Farrell vanished?" I asked her, without thinking about protocol. She snarled at me, her white teeth standing out against her dark tongue and brilliant lipstick.

Stan said, "Cooperate." At once her face smoothed out, all expression vanishing like wrinkles in a bedspread when you run your hand over it.

"I don't remember," she said finally. So Bill's ability to recall what he'd seen in minute detail was a personal gift. "I don't remember seeing Farrell more than a minute or two."

"Can you do the same thing to Rachel that you did to the barmaid?" Stan asked.

"No," I said immediately, my voice maybe a little too emphatic. "I can't read vampire minds at all. Closed books."

Bill said, "Can you remember a blond—one of us—who looks about sixteen years old? One with ancient blue tattooing on his arms and torso?"

"Oh, yes," red-haired Rachel said instantly. "The tattoos were from the time of the Romans, I think. They were crude but interesting. I wondered about him, because I hadn't seen him coming here to the house to ask Stan for hunting privileges."

So vamps passing through someone else's territory were required to sign in at the visitors' center, so to speak. I filed that away for future reference.

"He was with a human, or at least had some conversation with him," the red-haired vampire continued. She was wearing blue jeans and a green sweater that looked incredibly hot to me. But vamps don't worry about the actual temperature. She looked at Stan, then Bill, who made a beckoning gesture to indicate he wanted whatever memories she had. "The human was dark-haired, and had a mustache, if I am recalling him correctly." She made a gesture with her hands, an open-fingered sweep that seemed to say, "They're all so much alike!"

After Rachel left, Bill asked if there was a computer in the house. Stan said there was, and looked at Bill with actual curiosity when Bill asked if he could use it for a moment, apologizing for not having his laptop. Stan nodded. Bill was about to leave the room when he hesitated and looked back at me. "Will you be all right, Sookie?" he asked.

"Sure." I tried to sound confident.

Stan said, "She will be fine. There are more people for her to see."

I nodded, and Bill left. I smiled at Stan, which is what I do when I'm strained. It's not a happy smile, but it's better than screaming.

"You and Bill have been together for how long?" Stan asked.

"For a few months." The less Stan knew about us, the happier I'd be.

"You are content with him?"

"Yes."

"You love him?" Stan sounded amused.

"None of your business," I said, grinning. "Did you mention there were more people I needed to check?"

Following the same procedure I had with Bethany, I held a variety of hands and checked a boring bunch of brains. Bethany had definitely been the most observant person in the bar. These people—another barmaid, the human bartender, and a frequent patron (a fangbanger) who'd actually volunteered for this—had dull, boring thoughts and limited powers of recollection. I did find out the bartender fenced stolen household goods on the side, and after the guy had left, I recommended to Stan that he get another employee behind the bar, or he'd be sucked into any police investigation. Stan seemed more impressed by this than I hoped he'd be. I didn't want him to get too enamored of my services.

Bill returned as I finished up the last bar employee, and he looked just a little pleased, so I concluded he'd been successful. Bill had been spending most of his waking hours on the computer lately, which had not been too popular an idea with me.

"The tattooed vampire," Bill said when Stan and I were the only two left in the room, "is named Godric, though for the past century he's gone by Godfrey. He's a renouncer." I don't know about Stan, but I was impressed. A few minutes on the computer, and Bill had done a neat piece of detective work.

Stan looked appalled, and I suppose I looked puzzled.

"He's allied himself with radical humans. He plans to commit suicide," Bill told me in a soft voice, since Stan was wrapped in thought. "This Godfrey plans to meet the sun. His existence has turned sour on him."

"So he's gonna take someone with him?" Godfrey would expose Farrell along with himself?

"He has betrayed us to the Fellowship," Stan said.

Betrayed is a word that packs a lot of melodrama, but I didn't dream of smirking when Stan said it. I'd heard of the Fellowship, though I'd never met anyone who claimed to actually belong to it. What the Klan was to African Americans, the Fellowship of the Sun was to vampires. It was the fastest-growing cult in America.

Once again, I was in deeper waters than I could swim in.

5 ~

THERE WERE LOTS OF HUMANS WHO HADN'T LIKED DIS-
covering they shared the planet with vampires. Despite
the fact that they had always done so—without knowing
it—once they believed that vampires were real, these
people were bent on the vampires' destruction. They
weren't any choosier about their methods of murder than
a rogue vampire was about his.

Rogue vampires were the backward-looking undead;
they hadn't wanted to be made known to humans any
more than the humans wanted to know about them.
Rogues refused to drink the synthetic blood that was the
mainstay of most vampires' diets these days. Rogues believed the only future for vampires lay in a return to secrecy and invisibility. Rogue vampires would slaughter

humans for the fun of it, now, because they actually welcomed a return of persecution of their own kind. Rogues saw it as a means of persuading mainstream vampires that secrecy was best for the future of their kind; and then, too, persecution was a form of population control.

Now I learned from Bill that there were vampires who became afflicted with terrible remorse, or perhaps ennui, after a long life. These renouncers planned to "meet the sun," the vampire term for committing suicide by staying out past daybreak.

Once again, my choice of boyfriend had led me down paths I never would have trod otherwise. I wouldn't have needed to know any of this, would never have even dreamed of dating someone definitely deceased, if I hadn't been born with the disability of telepathy. I was kind of a pariah to human guys. You can imagine how impossible it is to date someone whose mind you can read. When I met Bill, I began the happiest time of my life. But I'd undoubtedly encountered more trouble in the months I'd known him than I had in my entire twenty-six years previously. "So, you're thinking Farrell is already dead?" I asked, forcing myself to focus on the current crisis. I hated to ask, but I needed to know.

"Maybe," Stan said after a long pause.

"Possibly they're keeping him somewhere," said Bill. "You know how they invite the press to these . . . ceremonies."

Stan stared into space for a long moment. Then he stood. "The same man was in the bar and at the airport," he said, almost to himself. Stan, the geeky head vampire of Dallas, was pacing now, up and down the room. It was making me nuts, though saying so was out of the question. This was Stan's house, and his "brother" was missing. But I'm not one for long, brooding silences. I was tired, and I wanted to go to bed.

"So," I said, doing my best to sound brisk, "how'd they know I was going to be there?"

If there's anything worse than having a vampire stare at you, it's having two vampires stare at you.

"To know you were coming ahead of time . . . there is a traitor," Stan said. The air in the room began to tremble and crackle with the tension he was producing.

But I had a less dramatic idea. I picked up a notepad lying on the table and wrote, "MAYBE YOU'RE BUGGED." They both glared at me as if I'd offered them a Big Mac. Vampires, who individually have incredible and various powers, are sometimes oblivious to the fact that humans have developed some powers of their own. The two men gave each other a look of speculation, but neither of them offered any practical suggestion.

Well, to heck with them. I'd only seen this done in movies, but I figured if someone had planted a bug in this room, they'd done it in a hurry and they'd been scared to death. So the bug would be close and not well hidden. I shrugged off the gray jacket and kicked off my shoes. Since I was a human and had no dignity to lose in Stan's eyes, I dropped below the table and began crawling down its length, pushing the rolling chairs away as I went. For about the millionth time, I wished I'd worn slacks.

I'd gotten about two yards from Stan's legs when I saw something odd. There was a dark bump adhering to the underside of the blond wood of the table. I looked at it as closely as I could without a flashlight. It was not old gum.

Having found the little mechanical device, I didn't

know what to do. I crawled out, somewhat dustier for the experience, and found myself right at Stan's feet. He held out his hand and I took it reluctantly. Stan pulled gently, or it seemed gently, but suddenly I was on my feet facing him. He wasn't very tall, and I looked more into his eyes than I really wanted. I held up my finger in front of my face to be sure he was paying attention. I pointed under the table.

Bill left the room in a flash. Stan's face grew even whiter, and his eyes blazed. I looked anywhere but directly at him. I didn't want to be the sight filling his eyes while he digested the fact that someone had planted a bug in his audience chamber. He had indeed been betrayed, just not in the fashion he'd expected.

I cast around in my mind for something to do that would help. I beamed at Stan. Reaching up automatically to straighten my ponytail, I realized my hair was still in its roll on the back of my head, though considerably less neat. Fiddling with it gave me a good excuse to look down.

I was considerably relieved when Bill reappeared with Isabel and the dishwashing man, who was carrying a bowl of water. "I'm sorry, Stan," Bill said. "I'm afraid Farrell is already dead, if you go by what we have discovered this evening. Sookie and I will return to Louisiana tomorrow, unless you need us further." Isabel pointed to the table, and the man set the bowl down.

"You might as well," Stan replied, in a voice as cold as ice. "Send me your bill. Your master, Eric, was quite adamant about that. I will have to meet him someday." His tone indicated the meeting would not be pleasant for Eric.

Isabel said abruptly, "You stupid human! You've

spilled my drink!" Bill reached past me to snatch the bug from under the table and drop it in the water, and Isabel, walking even more smoothly to keep the water from slopping over the sides of the bowl, left the room. Her companion remained behind.

That had been disposed of simply enough. And it was at least possible that whoever had been listening in had been fooled by that little bit of dialogue. We all relaxed, now that the bug was gone. Even Stan looked a little less frightening.

"Isabel says you have reason to think Farrell might have been abducted by the Fellowship," the man said. "Maybe this young lady and I could go to the Fellowship Center tomorrow, and try to find out if there're plans for any kind of ceremony soon."

Bill and Stan regarded him thoughtfully.

"That's a good idea," Stan said. "A couple would seem less noticeable."

"Sookie?" Bill asked.

"Certainly none of you can go," I said. "I think maybe we could at least get the layout of the place. If you think there's really a chance Farrell's being held there." If I could find out more about the situation at the Fellowship Center, maybe I could keep the vampires from attacking. They sure weren't going to go down to the police station to file a missing persons report to prod the police into searching the Center. No matter how much the Dallas vampires wanted to remain within the boundaries of human law so they could successfully reap the benefits of mainstreaming, I knew that if a Dallas vampire was being held captive in the Center, humans would die right, left, and sideways. I could maybe prevent that from happening, and locate the missing Farrell, too.

"If this tattooed vampire is a renouncer and plans to meet the sun, taking Farrell with him, and if this is being arranged through the Fellowship, then this pretend priest who tried to grab you at the airport must work for them. They know you now," Bill pointed out. "You would have to wear your wig." He smiled with gratification. The wig had been his idea.

A wig in this heat. Oh, hell. I tried not to look petulant. After all, it would be better to have an itchy head than to be identified as a woman who associated with vampires, while I was visiting a Fellowship of the Sun Center. "It would be better if there were another human with me," I admitted, sorry as I was to involve anyone else in danger.

"This is Isabel's current man," Stan said. He was silent for a minute, and I guessed he was "beaming" at her, or however he contacted his underlings.

Sure enough, Isabel glided in. It must be handy, being able to summon people like that. You wouldn't need an intercom, or a telephone. I wondered how far away other vamps could be and still receive his message. I was kind of glad Bill couldn't signal me without words, because I'd feel too much like his slave girl. Could Stan summon humans the way he called his vamps? Maybe I didn't really want to know.

The man reacted to Isabel's presence the way a bird dog does when he senses quail. Or maybe it was more like a hungry man who gets served a big steak, and then has to wait for grace. You could almost see his mouth water. I hoped I didn't look like that when I was around Bill.

"Isabel, your man has volunteered to go with Sookie

to the Fellowship of the Sun Center. Can he be convincing as a potential convert?"

"Yes, I think he can," Isabel said, staring into the man's eyes.

"Before you go—are there visitors this evening?"

"Yes, one, from California."

"Where is he?"

"In the house."

"Has he been in this room?" Naturally, Stan would love the bug-planter to be a vamp or human he didn't know.

"Yes."

"Bring him."

A good five minutes later, Isabel returned with a tall blond vampire in tow. He must have been six foot four, or maybe even more. He was brawny, clean-shaven, and he had a mane of wheat-colored hair. I looked down at my feet immediately, just as I sensed Bill going immobile.

Isabel said, "This is Leif."

"Leif," Stan said smoothly, "welcome to my nest. This evening we have a problem here."

I stared at my toes, wishing more than I'd ever wished anything that I could be completely alone with Bill for two minutes and find out what the hell was going on, because this vampire wasn't any "Leif," and he wasn't from California.

It was Eric.

Bill's hand came into my line of vision and closed around mine. He gave my fingers a very careful little squeeze, and I returned it. Bill slid his arm around me, and I leaned against him. I needed to relax, by golly.

"How may I help you?" Eric—no, Leif, for the moment—asked courteously.

"It seems that someone has entered this room and performed an act of spying."

That seemed a nice way to put it. Stan wanted to keep the bugging a secret for right now, and in view of the fact that there surely was a traitor here, that was probably a great idea.

"I am a visitor to your nest, and I have no problem with you or any of yours."

Leif's calm and sincere denial was quite impressive, given that I knew for a fact that his whole presence was an imposture to further some unfathomable vampire purpose.

"Excuse me," I said, sounding as frail and human as I possibly could.

Stan looked quite irritated at the interruption, but screw him.

"The, uh, item, would have had to be put in here earlier than today," I said, trying to sound like I was sure Stan had already thought of this fact. "To get the details of our arrival in Dallas."

Stan was staring at me with no expression whatsoever.

In for a penny, in for a pound. "And excuse me, but I am really worn out. Could Bill take me back to the hotel now?"

"We will have Isabel take you back by yourself," Stan said dismissively.

"No, sir."

Behind the fake glasses, Stan's pale eyebrows flew up. "No?" He sounded as though he'd never heard the word.

"By the terms of my contract, I don't go anywhere without a vampire from my area. Bill is that vampire. I go nowhere without him, at night."

Stan gave me another good long stare. I was glad I had

found the bug and proved myself useful otherwise, or I wouldn't last long in Stan's bailiwick. "Go," he said, and Bill and I didn't waste any time. We couldn't help Eric if Stan came to suspect him, and we might quite possibly give him away. I would be by far the more likely to do that by some word or gesture, with Stan watching me. Vampires have studied humans for centuries, in the way predators learn as much as they can about their prey.

Isabel came out with us, and we got back into her Lexus for the ride back to the Silent Shore Hotel. The streets of Dallas, though not empty, were at least much quieter than when we'd arrived at the nest hours earlier. I estimated it was less than two hours until dawn.

"Thank you," I said politely when we pulled under the porte cochere of the hotel.

"My human will come to get you at three o'clock in the afternoon," Isabel told me.

Repressing the urge to say, "Yes, ma'am!" and click my heels together, I just told her that would be fine. "What's his name?" I asked.

"His name is Hugo Ayres," she said.

"Okay." I already knew that he was a quick man with an idea. I went into the lobby and waited for Bill. He was only seconds behind me, and we went up in the elevator in silence.

"Do you have your key?" he asked me at the room door.

I had been half-asleep. "Where's yours?" I asked, none too graciously.

"I'd just like to see you recover yours," he said.

Suddenly I was in a better mood. "Maybe you'd like to find it," I suggested.

A male vampire with a waist-length black mane

strolled down the hall, his arm around a plump girl with a head of curly red hair. When they'd entered a room farther down the hall, Bill began searching for the key.

He found it pretty fast.

Once we'd gotten inside, Bill picked me up and kissed me at length. We needed to talk, since a lot had happened during this long night, but I wasn't in the mood and he wasn't, either.

The nice thing about skirts, I discovered, was that they just slide up, and if you were only wearing a thong underneath, it could vanish in a jiffy. The gray jacket was on the floor, the white shell was discarded, and my arms were locked around Bill's neck before you could say, "Screw a vampire."

Bill was leaning against the sitting room wall trying to open his slacks with me still wrapped around him when there was a knock at the door.

"Damn," he whispered in my ear. "Go away," he said, somewhat louder. I wriggled against him and his breath caught in his throat. He pulled the bobby pins and the Hairagami out of my hair to let it roll down my back.

"I need to talk to you," said a familiar voice, somewhat muffled by the thick door.

"No," I moaned. "Say it isn't Eric." The only creature in the world we *had* to admit.

"It's Eric," said the voice.

I unlocked my legs from around Bill's waist, and he gently lowered me to the floor. In a real snit, I stomped into the bedroom to put on my bathrobe. To hell with re-buttoning all those clothes.

I came back out as Eric was telling Bill that Bill had done well this evening.

"And, of course, you were marvelous, Sookie," Eric said, taking in the pink, short bathrobe with a comprehensive glance. I looked up at him—and up, and up—and wished him at the bottom of the Red River, spectacular smile, golden hair, and all.

"Oh," I said malignantly, "thanks so much for coming up to tell us this. We couldn't have gone to bed without a pat on the back from *you*."

Eric looked as blandly delighted as he possibly could. "Oh, dear," he said. "Did I interrupt something? Would these—well, this—be yours, Sookie?" He held up the black string that had formerly been one side of my thong.

Bill said, "In a word, yes. Is there anything else you would like to discuss with us, Eric?" Ice would've been surprised by how cold Bill could sound.

"We haven't got time tonight," Eric said regretfully, "since daylight is so soon, and there are things I need to see to before I sleep. But tomorrow night we must meet. When you find out what Stan wants you to do, leave me a note at the desk, and we'll make an arrangement."

Bill nodded. "Good-bye, then," he said.

"You don't want a nightcap?" Was he hoping to be offered a bottle of blood? Eric's eyes went to the refrigerator, then to me. I was sorry I was wearing a thin nylon robe instead of something bulky and chenille. "Warm from the vessel?" Bill maintained a stony silence.

His gaze lingering on me until the last minute, Eric stepped through the door and Bill locked it behind him.

"You think he's listening outside?" I asked Bill, as he untied the sash of my robe.

"I don't care," Bill said, and bent his head to other things.

* * *

When I got up, about one o'clock in the afternoon, the hotel had a silent feel to it. Of course, most of the guests were sleeping. Maids would not come into a room during the day. I had noted the security last night—vampire guards. The daytime would be different, since daytime guarding was what the guests were paying so heavily for. I called room service for the first time in my life and ordered breakfast. I was as hungry as a horse, since I hadn't eaten last night at all. I was showered and wrapped up in my robe when the waiter knocked on the door, and after I'd made sure he was who he said he was, I let him in.

After my attempted abduction at the airport the day before, I wasn't taking anything for granted. I held the pepper spray down by my side as the young man laid out the food and the coffeepot. If he took one step toward the door behind which Bill slept in his coffin, I would zap him. But this fellow, Arturo, had been well trained, and his eyes never even strayed toward the bedroom. He never looked directly at me, either. He was thinking about me, though, and I wished I'd put on a bra before I let him in.

When he'd gone—and as Bill had instructed me, I'd added a tip to the room ticket I signed—I ate everything he'd brought: sausage and pancakes and a bowl of melon balls. Oh gosh, it tasted good. The syrup was real maple syrup, and the fruit was just ripe enough. The sausage was wonderful. I was glad Bill wasn't around to watch and make me feel uncomfortable. He didn't really like to see me eat, and he hated it if I ate garlic.

I brushed my teeth and hair and got my makeup situated. It was time to prepare for my visit to the Fellowship Center. I sectioned my hair and pinned it up, and got the wig out of its box. It was short and brown and really undistinguished. I had thought Bill was nuts when he'd suggested I get a wig, and I still wondered why it had occurred to him I might need one, but I was glad to have it. I had a pair of glasses like Stan's, serving the same camouflaging purpose, and I put them on. There was a little magnification in the bottom part, so I could legitimately claim they were reading glasses.

What did fanatics wear to go to a fanatic gathering place? In my limited experience, fanatics were usually conservative in dress, either because they were too preoccupied with other concerns to think about it or because they saw something evil in dressing stylishly. If I'd been at home, I'd have run to Wal-Mart and been right on the money, but I was here in the expensive, windowless Silent Shores. However, Bill had told me to call the front desk for anything I needed. So I did.

"Front desk," said a human who was trying to copy the smooth, cool voice of an older vampire. "How may I help you?" I felt like telling him to give it up. Who wants an imitation when the real thing is under the roof?

"This is Sookie Stackhouse in three-fourteen. I need a long denim skirt, size eight, and a pastel flowered blouse or knit top, same size."

"Yes, ma'am," he said, after a longish pause. "When shall I have those for you?"

"Soon." Gee, this was a lot of fun. "As a matter of fact, the sooner the better." I was getting into this. I loved being on someone else's expense account.

I watched the news while I waited. It was the typical news of any American city: traffic problems, zoning problems, homicide problems.

"A woman found dead last night in a hotel Dumpster has been identified," said a newscaster, his voice appropriately grave. He bent down the corners of his mouth to show serious concern. "The body of twenty-one-year-old Bethany Rogers was found behind the Silent Shore Hotel, famous for being Dallas's first hotel catering to the undead. Rogers had been killed by a single gunshot wound to the head. Police described the murder as 'execution-style.' Detective Tawny Kelner told our reporter that police are following up several leads." The screen image shifted from the artificially grim face to a genuinely grim one. The detective was in her forties, I thought, a very short woman with a long braid down her back. The camera shot swiveled to include the reporter, a small dark man with a sharply tailored suit. "Detective Kelner, is it true that Bethany Rogers worked at a vampire bar?"

The detective's frown grew even more formidable. "Yes, that's true," she said. "However, she was employed as a waitress, not an entertainer." An entertainer? What did entertainers do at the Bat's Wing? "She had only been working there a couple of months."

"Doesn't the site used to dump her body indicate that there's some kind of vampire involvement?" The reporter was more persistent than I would've been.

"On the contrary, I believe the site was chosen to send a message to the vampires," Kelner snapped, and then looked as if she regretted speaking. "Now, if you'll excuse me . . ."

"Of course, detective," the reporter said, a little dazed. "So, Tom," and he turned to face the camera, as if he could see through it back to the anchor in the station, "that's a provocative issue."

Huh?

The anchor realized the reporter wasn't making any sense, too, and quickly moved to another topic.

Poor Bethany was dead, and there wasn't anyone I could discuss that with. I pushed back tears; I hardly felt I had a right to cry for the girl. I couldn't help but wonder what had happened to Bethany Rogers last night after she'd been led from the room at the vampire nest. If there'd been no fang marks, surely a vampire hadn't killed her. It would be a rare vampire who could pass up the blood.

Sniffling from repressed tears and miserable with dismay, I sat on the couch and hunted through my purse to find a pencil. At last, I unearthed a pen. I used it to scratch up under the wig. Even in the air-conditioned dark of the hotel, it itched. In thirty minutes, there was a knock at the door. Once again, I looked through the peephole. There was Arturo again, with garments draped across his arm.

"We'll return the ones you don't want," he said, handing me the bundle. He tried not to stare at my hair.

"Thanks," I said, and tipped him. I could get used to this in a hurry.

It wasn't long until I was supposed to be meeting the Ayres guy, Isabel's honey bun. Dropping the robe where I stood, I looked at what Arturo'd brought me. The pale peachy blouse with the off-white flowers, that would do, and the skirt . . . hmmm. He hadn't been able to find denim, apparently, and the two he'd brought were khaki. That would be all right, I figured, and I pulled one on. It looked too tight for the effect I needed, and I was glad he'd brought another style. It was just right for the image.

I slid my feet into flat sandals, put some tiny earrings in my pierced ears, and I was good to go. I even had a battered straw purse to carry with the ensemble. Unfortunately, it was my regular purse. But it fit right in. I dumped out my identifying items, and wished I had thought of that earlier instead of at the last minute. I wondered what other crucial safety measures I might have forgotten.

I stepped out into the silent corridor. It was exactly as it had been the night before. There were no mirrors and no windows, and the feeling of enclosure was complete. The dark red of the carpet and the federal blue, red, and cream of the wallpaper didn't help. The elevator snicked open when I touched the call button, and I rode down by myself. No elevator music, even. The Silent Shore was living up to its name.

There were armed guards on either side of the elevator when I reached the lobby. They were looking at the main doors to the hotel. Those doors were obviously locked. There was a television set mounted by the doors, and it showed the sidewalk outside of the doors. Another television set showed a wider view.

I thought a terrible attack must be imminent and I froze, my heart racing, but after a few seconds of calm I figured out they must be there all the time. This was why vampires stayed here, and at other similar specialty hotels. No one would get past these guards to the elevators. No one would make it into the hotel rooms where sleeping and helpless vampires lay. This was why the fee for the hotel was exorbitant. The two guards on duty at the moment were both huge, and wearing the black livery of the hotel. (Ho, hum. Everyone seemed to think vampires were obsessed with black.) The guards' sidearms seemed gigantic to me, but then, I'm not too familiar with guns. The men glanced at me and then went back to their bored forward stare.

Even the desk clerks were armed. There were shotguns on racks behind the counter. I wondered how far they would go to protect their guests. Would they really shoot other humans, intruders? How would the law handle it?

A man wearing glasses sat in one of the padded chairs that punctuated the marble floor of the lobby. He was about thirty, tall and lanky, with sandy hair. He was wearing a suit, a lightweight summer khaki suit, with a conservative tie and penny loafers. The dishwasher, sure enough.

"Hugo Ayres?" I asked.

He sprang up to shake my hand. "You must be Sookie? But your hair . . . last night, you were blond?"

"I am. I'm wearing a wig."

"It looks very natural."

"Good. Are you ready?"

"My car's outside." He touched my back briefly to point me in the right direction, as if I wouldn't see the doors otherwise. I appreciated the courtesy, if not the implication. I was trying to get a feel for Hugo Ayres. He wasn't a broadcaster.

"How long have you been dating Isabel?" I asked as we buckled up in his Caprice.

"Ah, um, I guess about eleven months," Hugo Ayres said. He had big hands, with freckles on the back. I was surprised he wasn't living in the suburbs with a wife with streaked hair and two sandy children.

"Are you divorced?" I asked impulsively. I was sorry when I saw the grief cross his face.

"Yes," he said. "Pretty recently."

"Too bad." I started to ask about the children, decided it was none of my business. I could read him well enough to know he had a little girl, but I couldn't discover her name and age.

"Is it true you can read minds?" he asked.

"Yes, it's true."

"No wonder you're so attractive to them."

Well, *ouch*, Hugo. "That's probably a good part of the reason," I said, keeping my voice flat and even. "What's your day job?"

"I'm a lawyer," Hugo said.

"No wonder you're so attractive to them," I said, in the most neutral voice I could manage.

After a longish silence, Hugo said, "I guess I deserved that."

"Let's move on past it. Let's get a cover story."

"Could we be brother and sister?"

"That's not out of the question. I've seen brother and sister teams that looked less like each other than we do. But I think boyfriend-girlfriend would account for the gaps in our knowledge of each other more, if we get separated and questioned. I'm not predicting that'll happen, and I'd be amazed if it did, but as brother and sister we'd have to know all about each other."

"You're right. Why don't we say that we met at church? You just moved to Dallas, and I met you in Sunday school at Glen Craigie Methodist. That's actually my church."

"Okay. How about I'm manager of a . . . restaurant?"

From working at Merlotte's, I thought I could be convincing in the role if I wasn't questioned too intensively.

He looked a little surprised. "That's just different enough to sound good. I'm not much of an actor, so if I just stick to being me, I'll be okay."

"How did you meet Isabel?" Of course I was curious.

"I represented Stan in court. His neighbors sued to have the vampires barred from the neighborhood. They lost." Hugo had mixed feelings about his involvement with a vampire woman, and wasn't entirely sure he should've won the court case, either. In fact, Hugo was deeply ambivalent about Isabel.

Oh, good, that made this errand much more frightening. "Did that get in the papers? The fact that you represented Stan Davis?"

He looked chagrined. "Yes, it did. Dammit, someone at the Center might recognize my name. Or me, from my picture being in the papers."

"But that might be even better. You can tell them you saw the error of your ways, after you'd gotten to know vampires."

Hugo thought that over, his big freckled hands moving restlessly on the steering wheel. "Okay," he said finally. "Like I said, I'm not much of an actor, but I think I can bring that off."

I acted all the time, so I wasn't too worried about myself. Taking a drink order from a guy while pretending you don't know whether he's speculating on whether you're blond all the way down can be excellent acting training. You can't blame people—mostly—for what they're thinking on the inside. You have to learn to rise above it.

I started to suggest to the lawyer that he hold my hand if things got tense today, to send me thoughts that I could act on. But his ambivalence, the ambivalence that wafted from him like a cheap cologne, gave me pause. He might be in sexual thrall to Isabel, he might even love her and the danger she represented, but I didn't think his heart and mind were wholly committed to her.

In an unpleasant moment of self-examination, I wondered if the same could be said of Bill and me. But now was not the time and place to ponder this. I was getting enough from Hugo's mind to wonder if he was completely trustworthy in terms of this little mission of ours. It was just a short step from there to wondering how safe I was in his company. I also wondered how much Hugo Ayres actually knew about me. He hadn't been in the room when I'd been working the night before. Isabel hadn't struck me as a chatterer. It was possible he didn't know much about me.

The four-lane road, running through a huge suburb, was lined with all the usual fast-food places and chain stores of all kinds. But gradually, the shopping gave way to residences, and the concrete to greenery. The traffic seemed unrelenting. I could never live in a place this size, cope with this on a daily basis.

Hugo slowed and put on his turn signal when we came to a major intersection. We were about to turn into the parking lot of a large church; at least, it had formerly been a church. The sanctuary was huge, by Bon Temps standards. Only Baptists could count that kind of attendance in my neck of the woods, and that's if all their congregations joined together. The two-story sanctuary was flanked by two long one-story wings. The whole building was white-painted brick, and all the windows were tinted. There was a chemically green lawn surrounding the whole, and a huge parking lot.

The sign on the well-tended lawn read THE FELLOWSHIP OF THE SUN CENTER—ONLY JESUS ROSE FROM THE DEAD.

I snorted as I opened my door and emerged from Hugo's car. "That right there is false," I pointed out to my companion. "Lazarus rose from the dead, too. Jerks can't even get their scripture right."

"You better banish that attitude from your head," Hugo warned me, as he got out and hit the lock button. "It'll make you careless. These people are dangerous. They've accepted responsibility, publicly, for handing over two vampires to the Drainers, saying at least humanity can benefit from the death of a vampire in some way."

"They deal with Drainers?" I felt sick. Drainers followed an extremely hazardous profession. They trapped vampires, wound them around with silver chains, and drained the blood from them for sale on the black market. "These people in here have handed over vampires to the Drainers?"

"That's what one of their members said in a newspaper interview. Of course, the leader was on the news the next day, denying the report vehemently, but I think that was just a smoke screen. The Fellowship kills vampires any way they can, thinks they're unholy and an abomination, and they're capable of anything. If you're a vampire's best friend, they can bring tremendous pressure to bear. Just remember that, every time you open your mouth in here."

"You, too, Mr. Ominous Warning."

We walked to the building slowly, looking it over as

we went. There were about ten other cars in the parking lot, ranging from aging and dented to brand new and up-scale. My favorite was a pearly white Lexus, so nice it might almost have belonged to a vampire.

"Someone's doing well out of the hate business," Hugo observed.

"Who's the head of this place?"

"Guy named Steve Newlin."

"Bet this is his car."

"That would account for the bumper sticker."

I nodded. It read TAKE THE UN OUT OF UNDEAD. Dangling from the mirror inside was a replica—well, maybe a replica—of a stake.

This was a busy place, for a Saturday afternoon. There were children using the swing set and jungle gym in a fenced yard to the side of the building. The kids were being watched by a bored teenager, who looked up every now and then from picking at his nails. Today was not as hot as the day before—summer was losing its doomed last stand, and thank God for that—and the door of the building was propped open to take advantage of the beautiful day and moderate temperature.

Hugo took my hand, which made me jump until I realized he was trying to make us look loverlike. He had zero interest in me personally, which was fine with me. After a second's adjustment we managed to look fairly natural. The contact made Hugo's mind just that more open to me, and I could tell that he was anxious but resolute. He found touching me distasteful, which was a little bit too strong a feeling for me to feel comfortable about; lack of attraction was peachy, but this actual distaste made me uneasy. There was something behind that feeling, some basic attitude . . . but there were people ahead of us, and I pulled my mind back to my job. I could feel my lips pull into their smile.

Bill had been careful to leave my neck alone last night, so I didn't have to worry about concealing any fang marks, and in my new outfit and on this lovely day it was easier to look carefree as we nodded at a middle-aged couple who were on their way out.

We passed into the dimness of the building, into what must have been the Sunday school wing of the church. There were fresh signs outside the rooms up and down the corridor, signs that read BUDGETING AND FINANCE, ADVERTISING, and most ominously, MEDIA RELATIONS.

A woman in her forties came out of a door farther down the hall, and turned to face us. She looked pleasant, even sweet, with lovely skin and short brown hair. Her definitely pink lipstick matched her definitely pink fingernails, and her lower lip was slightly pouty, which gave her an unexpectedly sensuous air; it sat with odd provocation on her pleasantly round body. A denim skirt and a knit shirt, neatly tucked in, were the echo of my own outfit, and I patted myself on the back mentally.

"Can I help you?" she asked, looking hopeful.

"We want to find out more about the Fellowship," Hugo said, and he seemed every bit as nice and sincere as our new friend. She had on a nametag, I noticed, which read S. NEWLIN.

"We're glad you're here," she said. "I'm the wife of the director, Steve Newlin. I'm Sarah." She shook hands with Hugo, but not with me. Some women don't believe in shaking hands with another woman, so I didn't worry about it.

We exchanged pleasedtomeetyou's, and she waved a manicured hand toward the double doors at the end of the hall. "If you'll just come with me, I'll show you where we get things done." She laughed a little, as if the idea of meeting goals was a touch ludicrous.

All of the doors in the hall were open, and within the rooms there was evidence of perfectly open activity. If the Newlins' organization was keeping prisoners or conducting covert ops, it was accomplishing its goals in some other part of the building. I looked at everything as hard as I could, determined to fill myself with information. But so far the interior of the Fellowship of the Sun was as blindingly clean as the outside, and the people hardly seemed sinister or devious.

Sarah covered ground ahead of us with an easy walk. She clutched a bundle of file folders to her chest and chattered over her shoulder as she moved at a pace that seemed relaxed, but actually was a bit challenging. Hugo and I, abandoning the handholding, had to step out to keep up.

This building was proving to be far larger than I'd estimated. We'd entered at the far end of one wing. Now we crossed the large sanctuary of the former church, set up for meetings like any big hall, and we passed into the other wing. This wing was divided into fewer and larger rooms; the one closest to the sanctuary was clearly the office of the former pastor. Now it had a sign on the door that read G. STEVEN NEWLIN, DIRECTOR.

This was the only closed door I'd seen in the building.

Sarah knocked and, having waited for a moment, entered. The tall, lanky man behind the desk stood to beam at us with an air of pleased expectancy. His head didn't seem quite big enough for his body. His eyes were a hazy blue, his nose was on the beaky side, and his hair was almost the same dark brown as his wife's, with a threading of gray. I don't know what I'd been expecting in a fanatic, but this man was not it. He seemed a little amused by his own life.

He'd been talking to a tall woman with iron gray hair. She was wearing a pair of slacks and a blouse, but she looked as if she'd have been more comfortable in a business suit. She was formidably made-up, and she was less than pleased about something—maybe our interruption.

"What can I do for you today?" Steve Newlin asked, indicating that Hugo and I should be seated. We took green leather armchairs pulled up opposite his desk, and Sarah, unasked, plopped down in a smaller chair that was against the wall on one side. "Excuse me, Steve," she said to her husband. "Listen, can I get you two some coffee? Soda?"

Hugo and I looked at each other and shook our heads.

"Honey, this is—oh, I didn't even ask your names?" She looked at us with charming ruefulness.

"I'm Hugo Ayres, and this is my girlfriend, Marigold."

Marigold? Was he *nuts*? I kept my smile pasted on my face with an effort. Then I saw the pot of marigolds on the table beside Sarah, and at least I could understand his selection. We'd certainly made a large mistake already; we should have talked about this on the drive over. It stood to reason that if the Fellowship was responsible for the bug, the Fellowship knew the name of Sookie Stackhouse. Thank God Hugo had figured that out.

"Don't we know Hugo Ayres, Sarah?" Steve Newlin's

face had the perfect quizzical expression—brow slightly wrinkled, eyebrows raised inquiringly, head tilted to one side.

"Ayres?" said the gray-haired woman. "By the way, I'm Polly Blythe, the Fellowship ceremonies officer."

"Oh, Polly, I'm sorry, I got sidetracked." Sarah tilted her head right back. Her forehead wrinkled, too. Then it smoothed out and she beamed at her husband. "Wasn't an Ayres the lawyer representing the vampires in University Park?"

"So he was," Steve said, leaning back in his chair and crossing his long legs. He waved to someone passing by in the corridor and wrapped his laced fingers around his knee. "Well, it's very interesting that you're paying us a call, Hugo. Can we hope that you've seen the other side of the vampire question?" Satisfaction rolled off Steve Newlin like scent off a skunk.

"It's appropriate that you should put it that way—" Hugo began, but Steve's voice just kept rolling on:

"The bloodsucking side, the dark side of vampire existence? Have you found that they want to kill us all, dominate us with their foul ways and empty promises?"

I knew my eyes were as round as plates. Sarah was nodding thoughtfully, still looking as sweet and bland as a vanilla pudding. Polly looked as if she were having some really grim kind of orgasm. Steve said—and he was still smiling—"You know, eternal life on this earth may sound good, but you'll lose your soul and eventually, when we catch up with you—maybe not me, of course, maybe my son, or eventually my granddaughter—we'll stake you and burn you and then you'll be in true hell. And it won't be any the better for having been put off.

God has a special corner for vampires who've used up humans like toilet tissue and then flushed . . ."

Well, ick. This was going downhill in a hurry. And what I was getting off of Steve was just this endless, gloating satisfaction, along with a heavy dash of cleverness. Nothing concrete or informative.

"Excuse me, Steve," said a deep voice. I swiveled in my chair to see a handsome black-haired man with a crewcut and a bodybuilder's muscles. He smiled at all of us in the room with the same goodwill they were all showing. It had impressed me earlier. Now, I thought it was just creepy. "Our guest is asking for you."

"Really? I'll be there in a minute."

"I wish you would come now. I'm sure your guests wouldn't mind waiting?" Black Crewcut glanced at us appealingly. Hugo was thinking of some deep place, a flash of thought which seemed very peculiar to me.

"Gabe, I'll be there when I've finished with our visitors," Steve said very firmly.

"Well, Steve . . ." Gabe wasn't willing to give up that easily, but he got a flash from Steve's eyes and Steve sat up and uncrossed his legs, and Gabe got the message. He shot Steve a look that was anything but worshipful, but he left.

That exchange was promising. I wondered if Farrell was behind some locked door, and I could picture myself returning to the Dallas nest, telling Stan exactly where his nest brother was trapped. And then . . .

Uh-oh. And then Stan would come and attack the Fellowship of the Sun and kill all the members and free Farrell, and then . . .

Oh dear.

*   *   *

"We just wanted to know if you have some upcoming events we can attend, something that'll give us an idea of the scope of the programs here." Hugo's voice sounded mildly inquiring, nothing more. "Since Miss Blythe is here, maybe she can answer that."

I noticed Polly Blythe glanced at Steve before she spoke, and I noticed that his face remained shuttered. Polly Blythe was very pleased to be asked to give information, and she was very pleased about Hugo and me being there at the Fellowship.

"We do have some upcoming events," the gray-haired woman said. "Tonight, we're having a special lock-in, and following that, we have a Sunday dawn ritual."

"That sounds interesting," I said. "Literally, at dawn?"

"Oh, yes, exactly. We call the weather service and everything," Sarah said, laughing.

Steve said, "You'll never forget one of our dawn services. It's inspiring beyond belief."

"What kind of—well, what happens?" Hugo asked.

"You'll see the evidence of God's power right before you," Steve said, smiling.

That sounded really, really ominous. "Oh, Hugo," I said. "Doesn't that sound exciting?"

"It sure does. What time does the lock-in start?"

"At six thirty. We want our members to get here before *they* rise."

For a second I envisioned a tray of rolls set in some warm place. Then I realized Steve meant he wanted members to get here before the vampires rose for the night.

"But what about when your congregation goes home?" I could not refrain from asking.

"Oh, you must not have gone to a lock-in as a

teenager!" Sarah said. "It's loads of fun. Everyone comes and brings their sleeping bags, and we eat and have games and Bible readings and a sermon, and we all spend the night actually in the church." I noticed that the Fellowship was a church, in Sarah's eyes, and I was pretty sure that reflected the view of the rest of the management. If it looked like a church, and functioned like a church, then it was a church, no matter what its tax status was.

I'd been to a couple of lock-ins as a teenager, and I'd scarcely been able to endure the experience. A bunch of kids locked in a building all night, closely chaperoned, provided with an endless stream of movies and junk food, activities and sodas. I had suffered through the mental bombardment of teenage hormone-fueled ideas and impulses, the shrieking and the tantrums.

This would be different, I told myself. These would be adults, and purposeful adults, at that. There weren't likely to be a million bags of chips around, and there might be decent sleeping arrangements. If Hugo and I came, maybe we'd get a chance to search around the building and rescue Farrell, because I was sure that he was the one who was going to get to meet the dawn on Sunday, whether or not he got to choose.

Polly said, "You'd be very welcome. We have plenty of food and cots."

Hugo and I looked at each other uncertainly.

"Why don't we just go tour the building now, and you can see all there is to see? Then you can make up your minds," Sarah suggested. I took Hugo's hand, got a wallop of ambivalence. I was filled with dismay at Hugo's torn emotions. He thought, *Let's get out of here.*

I jettisoned my previous plans. If Hugo was in such

turmoil, we didn't need to be here. Questions could wait until later. "We should go back to my place and pack our sleeping bags and pillows," I said brightly. "Right, baby?"

"And I've got to feed the cat," Hugo said. "But we'll be back here at . . . six thirty, you said?"

"Gosh, Steve, don't we have some bedrolls left in the supply room? From when that other couple came to stay here for a while?"

"We'd love to have you stay until everyone gets here," Steve urged us, his smile as radiant as ever. I knew we were being threatened, and I knew we needed to get out, but all I was receiving from the Newlins psychically was a wall of determination. Polly Blythe seemed to actually be almost—gloating. I hated to push and probe, now that I was aware they had some suspicion of us. If we could just get out of here right now, I promised myself I'd never come back. I'd give up this detecting for the vampires, I'd just tend bar and sleep with Bill.

"We really do need to go," I said with firm courtesy. "We are so impressed with you all here, and we want to come to the lock-in tonight, but there is still enough time before then for us to get some of our errands done. You know how it is when you work all week. All those little things pile up."

"Hey, they'll still be there when the lock-in ends to-morrow!" Steve said. "You need to stay, both of you."

There wasn't any way to get out of here without drag-ging everything out into the open. And I wasn't going to be the first one to do that, not while there was any hope left we could get out. There were lots of people around. We turned left when we came out of Steve Newlin's office, and with Steve ambling behind us, and Polly to our right, and Sarah ahead of us, we went down the hall. Every time we passed an open door, someone inside would call, "Steve, can I see you for a minute?" or "Steve, Ed says we have to change the wording on this!" But aside from a blink or a minor tremor in his smile, I could not see much reaction from Steve Newlin to these constant demands.

I wondered how long this movement would last if Steve were removed. Then I was ashamed of myself for thinking this, because what I meant was, if Steve were killed. I was beginning to think either Sarah or Polly would be able to step into his shoes, if they were allowed, because both seemed made of steel.

All the offices were perfectly open and innocent, if you considered the premise on which the organization was founded to be innocent. These all looked like average, rather cleaner-cut-than-normal Americans, and there were even a few people who were non-Caucasian.

And one nonhuman.

We passed a tiny, thin Hispanic woman in the hall, and as her eyes flicked over to us, I caught a mental signature I'd only felt once before. Then, it came from Sam Merlotte. This woman, like Sam, was a shapeshifter, and her big eyes widened as she caught the waft of "difference" from me. I tried to catch her gaze, and for a minute we stared at each other, me trying to send her a message, and her trying not to receive it.

"Did I tell you the first church to occupy this site was built in the early sixties?" Sarah was saying, as the tiny woman went on down the hall at a fast clip. She glanced back over her shoulder, and I met her eyes again. Hers were frightened. Mine said, "Help."

"No," I said, startled at the sudden turn in the conversation.

"Just a little bit more," Sarah coaxed. "We'll have seen the whole church." We'd come to the last door at the end of the corridor. The corresponding door on the other wing had led to the outside. The wings had seemed to be exactly balanced from the outside of the church. My observations had obviously been faulty, but still . . .

"It's certainly a large place," said Hugo agreeably. Whatever ambivalent emotions had been plaguing him seemed to have subsided. In fact, he no longer seemed at all concerned. Only someone with no psychic sense at all could fail to be worried about this situation.

That would be Hugo. No psychic sense at all. He looked only interested when Polly opened the last door, the door flat at the end of the corridor. It should have led outside.

Instead, it led down.

6 ~

Y OU KNOW, I HAVE A TOUCH OF CLAUSTROPHOBIA," I said instantly. "I didn't know many Dallas buildings had a basement, but I have to say, I just don't believe I want to see it." I clung to Hugo's arm and tried to smile in a charming but self-deprecating way.

Hugo's heart was beating like a drum because he was scared shitless—I'll swear he was. Faced with those stairs, somehow his calm was eroding again. What was with Hugo? Despite his fear, he gamely patted my shoulder and smiled apologetically at our companions. "Maybe we should go," he murmured.

"But I really think you should see what we've got underground. We actually have a bomb shelter," Sarah said, almost laughing in her amusement. "And it's fully equipped, isn't it, Steve?"

"Got all kinds of things down there," Steve agreed. He still looked relaxed, genial, and in charge, but I no longer saw those as benign characteristics. He stepped forward, and since he was behind us, I had to step forward or risk him touching me, which I found I very much did not want.

"Come on," Sarah said enthusiastically. "I'll bet Gabe's down here, and Steve can go on and see what Gabe wanted while we look at the rest of the facility." She trotted down the stairs as quickly as she'd moved down the hall, her round butt swaying in a way I probably would have considered cute if I hadn't been just on the edge of terrified.

Polly waved us down ahead of her, and down we went. I was going along with this because Hugo seemed absolutely confident that no harm would come to him. I was picking that up very clearly. His earlier fear had completely abated. It was as though he'd resigned himself to some program, and his ambivalence had vanished. Vainly, I wished he were easier to read. I turned my focus on Steve Newlin, but what I got from him was a thick wall of self-satisfaction.

We moved farther down the stairs, despite the fact that my steps had slowed, and then become slower again. I could tell Hugo was convinced that he would get to walk back up these stairs: after all, he was a civilized person. These were all civilized people.

Hugo really couldn't imagine that anything irreparable could happen to him, because he was a middle-class white American with a college education, as were all the people on the stairs with us.

I had no such conviction. I was not a wholly civilized person.

That was a new and interesting thought, but like many of my ideas that afternoon, it had to be stowed away, to be explored at leisure. If I ever had leisure again.

At the base of the stairs there was another door, and Sarah knocked on it in a pattern. Three fast, skip, two fast, my brain recorded. I heard locks shooting back.

Black Crewcut—Gabe—opened the door. "Hey, you brought me some visitors," he said enthusiastically. "Good show!" His golf shirt was tucked neatly into his pleated Dockers, his Nikes were new and spotless, and he was shaved as clean as a razor could get. I was willing to bet he did fifty push-ups every morning. There was an undercurrent of excitement in his every move and gesture; Gabe was really pumped about something.

I tried to "read" the area for life, but I was too agitated to concentrate.

"I'm glad you're here, Steve," Gabe said. "While Sarah is showing our visitors the shelter, maybe you can give our guest room a look-see." He nodded his head to the door in the right side of the narrow concrete hall. There was another door at the end of it, and a door to the left.

I hated it down here. I had pleaded claustrophobia to get out of this. Now that I had been coerced into coming down the stairs, I was finding that it was a true failing of mine. The musty smell, the glare of the artificial light, and the sense of enclosure . . . I hated it all. I didn't want to stay here. My palms broke out in a sweat. My feet felt anchored to the ground. "Hugo," I whispered. "I don't

want to do this." There was very little act in the despera-
tion in my voice. I didn't like to hear it, but it was there.

"She really needs to get back upstairs," Hugo said
apologetically. "If you all don't mind, we'll just go back
up and wait for you there."

I turned around, hoping this would work, but I found
myself looking up into Steve's face. He wasn't smiling
anymore. "I think you two need to wait in the other room
over there, until I'm through with my business. Then,
we'll talk." His voice brooked no discussion, and Sarah
opened the door to disclose a bare little room with two
chairs and two cots.

"No," I said, "I can't do that," and I shoved Steve as
hard as I could. I am very strong, very strong indeed,
since I've had vampire blood, and despite his size, he
staggered. I nipped up the stairs as fast as I could move,
but a hand closed around my ankle, and I fell most
painfully. The edges of the stairs hit me everywhere,
across my left cheekbone, my breasts, my hipbones, my
left knee. It hurt so much I almost gagged.

"Here, little lady," said Gabe, hauling me to my feet.

"What have you—how could you hurt her like that?"
Hugo was sputtering, genuinely upset. "We come here
thinking of joining your group, and this is the way you
treat us?"

"Drop the act," Gabe advised, and he twisted my arm
behind my back before I had gotten my wits back from
the fall. I gasped with the new pain, and he propelled me
into the room, at the last minute grabbing my wig and
yanking it off my head. Hugo stepped in behind me,
though I gasped, *"No!"* and then they shut the door behind him.

And we heard it lock.

And that was that.

"Sookie," Hugo said, "there's a dent across your cheek-bone."

"No shit," I muttered weakly.

"Are you badly hurt?"

"What do you think?"

He took me literally. "I think you have bruises and maybe a concussion. You didn't break any bones, did you?"

"Not but one or two," I said.

"And you're obviously not hurt badly enough to cut out the sarcasm," Hugo said. If he could be angry with me, it would make him feel better, I could tell, and I wondered why. But I didn't wonder too hard. I was pretty sure I knew.

I was lying on one of the cots, an arm across my face, trying to keep private and do some thinking. We hadn't been able to hear much happening in the hall outside. Once I thought I'd heard a door opening, and we'd heard muted voices, but that was all. These walls were built to withstand a nuclear blast, so I guess the quiet was to be expected.

"Do you have a watch?" I asked Hugo.

"Yes. It's five thirty."

A good two hours until the vampires rose.

I let the quiet go on. When I knew hard-to-read Hugo must have relapsed into his own thoughts, I opened my mind and I listened with complete concentration.

Not supposed to happen like this, don't like this, surely everything'll be okay, what about when we need to go to

the bathroom, I can't haul it out in front of her, maybe Is-
abel won't ever know, I should have known after that girl
last night, how can I get out of this still practicing law, if
I begin to distance myself after tomorrow maybe I can
kind of ease out of it . . .

I pressed my arm against my eyes hard enough to hurt,
to stop myself from jumping up and grabbing a chair and
beating Hugo Ayres senseless. At present, he didn't fully
understand my telepathy, and neither did the Fellowship,
or they wouldn't have left me in here with him.

Or maybe Hugo was as expendable to them as he was
to me. And he certainly would be to the vampires; I
could hardly wait to tell Isabel that her boy toy was a
traitor.

That sobered up my bloodlust. When I realized what
Isabel would do to Hugo, I realized that I would take no
real satisfaction in it if I witnessed it. In fact, it would ter-
rify me and sicken me.

But part of me thought he richly deserved it.

To whom did this conflicted lawyer owe fealty?

One way to find out.

I sat up painfully, pressed my back against the wall. I
would heal pretty fast—the vampire blood, again—but I
was still a human, and I still felt awful. I knew my face
was badly bruised, and I was willing to believe my cheekbone was fractured. The left side of my face was swelling
something fierce. But my legs weren't broken, and I
could still run, given the chance; that was the main thing.

Once I was braced and as comfortable as I was going
to get, I said, "Hugo, how long have you been a traitor?"

He flushed an incredible red. "To whom? To Isabel, or
to the human race?"

"Take your pick."

"I betrayed the human race when I took the side of the vampires in court. If I'd had any idea of what they were . . . I took the case sight unseen, because I thought it would be an interesting legal challenge. I have always been a civil rights lawyer, and I was convinced vampires had the same civil rights as other people."

Mr. Floodgates. "Sure," I said.

"To deny them the right to live anywhere they wanted to, that was un-American, I thought," Hugo continued. He sounded bitter and world-weary.

He hadn't *seen* bitter, yet.

"But you know what, Sookie? Vampires aren't American. They aren't even black or Asian or Indian. They aren't Rotarians or Baptists. They're all just plain vampires. That's their color and their religion and their nationality."

Well, that was what happened when a minority went underground for thousands of years. Duh.

"At the time, I thought if Stan Davis wanted to live on Green Valley Road, or in the Hundred Acre Wood, that was his right as an American. So I defended him against the neighborhood association, and I won. I was real proud of myself. Then I got to know Isabel, and I took her to bed one night, feeling real daring, really the big man, the emancipated thinker."

I stared at him, not blinking or saying a word.

"As you know, the sex is great, the best. I was in thrall to her, couldn't get enough. My practice suffered. I started seeing clients only in the afternoon, because I couldn't get up in the morning. I couldn't make my court dates in the morning. I couldn't leave Isabel after dark."

This sounded like an alcoholic's tale, to me. Hugo had become addicted to vampiric sex. I found the concept fascinating and repellent.

"I started doing little jobs she found for me. This past month, I've been going over there and doing the housekeeping chores, just so I can hang around Isabel. When she wanted me to bring the bowl of water into the dining room, I was excited. Not at doing such a menial task—I'm a *lawyer*, for God's sake! But because the Fellowship had called me, asked me if I could give them any insight into what the vampires of Dallas intended to do. At the time they called, I was mad at Isabel. We'd had a fight about the way she treated me. So I was open to listening to them. I'd heard your name pass between Stan and Isabel, so I passed it on to the Fellowship. They have a guy who works for Anubis Air. He found out when Bill's plane was coming in, and they tried to grab you at the airport so they could find out what the vamps wanted with you. What they'd do to get you back. When I came in with the bowl of water, I heard Stan or Bill call you by name, so I knew they'd missed you at the airport. I felt like I had something to tell them, to make up for losing the bug I'd put in the conference room."

"You betrayed Isabel," I said. "And you betrayed me, though I'm human, like you."

"Yes," he said. He didn't look me in the eyes.

"What about Bethany Rogers?"

"The waitress?" He was stalling.

"The dead waitress," I said.

"They took her," he said, shaking his head from side to

side, as if he were actually saying, No, they couldn't have done what they did. "They took her, and I didn't know what they were going to do. I knew she was the only one who'd seen Farrell with Godfrey, and I'd told them that. When I got up today and I heard she'd been found dead, I just couldn't believe it."

"They abducted her after you told them she'd been at Stan's. After you told them she was the only true witness."

"Yes, they must have."

"You called them last night."

"Yes, I have a cell phone. I went out in the backyard and I called. I was really taking a chance, because you know how well the vamps can hear, but I called." He was trying to convince himself that had been a brave, bold thing to do. Place a phone call from vamp headquarters to lay the finger on poor, pathetic Bethany, who'd ended up shot in an alley.

"She was shot after you betrayed her."

"Yes, I . . . I heard that on the news."

"Guess who did that, Hugo."

"I . . . just don't know."

"Sure you do, Hugo. She'd been an eyewitness. And she was a lesson, a lesson to the vampires. 'This is what we'll do to people who work for you or make their living from you, if they go against the Fellowship.' What do you think they're going to do with you, Hugo?"

"I've been helping them," he said, surprised.

"Who else knows that?"

"No one."

"So who would die? The lawyer that helped Stan Davis live where he wanted."

Hugo was speechless.

"If you're so all-fired important to them, how come you're in this room with me?"

"Because up until now, you didn't know what I'd done," he pointed out. "Up until now, it was possible you would give me other information we could use against them."

"So now, now that I know what you are, they'll let you out. Right? Why don't you try it and see? I'd much rather be alone."

Just then a small aperture in the door opened. I hadn't even known it was there, having been preoccupied while I was out in the hall. A face appeared at the opening, which measured perhaps ten inches by ten inches.

It was a familiar face. Gabe, grinning. "How you doing in there, you two?"

"Sookie needs a doctor," Hugo said. "She's not complaining, but I think her cheekbone is broken." He sounded reproachful. "And she knows about my alliance with the Fellowship, so you might as well let me out."

I didn't know what Hugo thought he was doing, but I tried to look as beaten as possible. That was pretty easy.

"I have me an idea," Gabe said. "I've gotten kind of bored down here, and I don't expect Steve or Sarah—or even old Polly—will be coming back down here any time soon. We got another prisoner over here, Hugo, might be glad to see you. Farrell? You meet him over at the headquarters of the Evil Ones?"

"Yes," said Hugo. He looked very unhappy about this turn of the conversation.

"You know how fond Farrell's gonna be of you? And he's gay, too, a queer bloodsucker. We're so deep underground that he's been waking up early. So I thought I might just put you in there with him, while I have me a little fun with the female traitor, here." And Gabe smiled at me in a way that made my stomach lurch.

Hugo's face was a picture. A real picture. Several things crossed my mind, pertinent things to say. I forewent the doubtful pleasure. I needed to save my energy.

One of my Gran's favorite adages popped into my mind irresistibly as I looked at Gabe's handsome face. "Pretty is as pretty does," I muttered, and began the painful process of getting to my feet to defend myself. My legs might not be broken, but my left knee was surely in bad shape. It was already badly discolored and swollen.

I wondered if Hugo and I together could take Gabe down when he opened the door, but as soon as it swung outward, I saw he'd armed himself with a gun and a black, menacing-looking object I decided might be a stun gun.

"Farrell!" I called. If he were awake, he'd hear me; he was a vampire.

Gabe jumped, looked at me suspiciously.

"Yes?" came a deep voice from the room farther down the hall. I heard chains clink as the vampire moved. Of course, they'd have to chain him with silver. Otherwise he could rip the door off its hinges.

"Stan sent us!" I yelled, and then Gabe backhanded me with the hand that held the gun. Since I was against the wall, my head bounced off it. I made an awful noise, not quite a scream but too loud for a moan.

"Shut up, bitch!" Gabe screamed. He was pointing the gun at Hugo and had the stun gun held at the ready a few inches from me. "Now, Lawyer, you get out here in the hall. Keep away from me, you hear?"

Hugo, sweat pouring down his face, edged past Gabe and into the hall. I was having a hard time tracking what was happening, but I noticed that in the narrow width Gabe had to maneuver, he came very close to Hugo on his way to open Farrell's cell. Just when I thought he was far enough down the hall for me to make it, he told Hugo to close my cell door, and though I frantically shook my head at Hugo, he did so.

I don't think Hugo even saw me. He was turned completely inward. Everything inside him was collapsing, his thoughts were in chaos. I'd done my best for him by telling Farrell we were from Stan, which in Hugo's case was stretching it considerably, but Hugo was too frightened or disillusioned or ashamed to show any backbone. Considering his deep betrayal, I was very surprised I'd bothered. If I hadn't held his hand and seen the images of his daughter, I wouldn't have.

"There's nothing to you, Hugo," I said. His face reappeared at the still-open window momentarily, his face white with distress of all kinds, but then he vanished. I heard a door open, I heard the clink of chains, and I heard a door close.

Gabe had forced Hugo into Farrell's cell. I took deep breaths, one right after another, until I felt I might hyperventilate. I picked up one of the chairs, a plastic one with four metal legs, the kind you've sat on a million times in churches and meetings and classrooms. I held it lion-tamer style, with the legs facing outward. It was all I could think of to do. I thought of Bill, but that was too painful. I thought of my brother, Jason, and I wished he were there with me. It had been a long time since I'd wished that about Jason.

The door opened. Gabe was already smiling as he came in. It was a nasty smile, letting all the ugliness leak out of his soul through his mouth and eyes. This really was his idea of a good time.

"You think that little chair is going to keep you safe?" he asked.

I wasn't in the mood for talking, and I didn't want to listen to the snakes in his mind. I closed myself off, contained myself tightly, bracing myself.

He'd holstered the gun, but kept the stun gun in his hand. Now, such was his confidence, he put it in a little leather pouch on his belt, on the left side. He seized the legs of the chair and began to yank the chair from side to side.

I charged.

I almost had him out the door, so unexpected was my strong counterattack, but at the last minute he managed to twist the legs sideways, so that they couldn't pass through the narrow doorway. He stood against the wall on the other side of the hall, panting, his face red.

"Bitch," he hissed, and came at me again, and this time he tried to pull the chair out of my hands altogether. But as I've said before, I've had vampire blood, and I didn't let him have it. And I didn't let him have me.

Without my seeing it, he'd drawn the stun gun and, quick as a snake, he reached over the chair and touched it to my shoulder.

I didn't collapse, which he expected, but I went down on my knees, still holding the chair. While I was still trying to figure out what had happened to me, he yanked the chair from my hands, and knocked me backwards.

I could hardly move, but I could scream and lock my legs together, and I did.

"Shut up!" he yelled, and since he was touching me, I could tell that he really wanted me unconscious, he would enjoy raping me while I was unconscious; in fact, that was his ideal.

"Don't like your women awake," I panted, "do you?" He stuck a hand between us and yanked open my blouse.

I heard Hugo's voice, yelling, as if that would do any good. I bit at Gabe's shoulder.

He called me a bitch again, which was getting old. He'd opened his own pants, now he was trying to pull up my skirt. I was fleetingly glad I'd bought a long one.

"You afraid they'll complain, if they're awake?" I yelled. "Let me go, get off me! Get off, get off, *get off!*" Finally, I'd unpinned my arms. In a moment, they'd recovered enough from the electric jolt to function. I formed two cups with my hands. As I screamed at him, I clapped my hands over his ears.

He roared, and reared back, his own hands going to his head. He was so full of rage it escaped him and washed over me; it felt like bathing in fury. I knew then that he would kill me if he could, no matter what reprisals he faced. I tried to roll to one side, but he had me pinned with his legs. I watched as his right hand formed a fist, which seemed as big as a boulder to me. And with a sense of doom, I watched the arc of that fist as it descended to my face, knowing this one would knock me out and it would be all over. . . .

And it didn't happen.

Up in the air Gabe went, pants open and dick hanging out, his fist landing on air, his shoes kicking at my legs.

A short man was holding Gabe up in the air; not a man, I realized at second glance, a teenager. An ancient teenager.

He was blond and shirtless, and his arms and chest were covered with blue tattoos. Gabe was yelling and flailing, but the boy stood calmly, his face expressionless, until Gabe ran down. By the time Gabe was silent, the boy had transferred his grip to a kind of bear hug encircling Gabe's waist, and Gabe was hanging forward.

The boy looked down at me dispassionately. My blouse had been torn open, and my bra was ripped down the middle.

"Are you badly hurt?" the boy asked, almost reluctantly.

I had a savior, but not an enthusiastic one.

I stood up, which was more of a feat than it sounds. It took me quite a while. I was trembling violently from the emotional shock. When I was upright, I was on an eye level with the boy. In human years, he would've been about sixteen when he'd been made vampire. There was no telling how many years ago that had been. He must be older than Stan, older than Isabel. His English was clear, but heavily accented. I had no idea what kind of accent it was. Maybe his original language was not even spoken anymore. What a lonely feeling that would be.

"I'll mend," I said. "Thank you." I tried to rebutton my blouse—there were a few remaining buttons—but my hands were shaking too badly. He wasn't interested in seeing my skin, anyway. It didn't do a thing for him. His eyes were quite dispassionate.

"Godfrey," Gabe said. His voice was thready. "Godfrey, she was trying to escape."

Godfrey shook him, and Gabe shut up.

So, Godfrey was the vampire I had seen through Bethany's eyes—the eyes that had vividly remembered seeing him at the Bat's Wing that evening. The eyes that were no longer seeing anything.

"What do you intend to do?" I asked him, keeping my voice quiet and even.

Godfrey's pale blue eyes flickered. He didn't know.

He'd gotten the tattoos while he was alive, and they were very strange. Symbols whose meanings had been lost centuries ago, I was willing to bet. Probably some scholar would give his eyeteeth to have a look at those tattoos. Lucky me, I was getting to see them for nothing.

"Please let me out," I said with as much dignity as I could muster. "They'll kill me."

"But you consort with vampires," he said.

My eyes darted from one side to another, as I tried to figure this one out.

"Ah," I said hesitantly. "You're a vampire, aren't you?"

"Tomorrow I atone for my sin publicly," Godfrey said. "Tomorrow I greet the dawn. For the first time in a thousand years, I will see the sun. Then I will see the face of God."

Okay. "You chose," I said.

"Yes."

"But I didn't. I don't want to die." I spared a glance for Gabe's face, which was quite blue. In his agitation, Godfrey was squeezing Gabe much tighter than he ought to. I wondered if I should say something.

"You do consort with vampires," Godfrey accused, and I switched my gaze back to his face. I knew I'd better not let my concentration wander again.

"I'm in love," I said.

"With a vampire."

"Yes. Bill Compton."

"All vampires are damned, and should all meet the sun. We're a taint, a blot on the face of the earth."

"And these people"—I pointed upward to indicate I meant the Fellowship—"these people are better, Godfrey?"

The vampire looked uneasy and unhappy. He was starving, I noticed; his cheeks were almost concave, and they were as white as paper. His blond hair almost floated around his head, it was so electric, and his eyes looked like blue marbles against his pallor. "They, at least, are human, part of God's plan," he said quietly. "Vampires are an abomination."

"Yet you've been nicer to me than this human." Who was dead, I realized, as I glanced down at his face. I tried not to flinch, and refocused on Godfrey, who was much more important to my future.

"But we take the blood of the innocents." Godfrey's pale blue eyes fixed on mine.

"Who is innocent?" I asked rhetorically, hoping I

didn't sound too much like Pontius Pilate asking, What is truth? when he knew damn well.

"Well, children," Godfrey said.

"Oh, you . . . fed on children?" I put my hand over my mouth.

"I killed children."

I couldn't think of a thing to say for a long time. Godfrey stood there, looking at me sadly, holding Gabe's body in his arms, forgotten.

"What stopped you?" I asked.

"Nothing will stop me. Nothing but my death."

"I'm so sorry," I said inadequately. He was suffering, and I was truly sorry for that. But if he'd been human, I'd have said he deserved the electric chair without thinking twice.

"How soon is it until dark?" I asked, not knowing what else to say.

Godfrey had no watch, of course. I assumed he was up only because he was underground and he was very old. Godfrey said, "An hour."

"Please let me go. If you help me, I can get out of here."

"But you will tell the vampires. They will attack. I will be prevented from meeting the dawn."

"Why wait till the morning?" I asked, suddenly irritated. "Walk outside. Do it now."

He was astounded. He dropped Gabe, who landed with a thud. Godfrey didn't even spare him a glance. "The ceremony is planned for dawn, with many believers there to witness it," he explained. "Farrell will also be brought up to face the sun."

"What part would I have played in this?"

He shrugged. "Sarah wanted to see if the vampires would exchange one of their own for you. Steve had other plans. His idea was to lash you to Farrell, so that when he burned, so would you."

I was stunned. Not that Steve Newlin had had the idea, but that he thought it would appeal to his congregation, for that was what they were. Newlin was further over the top than even I had guessed. "And you think lots of people would enjoy seeing that, a young woman executed without any kind of trial? That they would think it was a valid religious ceremony? You think the people who planned this terrible death for me are truly religious?"

For the first time, he seemed a shade doubtful. "Even for humans, that seems a little extreme," he agreed. "But Steve thought it would be a powerful statement."

"Well, sure it would be a powerful statement. It would say, 'I'm nuts.' I know this world has plenty of bad people and bad vampires, but I don't believe the majority of the people in this country, or for that matter just here in Texas, would be edified by the sight of a screaming woman burning to death."

Godfrey looked doubtful. I could see I was voicing thoughts that had occurred to him, thoughts he had denied to himself he was entertaining. "They have called the media," he said. It was like the protest of a bride slated to marry a groom she suddenly doubted. But the invitations have been sent out, Mother.

"I'm sure they have. But it'll be the end of their organization, I can tell you that flat out. I repeat, if you really want to make a statement that way, a big 'I'm sorry,' then you walk out of this church right now and stand on the lawn. God'll be watching, I promise you. That's who you should care about."

He struggled with it; I'll give him that.

"They have a special white robe for me to wear," he said. (But I've already bought the dress and reserved the church.)

"Big damn deal. If we're arguing clothes, you don't really want to do it. I bet you'll chicken out."

I had definitely lost sight of my goal. When the words came out of my mouth, I regretted them.

"You will see," he said firmly.

"I don't want to see, if I'm tied to Farrell at the time. I am not evil, and I don't want to die."

"When was the last time you were in church?" He was issuing me a challenge.

"About a week ago. And I took Communion, too." I was never happier to be a churchgoer, because I couldn't have lied about that.

"Oh." Godfrey looked dumbfounded.

"See?" I felt I was robbing him of all his wounded majesty by this argument, but dammit, I didn't want to die by burning. I wanted Bill, wanted him with a longing so intense I hoped it would pop his coffin open. If only I could tell him what was going on. . . . "Come on," said Godfrey, holding out his hand.

I didn't want to give him a chance to rethink his position, not after this long do-si-do, so I took his hand and stepped over Gabe's prone form out into the hall. There was an ominous lack of conversation from Farrell and

Hugo, and to tell the truth, I was too scared to call out to find out what was going on with them. I figured if I could get out, I could rescue them both, anyway.

Godfrey sniffed the blood on me, and his face was swept with longing. I knew that look. But it was devoid of lust. He didn't care a thing for my body. The link between blood and sex is very strong for all vampires, so I considered myself lucky that I was definitely adult in form. I inclined my face to him out of courtesy. After a long hesitation, he licked the trickle of blood from the cut on my cheekbone. He closed his eyes for a second, savoring the taste, and then we started for the stairs.

With a great deal of help from Godfrey, I made it up the steep flight. He used his free arm to punch in a combination on the door, and swung it open. "I've been staying down here, in the room at the end," he explained, in a voice that was hardly more than a disturbance of the air.

The corridor was clear, but any second someone might come out of one of the offices. Godfrey didn't seem to fear that at all, but I did, and I was the one whose freedom was at stake. I didn't hear any voices; apparently the staff had gone home to get ready for the lock-in, and the lock-in guests had not yet started arriving. Some of the office doors were closed, and the windows in the offices were the only means of sunlight getting to the hall. It was dark enough for Godfrey to be comfortable, I assumed, since he didn't even wince. There was bright artificial light coming from under the main office door.

We hurried, or at least tried to, but my left leg was not very cooperative. I wasn't sure what door Godfrey was

heading toward, perhaps the double doors I'd seen earlier at
the back of the sanctuary. If I could get safely out of those,
I wouldn't have to traverse the other wing. I didn't know
what I'd do when I got outside. But being outside would
definitely be better than being inside. Just as we reached
the open doorway of the next-to-last office on the left, the
one from which the tiny Hispanic woman had come, the
door to Steve's office opened. We froze. Godfrey's arm
around me felt like an iron band. Polly stepped out, still
facing into the room. We were only a couple of yards away.

". . . bonfire," she was saying.

"Oh, I think we've got enough," Sarah's sweet voice
said. "If everyone returned their attendance cards, we'd
know for sure. I can't believe how bad people are about not
replying. It's so inconsiderate, after we made it as easy as
possible for them to tell us whether or not they'd be here!"

An argument about etiquette. Gosh, I wished Miss
Manners were here to give me advice on this situation. *I
was an uninvited guest of a small church, and I left without saying good-bye. Am I obliged to write a thank-you
note, or may I simply send flowers?*

Polly's head began turning, and I knew any moment
she would see us. Even as the thought formed, Godfrey
pushed me into the dark empty office.

"Godfrey! What are you doing up here?" Polly didn't
sound frightened, but she didn't sound happy, either. It
was more like she'd found the yardman in the living
room, making himself at home.

"I came to see if there is anything more I need to do."

"Isn't it awfully early for you to be awake?"

"I am very old," he said politely. "The old don't need
as much sleep as the young."

Polly laughed. "Sarah," she said brightly, "Godfrey's up!"

Sarah's voice sounded closer, when she spoke. "Well, hey, Godfrey!" she said, in an identical bright tone. "Are you excited? I bet you are!"

They were talking to a thousand-year-old vampire like he was a child on his birthday eve.

"Your robe's all ready," Sarah said. "All systems go!"

"What if I changed my mind?" Godfrey asked.

There was a long silence. I tried to breathe very slowly and quietly. The closer it got to dark the more I could imagine I had a chance of getting out of this.

If I could telephone . . . I glanced over at the desk in the office. There was a telephone on it. But wouldn't the buttons in the offices light up, the buttons for that line, if I used the phone? At the moment, it would make too much noise.

"You changed your mind? Can this be possible?" Polly asked. She was clearly exasperated. "You came to us, remember? You told us about your life of sin, and the shame you felt when you killed children and . . . did other things. Has any of this changed?"

"No," Godfrey said, sounding more thoughtful than anything else. "None of this has changed. But I see no need to include any humans in this sacrifice of mine. In fact, I believe that Farrell should be left to make his own peace with God. We shouldn't force him into immolation."

"We need to get Steve back here," Polly said to Sarah in an undertone.

After that, I just heard Polly, so I assumed Sarah had gone back into the office to call Steve.

One of the lights on the phone lit up. Yep, that was what she was doing. She'd know if I tried to use one of the other lines. Maybe in a minute.

Polly was trying sweet reason with Godfrey. Godfrey was not talking much himself, and I had no idea what was going through his head. I stood helplessly, pressed against the wall, hoping no one would come into the office, hoping no one would go downstairs and raise the alarm, hoping Godfrey wouldn't have yet another change of heart.

Help, I said in my mind. If only I could call for help that way, through my other sense!

A flicker of an idea crossed my mind. I made myself stand calmly, though my legs were still trembling with shock, and my knee and face hurt like the six shades of hell. Maybe I *could* call someone: Barry, the bellboy. He was a telepath, like me. He could be able to hear me. Not that I'd ever made such an attempt before—well, I'd never met another telepath, had I? I tried desperately to locate myself in relation to Barry, assuming he was at work. This was about the same time we'd arrived from Shreveport, so he might be. I pictured my location on the map, which luckily I'd looked up with Hugo—though I knew now that he had been pretending not to know where the Fellowship Center was—and I figured we were south-west of the Silent Shore Hotel.

I was in new mental territory. I gathered up what energy I had and tried to roll it into a ball, in my mind. For a second, I felt absolutely ridiculous, but when I thought of getting free of this place and these people, there was very little to gain in not being ridiculous. I thought to Barry. It's hard to peg down exactly how I did it, but I projected. Knowing his name helped, and knowing his location helped.

I decided to start easy. *Barry Barry Barry Barry* . . .

What do you want? He was absolutely panicked. This had never happened to him before.

I've never done this, either. I hoped I sounded reassuring. *I need help. I'm in big trouble.*

Who are you?

Well, that would help. Stupid me. *I'm Sookie, the blonde who came in last night with the brown-haired vampire. Third-floor suite.*

The one with the boobs? Oh, sorry.

At least he'd apologized. *Yes. The one with the boobs. And the boyfriend.*

So, what's the matter?

Now, all this sounds very clear and organized, but it wasn't words. It was like we were sending each other emotional telegrams and pictures.

I tried to think how to explain my predicament. *Get my vampire as soon as he wakes.*

And then?

Tell him I'm in danger. Dangerdangerdanger . . .

Okay, I get the idea. Where?

Church. I figured that would be shorthand for the Fellowship Center. I couldn't think how to convey that to Barry.

He knows where?

He knows where. Tell him, Go down the stairs.

Are you for real? I didn't know there was anyone else . . .

I'm for real. Please, help me.

I could feel a complicated bundle of emotions racing through Barry's mind. He was scared of talking to a vampire, he was frightened that his employers would discover he had a "weird brain thing," he was just excited that there was someone like him. But mostly he was scared of this part of him that had puzzled and frightened him for so long.

I knew all those feelings. *It's okay, I understand,* I told him. *I wouldn't ask if I wasn't going to be killed.*

Fear struck him again, fear of his own responsibility in this. I should never have added that.

And then, somehow, he erected a flimsy barrier between us, and I wasn't sure what Barry was going to do.

While I'd been concentrating on Barry, things had been moving right along in the hall. When I began listening again, Steve had returned. He, too, was trying to be reasonable and positive with Godfrey.

"Now, Godfrey," he was saying, "if you didn't want to do this, all you had to do was say so. You committed to it, we all did, and we've moved forward with every expectation that you would keep to your word. A lot of people are going to be very disappointed if you lose your commitment to the ceremony."

"What will you do with Farrell? With the man Hugo, and the blond woman?"

"Farrell's a vampire," said Steve, still the voice of sweet reason. "Hugo and the woman are vampires' creatures. They should go to the sun, too, tied to a vampire. That is the lot they chose in their lives, and it should be their lot in death."

"I am a sinner, and I know it, so when I die my soul will go to God," Godfrey said. "But Farrell does not know this. When he dies, he won't have a chance. The man and woman, too, have not had a chance to repent their ways. Is it fair to kill them and condemn them to hell?"

"We need to go into my office," Steve said decisively.

And I realized, finally, that that was what Godfrey had been aiming for all along. There was a certain amount of foot shuffling, and I heard Godfrey murmur, "After you," with great courtesy.

He wanted to be last so he could shut the door behind him.

My hair finally felt dry, freed from the wig that had drenched it in sweat. It was hanging around my shoulders in separate locks, because I'd been silently unpinning it during the conversation. It had seemed a casual thing to be doing, while listening to my fate being settled, but I had to keep occupied. Now I cautiously pocketed the bobby pins, ran my fingers through the tangled mess, and prepared to sneak out of the church.

I peered cautiously from the doorway. Yes, Steve's door was closed. I tiptoed out of the dark office, took a left, and continued to the door leading into the sanctuary. I turned its knob very quietly and eased it open. I stepped into the sanctuary, which was very dusky. There was just enough light from the huge stained-glass windows to help me get down the aisle without falling over the pews.

Then I heard voices, getting louder, coming from the far wing. The lights in the sanctuary came on. I dove into a row and rolled under the pew. A family group came in, all talking loudly, the little girl whining about missing some favorite show on television because she had to go to the stinky old lock-in.

That got her a slap on the bottom, sounded like, and her father told her she was lucky she was going to get to see such amazing evidence of the power of God. She was going to see salvation in action.

Even under the circumstances, I took issue with that. I wondered if this father really understood that his leader planned for the congregation to watch two vampires burn to death, at least one of them clutching a human who would also burn. I wondered how the little girl's mental health would fare after that "amazing evidence of the power of God."

To my dismay, they proceeded to put their sleeping bags up against a wall on the far side of the sanctuary, still talking. At least this was a family that communicated. In addition to the whiny little girl, there were two older kids, a boy and a girl, and like true siblings they fought like cats and dogs.

A pair of small flat red shoes trotted by the end of my pew and disappeared through the door into Steve's wing. I wondered if the group in his office was still debating.

The feet went by again after a few seconds, this time going very fast. I wondered about that, too.

I waited about five more minutes, but nothing else happened.

From now on, there would be more people coming in. It was now or never. I rolled out from under the pew and got up. By my good fortune, they were all looking down at their task when I stood up, and I began walking briskly to the double doors at the back of the church. By their sudden silence, I knew they'd spotted me.

"Hi!" called the mother. She rose to her feet beside her bright blue sleeping bag. Her plain face was full of curiosity. "You must be new at the Fellowship. I'm Francie Polk."

"Yes," I called, trying to sound cheerful. "Gotta rush! Talk to you later!"

She drew closer. "Have you hurt yourself?" she asked. "You—excuse me—you look awful. Is that blood?"

I glanced down at my blouse. There were some small stains on my chest.

"I had a fall," I said, trying to sound rueful. "I need to go home and do a little first aid, change my clothes, like that. I'll be back!"

I could see the doubt on Francie Polk's face. "There's a first aid kit in the office, why don't I just run and get that?" she asked.

Because I don't want you to. "You know, I need to get a fresh blouse, too," I said. I wrinkled my nose to show my low opinion of going around in a spotted blouse all evening.

Another woman had come in the very doors I was hoping to go out of, and she stood listening to the conversation, her dark eyes darting back and forth from me to the determined Francie.

"Hey, girl!" she said in a lightly accented voice, and the little Hispanic woman, the shapeshifter, gave me a hug. I come from a hugging culture, and it was automatic to hug her right back. She gave me a meaningful pinch while we were clenched.

"How are you?" I asked brightly. "It's been too long."

"Oh, you know—same old, same old," she said. She beamed up at me, but there was caution in her eyes. Her hair was a very dark brown, rather than black, and it was coarse and abundant. Her skin was the color of a milky caramel, and she had dark freckles. Generous lips were painted an outstanding fuchsia. She had big white teeth, flashing at me in her wide smile. I glanced down at her feet. Flat red shoes.

"Hey, come outside with me while I have a cigarette," she said.

Francie Polk was looking more satisfied.

"Luna, can't you see your friend needs to go to the doctor?" she said righteously.

"You do have a few bumps and bruises," Luna said, examining me. "Have you fallen down again, girl?"

"You know Mama always tells me, 'Marigold, you're as clumsy as an elephant.'"

"That mama of yours," Luna said, shaking her head in disgust. "Like that would make you less clumsy!"

"What can you do?" I said, shrugging. "If you'll excuse us, Francie?"

"Well, sure," she said. "I'll see you later, I guess."

"Sure will," said Luna. "I wouldn't miss it for anything."

And with Luna, I strolled out of the Fellowship of the Sun meeting hall. I concentrated ferociously on keeping my gait even, so Francie wouldn't see me limp and become even more suspicious.

"Thank God," I said, when we were outside.

"You knew me for what I was," she said rapidly. "How did you know?"

"I have a friend who's a shapeshifter."

"Who is he?"

"He's not local. And I won't tell you without his consent."

She stared at me, all pretense of friendship dropped in that instant.

"Okay, I respect that," she said. "Why are you here?"

"What's it to you?"

"I just saved your ass."

She had a point, a good point. "Okay. I am a telepath, and I was hired by your vampire area leader to find out what had become of a missing vampire."

"That's better. But it ain't *my* area leader. I'm a supe, but I ain't no freaking vampire. What vamp did you deal with?"

"I don't need to tell you that."

She raised her eyebrows.

"I don't."

She opened her mouth as if to yell.

"Yell away. There're some things I just won't tell. What's a supe?"

"A supernatural being. Now, you listen to me," Luna said. We were walking through the parking lot now, and cars were beginning to pull in regularly from the road. She did a lot of smiling and waving, and I tried to at least look happy. But the limp was no longer concealable, and my face was swelling like a bitch, as Arlene would say.

Gosh, I was homesick all of a sudden. But I thrust that feeling away to pay attention to Luna, who clearly had things to tell me.

"You tell the vampires *we* have this place under surveillance—"

" 'We' being who?"

" 'We' being the shapeshifters of the greater Dallas area."

"You guys are organized? Hey, that's great! I'll have to tell . . . my friend."

She rolled her eyes, clearly not impressed with my intellect. "Listen here, missy, you tell the vampires that as soon as the Fellowship figures out about us, they will be on us, too. And we aren't going to mainstream. We're underground for good. Stupid freakin' vampires. So we're keeping an eye on the Fellowship."

"If you're keeping such a good eye, how come you didn't call the vampires and tell them about Farrell being in the basement? And about Godfrey?"

"Hey, Godfrey wants to kill himself, no skin off our teeth. He came to the Fellowship; they didn't go to him. They about peed their pants, they were so glad to have him, after they got over the shock of sitting in the same room with one of the damned."

"What about Farrell?"

"I didn't know who was down there," Luna admitted. "I knew they'd captured someone, but I'm not exactly in the inner circle yet, and I couldn't find out who. I even tried buttering up that asshole Gabe, but that didn't help."

"You'll be pleased to know that Gabe is dead."

"Hey!" She smiled genuinely for the first time. "That *is* good news."

"Here's the rest. As soon as I get in touch with the vampires, they're going to be here to get Farrell. So if I were you, I wouldn't go back to the Fellowship tonight."

She chewed on her lower lip for a minute. We were at the far end of the parking lot.

"In fact," I said, "it would be perfect if you would give me a lift to the hotel."

"Well, I'm not in the business of making your life perfect," she snarled, recalling her tough cookie persona. "I got to get back in that church before the shit hits the fan, and get some papers out. Think about this, girl. What are the vampires gonna do with Godfrey? Can they let him live? He's a child molester and a serial killer; so many times over you couldn't even count. He can't stop, and he knows it."

So there was a good side to the church . . . it gave vampires like Godfrey a venue to commit suicide while being watched?

"Maybe they should just put it on pay-per-view," I said.

"They would if they could." Luna was serious. "Those vampires trying to mainstream, they're pretty harsh to anyone who might upset their plan. Godfrey's no poster boy."

"I can't solve every problem, Luna. By the way, my real name is Sookie. Sookie Stackhouse. Anyway, I've done what I could. I did the job I was hired to do, and now I have to get back and report. Godfrey lives or Godfrey dies. I think Godfrey will die."

"You better be right," she said ominously.

I couldn't figure out why it was my fault if Godfrey changed his mind. I had just questioned his chosen venue. But maybe she was right. I might have some responsibility, here.

It was all just too much for me.

"Good-bye," I said, and began limping along the back of the parking lot to the road. I hadn't gotten far when I heard a hue and cry arise from the church, and all the outside lights popped on. The sudden glare was blinding.

"Maybe I won't go back in the Fellowship Center after all. Not a good idea," Luna said from the window of a Subaru Outback. I scrambled into the passenger's seat, and we sped toward the nearest exit onto the four-lane road. I fastened my seat belt automatically.

But as swiftly as we had moved, others had moved even more swiftly. Various family vehicles were being positioned to block the exits from the parking lot.

"Crap," said Luna.

We sat idling for a minute while she thought.

"They'll never let me out, even if we hide you somehow. I can't get you back into the church. They can search the parking lot too easily." Luna chewed on her lip some more.

"Oh, freak this job, anyway," she said, and threw the Outback into gear. She drove conservatively at first, trying to attract as little attention as possible. "These people wouldn't know what religion was if it bit them in the ass," she said. Up by the church, Luna drove over the curb separating the parking lot from the lawn. Then we were flooring it over the lawn, circling the fenced play area, and I discovered I was grinning from ear to ear, though it hurt to do so.

"Yee-hah!" I yelled, as we hit a sprinkler head on the lawn watering system. We flew across the front yard of the church, and, out of sheer shock, no one was pursuing us. They'd organize themselves in a minute, though, the diehards. Those people who didn't espouse the more extreme measures of this Fellowship were going to get a real wake-up call tonight.

Sure enough, Luna looked in her rearview mirror and

said, "They've unblocked the exits, and someone's coming after us." We pulled out into traffic on the road running in front of the church, another major four-lane road, and horns honked all around at our sudden entry into the traffic flow.

"Holy shit," Luna said. She slowed down to a reasonable speed and kept looking in her rearview mirror. "It's too dark now, I can't tell which headlights are them."

I wondered if Barry had alerted Bill.

"You got a cell phone?" I asked her.

"It's in my purse, along with my driver's license, which is still sitting in my office in the church. That's how I knew you were loose. I went in my office, smelled your scent. Knew you'd been hurt. So I went outside and scouted around, and when I couldn't find you, I came back in. We're damn lucky I had my keys in my pocket."

God bless shapeshifters. I felt wistful about the phone, but it couldn't be helped. I suddenly wondered where my purse was. Probably back in the Fellowship of the Sun office. At least I'd taken all my ID out of it.

"Should we stop at a pay phone, or the police station?"

"If you call the police, what are they going to do?" asked Luna, in the encouraging voice of someone leading a small child to wisdom.

"Go to the church?"

"And what will happen then, girl?"

"Ah, they'll ask Steve why he was holding a human prisoner?"

"Yep. And what will he say?"

"I don't know."

"He'll say, 'We never held her prisoner. She got into

some kind of argument with our employee Gabe, and he ended up dead. Arrest her!' "

"Oh. You think?"

"Yeah, I think."

"What about Farrell?"

"If the police start coming in, you can better believe they've got someone detailed to hustle down to the basement and stake him. By the time the cops get there, no more Farrell. They could do the same to Godfrey, if he wouldn't back them up. He would probably stand still for it. He wants to die, that Godfrey."

"Well, what about Hugo?"

"You think Hugo is going to explain how come he got locked in a basement there? I don't know what that jerk would say, but he won't tell the truth. He's led a double life for months now, and he can't say whether his head is on straight or not."

"So we can't call the police. Who can we call?"

"I got to get you with your people. You don't need to meet mine. They don't want to be known, you understand?"

"Sure."

"You have to be something weird yourself, huh? To recognize us."

"Yes."

"So what are you? Not a vamp, for sure. Not one of us, either."

"I'm a telepath."

"You are! No shit! Well, woooo woooo," Luna said, imitating the traditional ghost sound.

"No more woo woo than you are," I said, feeling I could be pardoned for sounding a bit testy.

"Sorry," she said, not meaning it. "Okay, here's the plan—"

But I didn't get to hear what the plan was, because at that moment we were hit from the rear.

The next thing I knew, I was hanging upside down in my seat belt. A hand was reaching in to pull me out. I recognized the fingernails; it was Sarah. I bit her.

With a shriek, the hand withdrew. "She's obviously out of it," I heard Sarah's sweet voice gabbling to someone else, someone unconnected with the church, I realized, and knew I had to act.

"Don't you listen to her. It was her car that hit us," I called. "Don't you let her touch me."

I looked over at Luna, whose hair now touched the ceiling. She was awake but not talking. She was wriggling around, and I figured she was trying to undo her seat belt.

There was lots of conversation outside the window, most of it contentious.

"I tell you, I am her sister, and she is just drunk," Polly was telling someone.

"I am not. I demand to have a sobriety test right now," I said, in as dignified a voice as I could manage, considering that I was shocked silly and hanging upside down. "Call the police immediately, please, and an ambulance."

Though Sarah began spluttering, a heavy male voice said, "Lady, doesn't sound like she wants you around. Sounds like she's got some good points."

A man's face appeared in the window. He was kneeling and bent sideways to see in. "I've called nine-one-

one," the heavy voice said. He was disheveled and stubbly and I thought he was beautiful.

"Please stay here till they come," I begged.

"I will," he promised, and his face vanished.

There were more voices now. Sarah and Polly were getting shrill. They'd hit our car. Several people had witnessed it. Them claiming to be sisters or whatever didn't go over well with this crowd. Also, I gathered, they had two Fellowship males with them who were being less than endearing.

"Then we'll just go," Polly said, fury in her voice.

"No, you won't," said my wonderful, belligerent male. "You gotta trade insurance with them, anyway."

"That's right," said a much younger male voice. "You just don't want to pay for getting their car fixed. And what if they're hurt? Don't you have to pay their hospital?"

Luna had managed to unbuckle herself, and she twisted when she fell to the roof that was now the floor of the car. With a suppleness I could only envy, she worked her head out of the open window, and then began to brace her feet against whatever purchase she could find. Gradually, she began to wriggle her way out of the window. One of the purchases happened to be my shoulder, but I didn't even peep. One of us needed to be free.

There were exclamations outside as Luna made her appearance, and then I heard her say, "Okay, which one of you was driving?"

Various voices chimed in, some saying one, some saying another, but they all knew Sarah and Polly and their henchmen were the perpetrators and Luna was a victim. There were so many people around that when yet another car of men from the Fellowship pulled up, there wasn't any way they could just haul us off. God bless the American spectator, I thought. I was in a sentimental mood.

The paramedic that ended up extricating me from the car was the cutest guy I'd ever seen. His name was Salazar, according to his bar pin, and I said, "Salazar," just to be sure I could say it. I had to sound it out carefully.

"Yep, that's me," he said while lifting my eyelid to look at my eye. "You're kinda banged up, lady."

I started to tell him that I'd had some of these injuries before the car accident, but then I heard Luna say, "My calendar flew off the dashboard and hit her in the face."

"Be a lot safer if you'd keep your dash clear, ma'am," said a new voice with a flat twang to it.

"I hear you, Officer."

Officer? I tried to turn my head and got admonished by Salazar. "You just keep still till I finish looking you over," he said sternly.

"Okay." After a second I said, "The police are here?"

"Yes, ma'am. Now, what hurts?"

We went through a whole list of questions, most of which I was able to answer.

"I think you're going to be fine, ma'am, but we need to take you and your friend to the hospital just to check you out." Salazar and his partner, a heavy Anglo woman, were matter-of-fact about this necessity.

"Oh," I said anxiously, "we don't need to go to the hospital, do we, Luna?"

"Sure," she said, as surprised as she could be. "We have to get you X-rayed, honey bunch. I mean, that cheek of yours looks bad."

"Oh." I was a little stunned by this turn of events. "Well, if you think so."

"Oh, yeah."

So Luna walked to the ambulance, and I was loaded in on a gurney, and with siren blaring, we started off. My last view before Salazar shut the doors was of Polly and Sarah talking to a very tall policeman. Both of them looked very upset. That was good.

The hospital was like all hospitals. Luna stuck to me like white to rice, and when we were in the same cubicle and a nurse entered to take down still more details, Luna said, "Tell Dr. Josephus that Luna Garza and her sister are here."

The nurse, a young African American woman, gave Luna a doubtful look, but said, "Okay," and left immediately.

"How'd you do that?" I asked.

"Get a nurse to stop filling out charts? I asked for this hospital on purpose. We've got someone at every hospital in the city, but I know our man here best."

"Our?"

"Us. The Two-Natured."

"Oh." The shapeshifters. I could hardly wait to tell Sam about this.

"I'm Dr. Josephus," said a calm voice. I raised my head to see that a spare, silver-haired man had stepped into our curtained area. His hair was receding and he had a sharp nose on which a pair of wire-rimmed glasses perched. He had intent blue eyes, magnified by his glasses.

"I'm Luna Garza, and this is my friend, ah, Marigold." Luna said this as if she were a different person. In fact, I glanced over to see if it was the same Luna. "We met with misfortune tonight in the line of duty."

The doctor looked at me with some mistrust.

"She is worthy," Luna said with great solemnity. I didn't want to ruin the moment by giggling, but I had to bite the inside of my mouth.

"You need X-rays," the doctor said after looking at my face and examining my grotesquely swollen knee. I had various abrasions and bruises, but those were my only really significant injuries.

"Then we need them very quickly, and then we need out of here in a secure way," Luna said in a voice that would brook no denial.

No hospital had ever moved so quickly. I could only suppose that Dr. Josephus was on the board of directors. Or maybe he was the chief of staff. The portable X-ray machine was wheeled in, the X-rays were taken, and in a few minutes Dr. Josephus told me that I had a hairline fracture of the cheekbone that would mend on its own. Or I could see a plastic surgeon when the swelling had gone down. He gave me a prescription for pain pills, a lot of advice, and an ice pack for my face and another for my knee, which he called "wrenched."

Within ten minutes after that, we were on our way out of the hospital. Luna was pushing me in a wheelchair, and Dr. Josephus was leading us through a kind of service tunnel. We passed a couple of employees on their way in. They appeared to be poor people, the kind who take low-paying jobs like hospital janitor and cook. I couldn't believe the massively self-assured Dr. Josephus had ever come down this tunnel before, but he seemed to know his way, and the staff didn't act startled at the sight of him. At the end of the tunnel, he pushed open a heavy metal door.

Luna Garza nodded to him regally, said, "Many thanks," and wheeled me out into the night. There was a big old car parked out there. It was dark red or dark brown. As I looked around a little more, I realized that we were in an alley. There were big trash bins lining the wall, and I saw a cat pouncing on something—I didn't want to know what—between two of the bins. After the door whooshed pneumatically shut behind us, the alley was quiet. I began to feel afraid again.

I was incredibly tired of being afraid.

Luna went over to the car, opened the rear door, and said something to whoever was inside. Whatever answer she got, it made her angry. She expostulated in another language.

There was further argument.

Luna stomped back to me. "You have to be blind-folded," she said, obviously certain I would take great offense.

"No problem," I said, with a sweep of one hand to indicate how trifling a matter this was.

"You don't mind?"

"No. I understand, Luna. Everyone likes his privacy."

"Okay, then." She hurried back to the car and returned with a scarf in her hands, of green and peacock blue silk. She folded it as if we were going to play pin-the-tail, and tied it securely behind my head. "Listen to me," she said in my ear, "these two are tough. You watch it." Good. I wanted to be more frightened.

She rolled me over to the car and helped me in. I guess she wheeled the chair back to the door to await pickup;

anyway, after a minute she got in the other side of the car.

There were two presences in the front seat. I felt them mentally, very delicately, and discovered both were shapeshifters; at least, they had the shapeshifter feel to their brains, the semiopaque snarly tangle I got from Sam and Luna. My boss, Sam, usually changes into a collie. I wondered what Luna preferred. There was a difference about these two, a pulsing sort of heaviness. The outline of their heads seemed subtly different, not exactly human.

There was only silence for a few minutes, while the car bumped out of the alley and drove through the night.

"Silent Shore Hotel, right?" said the driver. She sounded kind of growly. Then I realized it was almost the full moon. Oh, hell. They had to change at the full moon. Maybe that was why Luna had kicked over the traces so readily at the Fellowship tonight, once it got dark. She had been made giddy by the emergence of the moon.

"Yes, please," I said politely.

"Food that talks," said the passenger. His voice was even closer to a growl.

I sure didn't like that, but had no idea how to respond. There was just as much for me to learn about shapeshifters as there was about vampires, apparently.

"You two can it," Luna said. "This is my guest."

"Luna hangs with puppy chow," said the passenger. I was beginning to really not like this guy.

"Smells more like hamburger to me," said the driver. "She's got a scrape or two, doesn't she, Luna?"

"Y'all are giving her a great impression of how civilized we are," Luna snapped. "Show some control. She's already had a bad night. She's got a broken bone, too."

And the night wasn't even halfway over yet. I shifted the ice pack I was holding to my face. You can only stand so much freezing cold on your sinus cavity.

"Why'd Josephus have to send for freakin' werewolves?" Luna muttered into my ear. But I knew they'd heard; Sam heard everything, and he was by no means as powerful as a true werewolf. Or at least, that was my evaluation. To tell you the truth, until this moment, I hadn't been sure werewolves actually existed.

"I guess," I said tactfully and audibly, "he thought they could defend us best if we're attacked again."

I could feel the creatures in the front seat prick up their ears. Maybe literally.

"We were doing okay," Luna said indignantly. She twitched and fidgeted on the seat beside me like she'd drunk sixteen cups of coffee.

"Luna, we got rammed and your car got totaled. We were in the emergency room. 'Okay' in what sense?"

Then I had to answer my own question. "Hey, I'm sorry, Luna. You got me out of there when they would've killed me. It's not your fault they rammed us."

"You two have a little roughhouse tonight?" asked the passenger, more civilly. He was spoiling for a fight. I didn't know if all werewolves were as feisty as this guy, or if it was just his nature.

"Yeah, with the fucking Fellowship," Luna said, more than a trace of pride in her voice. "They had this chick stuck in a cell. In a dungeon."

"No shit?" asked the driver. She had the same hyper pulsing to her—well, I just had to call it her aura, for lack of a better word.

"No shit," I said firmly. "I work for a shifter, at home," I added, to make conversation.

"No kidding? What's the business?"

"A bar. He owns a bar."

"So, are you far from home?"

"Too far," I said.

"This little bat saved your life tonight, for real?"

"Yes." I was absolutely sincere about that. "Luna saved my life." Could they mean that literally? Did Luna shapeshift into a . . . oh golly.

"Way to go, Luna." There was a fraction more respect in the deeper growly voice.

Luna found the praise pleasant, as she ought to, and she patted my hand. In a more agreeable silence, we drove maybe five more minutes, and then the driver said, "The Silent Shore, coming up."

I breathed out a long sigh of relief.

"There's a vampire out front, waiting."

I almost ripped off the blindfold, before I realized that would be a really tacky thing to do. "What does he look like?"

"Very tall, blond. Big head of hair. Friend or foe?"

I had to think about that. "Friend," I said, trying not to sound doubtful.

"Yum, yum," said the driver. "Does he cross-date?"

"I don't know. Want me to ask?"

Luna and the passenger both made gagging sounds. "You can't date a deader!" Luna protested. "Come on, Deb—uh, girl!"

"Oh, okay," said the driver. "Some of them aren't so bad. I'm pulling into the curb, little Milkbone."

"That would be you," Luna said in my ear.

We came to a stop, and Luna leaned over me to open my door. As I stepped out, guided and shoved by her hands, I heard an exclamation from the sidewalk. Quick as a wink Luna slammed the door shut behind me. The car full of shapeshifters pulled away from the curb with a screech of tires. A howl trailed behind it in the thick night air.

"Sookie?" said a familiar voice.

"Eric?"

I was fumbling with the blindfold, but Eric just grabbed the back of it and pulled. I had acquired a beautiful, if somewhat stained, scarf. The front of the hotel, with its heavy blank doors, was brilliantly lit in the dark night, and Eric looked remarkably pale. He was wearing an absolutely conventional navy blue pinstripe suit, of all things.

I was actually glad to see him. He grabbed my arm to keep me from wobbling and looked down at me with an unreadable face. Vampires were good at that. "What has happened to you?" he said.

"I got . . . well, it's hard to explain in a second. Where is Bill?"

"First he went to the Fellowship of the Sun to get you out. But we heard along the way, from one of us who is a policeman, that you had been involved in an accident and gone to a hospital. So then he went to the hospital. At the hospital, he found out you had left outside the proper channels. No one would tell him anything, and he couldn't threaten them properly." Eric looked extremely frustrated. The fact that he had to live within human laws was a constant irritant to Eric, though he greatly enjoyed the benefits. "And then there was no trace of you. The doorman had only heard the once from you, mentally."

"Poor Barry. Is he all right?"

"The richer for several hundred dollars, and quite happy about it," Eric said in a dry voice. "Now we just need Bill. What a lot of trouble you are, Sookie." He pulled a cell phone out of his pocket and punched in a number. After what seemed a long time, it was answered.

"Bill, she is here. Some shapeshifters brought her in." He looked me over. "Battered, but walking." He listened some more. "Sookie, do you have your key?" he asked. I felt in the pocket of my skirt where I'd stuffed the plastic rectangle about a million years ago.

"Yes," I said, and simply could not believe that something had gone right. "Oh, wait! Did they get Farrell?"

Eric held up his hand to indicate he'd get to me in a minute. "Bill, I'll take her up and start doctoring." Eric's back stiffened. "Bill," he said and there was a world of threat in his voice. "All right then. Good-bye." He turned back to me as if there'd been no interruption.

"Yes, Farrell is safe. They raided the Fellowship."

"Did . . . did many people get hurt?"

"Most of them were too frightened to approach. They scattered and went home. Farrell was in an underground cell with Hugo."

"Oh, yes, Hugo. What happened to Hugo?"

My voice must have been very curious, because Eric looked at me sideways while we were progressing toward the elevator. He was matching my pace, and I was limping very badly.

"May I carry you?" he asked.

"Oh, I don't think so. I've made it this far." I would've taken Bill up on the offer instantly. Barry, at the bell captain's desk, gave me a little wave. He would've run up to me if I hadn't been with Eric. I gave him what I hoped was a significant look, to say I'd talk to him again later, and then the elevator door dinged open and we got on. Eric punched the floor button and leaned against the mirrored wall of the car opposite me. In looking at him, I got a look at my own reflection.

"Oh, no," I said, absolutely horrified. "Oh, no." My hair had been flattened by the wig, and then combed out with my fingers, so it was a disaster. My hands went up to it, helplessly and painfully, and my mouth shook with suppressed tears. And my hair was the least of it. I had visible bruises ranging from mild to severe on most of my body, and that was just the part you could see. My face was swollen and discolored on one side. There was a cut in the middle of the bruise over my cheekbone. My blouse was missing half its buttons, and my skirt was ripped and filthy. My right arm was ridged with bloody lumps.

I began crying. I looked so awful; it just broke what was left of my spirit.

To his credit, Eric didn't laugh, though he may have wanted to. "Sookie, a bath and clean clothes and you will be put to rights," he said as if he were talking to a child. To tell you the truth, I didn't feel much older at the moment.

"The werewolf thought you were cute," I said, and sobbed some more. We stepped out of the elevator.

"The werewolf? Sookie, you have had adventures tonight." He gathered me up like an armful of clothes and held me to him. I got his lovely suit jacket wet and snotty, and his pristine white shirt was spotless no more.

"Oh, I'm so sorry!" I held back and looked at his ensemble. I swabbed it with the scarf.

"Don't cry again," he said hastily. "Just don't start crying again, and I won't mind taking this to the cleaners. I won't even mind getting a whole new suit."

I thought it was pretty amusing that Eric, the dread master vampire, was afraid of weeping women. I sniggered through the residual sobs.

"Something funny?" he asked.

I shook my head.

I slid my key in the door and we went in. "I'll help you into the tub if you like, Sookie," Eric offered.

"Oh, I don't think so." A bath was what I wanted more than anything else in the world, that and to never put on these clothes again, but I sure wasn't taking a bath with Eric anywhere around.

"I'll bet you are a treat, naked," Eric said, just to boost my spirits.

"You know it. I'm just as tasty as a big éclair," I said, and carefully settled into a chair. "Though at the moment I feel more like boudain." Boudain is Cajun sausage, made of all kinds of things, none of them elegant. Eric pushed over a straight chair and lifted my leg to elevate the knee. I resettled the ice pack on it and closed my eyes. Eric called down to the desk for some tweezers, a bowl, and some antiseptic ointment, plus a rolling chair. The items arrived within ten minutes. This staff was good.

There was a small desk by one wall. Eric moved it over to the right side of my chair, lifted my arm, and laid it over the top of the desk. He switched on the lamp. After swabbing off my arm with a wet washcloth, Eric began removing the lumps. They were tiny pieces of glass from Luna's Outback's window. "If you were an ordinary girl, I could glamour you and you wouldn't feel this," he commented. "Be brave." It hurt like a bitch, and tears streamed down my face the whole time he worked. I worked hard keeping silent.

At last, I heard another key in the door, and I opened my eyes. Bill glanced at my face, winced, and then examined what Eric was doing. He nodded approvingly to Eric.

"How did this happen?" he asked, laying the lightest of touches on my face. He pulled the remaining chair closer and sat in it. Eric continued with his work.

I began to explain. I was so tired my voice faltered from time to time. When I got to the part about Gabe, I didn't have enough wits to tone the episode down, and I could see Bill was holding on to his temper with iron control. He gently lifted my blouse to peer at the ripped bra and the bruises on my chest, even with Eric there. (He looked, of course.)

"What happened to this Gabe?" Bill asked, very quietly.

"Well, he's dead," I said. "Godfrey killed him."

"You saw Godfrey?" Eric leaned forward. He hadn't said a thing up till this point. He'd finished doctoring my arm. He'd put antibiotic ointment all over it as if he were protecting a baby from diaper rash.

"You were right, Bill. He was the one who kidnapped Farrell, though I didn't get any details. And Godfrey stopped Gabe from raping me. Though I got to say, I had gotten in a few good licks myself."

"Don't brag," said Bill with a small smile. "So, the man is dead." But he didn't seem satisfied.

"Godfrey was very good in stopping Gabe and helping me get out. Specially since he just wanted to think about meeting the dawn. Where is he?"

"He ran into the night during our attack on the Fellowship," Bill explained. "None of us could catch him."

"What happened at the Fellowship?"

"I'll tell you, Sookie. But let's say good night to Eric, and I will tell you while I bathe you."

"Okay," I agreed. "Good night, Eric. Thanks for the first aid."

"I think those are the main points," Bill said to Eric. "If there is more, I'll come to your room later."

"Good." Eric looked at me, his eyes half-open. He'd had a lick or two at my bloody arm while he doctored it, and the taste seemed to have intoxicated him. "Rest well, Sookie."

"Oh," I said, my eyes opening all the way suddenly. "You know, we owe the shapeshifters."

Both the vampires stared at me. "Well, maybe not you guys, but I sure do."

"Oh, they'll put in a claim," Eric predicted. "Those shapeshifters never perform any service for free. Good night, Sookie. I am glad you weren't raped and killed." He gave his sudden flashing grin, and looked a lot more like himself.

"Gee, thanks a lot," I said, my eyes closing again. "Night."

When the door had closed behind Eric, Bill gathered me up out of the chair and took me in the bathroom. It was about as big as most hotel bathrooms, but the tub was adequate. Bill ran it full of hot water and very carefully took off my clothes.

"Just toss 'em, Bill," I said.

"Maybe I will, at that." He was eyeing the bruises again, his lips pressed together in a straight line.

"Some of these are from the fall on the stairs, and some are from the car accident," I explained.

"If Gabe wasn't dead, I would find him and kill him," Bill said, mostly to himself. "I would take my time." He lifted me as easily as if I were a baby and put me in the bath, and began washing me with a cloth and a bar of soap.

"My hair is so nasty."

"Yes, it is, but we may have to take care of your hair in the morning. You need sleep."

Beginning with my face, Bill gently scrubbed me all the way down. The water became discolored with dirt and old blood. He checked my arm thoroughly, to make sure Eric had gotten all the glass. Then he emptied the tub and refilled it, while I shivered. This time, I got clean. After I moaned about my hair a second time, he gave in. He wet my head and shampooed my hair, rinsing it laboriously. There is nothing more wonderful than feeling head-to-toe clean after you've been filthy, having a comfortable bed with clean sheets, being able to sleep in it in safety.

"Tell me about what happened at the Fellowship," I said as he carried me to the bed. "Keep me company."

Bill inserted me under the sheet and crawled in the other side. He slid his arm under my head and scooted close. I carefully touched my forehead to his chest and rubbed it.

"By the time we got there, it was like a disrupted anthill," he said. "The parking lot was full of cars and people, and more kept arriving for the—all-night sleepover?"

"Lock-in," I murmured, carefully turning on my right side to burrow against him.

"There was a certain amount of turmoil when we arrived. Almost all of them piled into their cars and left as fast as traffic would allow. Their leader, Newlin, tried to deny us entrance to the Fellowship hall—surely that was a church at one time?—and he told us we would burst into flames if we entered, because we were the damned." Bill snorted. "Stan picked him up and set him aside. And into the church we went, Newlin and his woman trailing right behind us. Not a one of us burst into flames, which seemed to shake up the people a great deal."

"I'll bet," I mumbled into his chest.

"Barry told us that when he communicated with you, he had the sense you were 'down'—below ground level. He thought he picked up the word 'stairs' from you. There were six of us—Stan, Joseph Velasquez, Isabel, and others—and it took us perhaps six minutes to eliminate all the possibilities and find the stairs."

"What did you do about the door?" It had had stout locks, I remembered.

"We ripped it from its hinges."

"Oh." Well, that would provide quick access, sure enough.

"I thought you were still down there, of course. When I found the room with the dead man, who had his pants open . . ." He paused a long moment. "I was sure you had been there. I could smell you in the air still. There was a smear of blood on him, your blood, and I found other traces of it around. I was very worried."

I patted him. I felt too tired and weak to pat very vigorously, but it was the only consolation I had to offer at the moment.

"Sookie," he said very carefully, "is there anything more you want to tell me?"

I was too sleepy to figure this one through. "No," I said and yawned. "I think I pretty much covered my adventures earlier."

"I thought maybe since Eric was in the room earlier, you wouldn't want to say everything?"

I finally heard the other shoe drop. I kissed his chest, over his heart. "Godfrey really was in time."

There was a long silence. I looked up to see Bill's face set so rigidly that he looked like a statue. His dark eyelashes stood out against his pallor with amazing clarity. His dark eyes seemed bottomless. "Tell me the rest," I said.

"Then we went farther into the bomb shelter and found the larger room, along with an extended area full of supplies—food and guns—where it was obvious another vampire had been staying."

I hadn't seen that part of the bomb shelter, and I certainly had no plans to revisit it to view what I'd missed.

"In the second cell we found Farrell and Hugo."

"Was Hugo alive?"

"Just barely." Bill kissed my forehead. "Luckily for Hugo, Farrell likes his sex with younger men."

"Maybe that was why Godfrey chose Farrell to abduct, when he decided to make an example of another sinner."

Bill nodded. "That is what Farrell said. But he had

been without sex and blood for a long time, and he was hungry in every sense. Without the silver manacles, Hugo would have . . . had a bad time. Even with silver on his wrists and ankles, Farrell was able to feed from Hugo."

"Did you know that Hugo was the traitor?"

"Farrell heard your conversation with him."

"How—oh, right, vampire hearing. Stupid me."

"Farrell would also like to know what you did to Gabe to make him scream."

"Clapped him over the ears." I cupped one hand to show him.

"Farrell was delighted. This Gabe was one of those men who enjoys power over others. He subjected Farrell to many indignities."

"Farrell's just lucky he's not a woman," I said. "Where is Hugo now?"

"He is somewhere safe."

"Safe for who?"

"Safe for vampires. Away from the media. They would enjoy Hugo's story all too much."

"What are they gonna do with him?"

"That's for Stan to decide."

"Remember the deal we had with Stan? If humans are found guilty by evidence of mine, they don't get killed."

Bill obviously didn't want to debate me on this now. His face shut down. "Sookie, you have to go to sleep now. We'll talk about it when you get up."

"But by then he may be dead."

"Why should you care?"

"Because that was the deal! I know Hugo is a shit, and I hate him, too, but I feel sorry for him; and I don't think I can be implicated in his death and live with a clear conscience."

"Sookie, he will still be alive when you get up. We'll talk about it then."

I felt sleep pulling me under like the undertow of the surf. It was hard to believe it was only two o'clock in the morning.

"Thanks for coming after me."

Bill said, after a pause, "First you weren't at the Fellowship, just traces of your blood and dead rapist. When I found you weren't at the hospital, that you had been spirited out of there somehow . . ."

"Mmmmh?"

"I was very, very scared. No one had any idea where you were. In fact, while I stood there talking to the nurse who admitted you, your name went off the computer screen."

I was impressed. Those shapeshifters were organized to an amazing degree. "Maybe I should send Luna some flowers," I said, hardly able to get the words out of my mouth.

Bill kissed me, a very satisfying kiss, and that was the last thing I remembered.

1~

I TURNED OVER LABORIOUSLY AND PEERED AT THE ILLU-
minated clock on the bedside table. It was not yet dawn,
but dawn would come soon. Bill was in his coffin already: the lid was closed. Why was I awake? I thought it
over.

There was something I had to do. Part of me stood
back in amazement at my own stupidity as I pulled on
some shorts and a T-shirt and slid my feet into sandals. I
looked even worse in the mirror, to which I gave only a
sideways glance. I stood with my back to it to brush my
hair. To my astonishment and pleasure, my purse was sitting on the table in the sitting room. Someone had re-
trieved it from the Fellowship headquarters the night
before. I stuck my plastic key in it and made my way

painfully down the silent halls.

Barry was not on duty anymore, and his replacement was too well trained to ask me what the hell I was doing going around looking like something a train had dragged in. He got me a cab and I told the driver where I needed to go. The driver looked at me in the rearview mirror. "Wouldn't you rather go to a hospital?" he suggested uneasily.

"No. I've already been." That hardly seemed to reassure him.

"Those vampires treat you so bad, why do you hang around them?"

"People did this to me," I said. "Not vampires."

We drove off. Traffic was light, it being nearly dawn on a Sunday morning. It only took fifteen minutes to get to the same place I'd been the night before, the Fellowship parking lot.

"Can you wait for me?" I asked the driver. He was a man in his sixties, grizzled and missing a front tooth. He wore a plaid shirt with snaps instead of buttons.

"I reckon I can do that," he said. He pulled a Louis L'Amour Western out from under his seat and switched on a dome light to read.

Under the glare of the sodium lights, the parking lot showed no visible traces of the events of the night before. There were only a couple of vehicles remaining, and I figured they'd been abandoned the night before. One of these cars was probably Gabe's. I wondered if Gabe had had a family; I hoped not. For one thing, he was such a sadist he must have made their lives miserable, and for another, for the rest of their lives they'd have to wonder how and why he'd died. What would Steve and Sarah

Newlin do now? Would there be enough members left of their Fellowship to carry on? Presumably the guns and provisions were still in the church. Maybe they'd been stockpiling against the apocalypse.

Out of the dark shadows next to the church a figure emerged. Godfrey. He was still bare-chested, and he still looked like a fresh-faced sixteen. Only the alien character of the tattoos and his eyes gave the lie to his body.

"I came to watch," I said, when he was close to me, though maybe "bear witness" would have been more accurate.

"Why?"

"I owe it to you."

"I am an evil creature."

"Yes, you are." There just wasn't any getting around that. "But you did a good thing, saving me from Gabe."

"By killing one more man? My conscience hardly knew the difference. There have been so many. At least I spared you some humiliation."

His voice grabbed at my heart. The growing light in the sky was still so faint that the parking lot security lights remained on, and by their glow I examined the young, young face.

All of a sudden, absurdly, I began to cry.

"That's nice," Godfrey said. His voice was already remote. "Someone to cry for me at the end. I had hardly expected that." He stepped back to a safe distance.

And then the sun rose.

When I got back in the cab, the driver stowed away his book.

"They have a fire going over there?" he asked. "I

thought I saw some smoke. I almost came to see what was happening."

"It's out now," I said.

I mopped at my face for a mile or so, and then I stared out the window as the stretches of city emerged from the night.

Back at the hotel, I let myself into our room again. I pulled off my shorts, lay down on the bed, and just as I was preparing myself for a long period of wakefulness, I fell deep asleep.

Bill woke me up at sundown, in his favorite way. My T-shirt was pushed up, and his dark hair brushed my chest. It was like waking up halfway down the road, so to speak; his mouth was sucking so tenderly on half of what he told me was the most beautiful pair of breasts in the world. He was very careful of his fangs, which were fully down. That was only one of the evidences of his arousal. "Do you feel up to doing this, enjoying it, if I am very, very careful?" he whispered against my ear.

"If you treat me like I was made of glass," I murmured, knowing that he could.

"But that doesn't feel like glass," he said, his hand moving gently. "That feels warm. And wet."

I gasped.

"That much? Am I hurting you?" His hand moved more forcefully.

"Bill" was all I could say. I put my lips on his, and his tongue began a familiar rhythm.

"Lie on your side," he whispered. "I will take care of everything."

And he did.

"Why were you partly dressed?" he asked, later. He'd gotten up to get a bottle of blood from the refrigerator in the room, and he'd warmed it in the microwave. He hadn't taken any of my blood, in consideration of my weakened state.

"I went to see Godfrey die."

His eyes glowed down at me. "What?"

"Godfrey met the dawn." The phrase I had once considered embarrassingly melodramatic flowed quite naturally from my mouth.

There was a long silence.

"How did you know he would? How did you know where?"

I shrugged as much as you can while you're lying in a bed. "I just figured he'd stick with his original plan. He seemed pretty set on it. And he'd saved my life. It was the least I could do."

"Did he show courage?"

I met Bill's eyes. "He died very bravely. He was eager to go."

I had no idea what Bill was thinking. "We have to go see Stan," he said. "We'll tell him."

"Why do we have to go see Stan again?" If I hadn't been such a mature woman, I would've pouted. As it was, Bill gave me one of those looks.

"You have to tell him your part, so he can be convinced we've performed our service. Also, there's the matter of Hugo."

That was enough to make me gloomy. I was so sore the idea of any more clothes than necessary touching my skin made me feel ill, so I pulled on a long, sleeveless taupe dress made out of a soft knit and slid my feet care-fully into sandals, and that was my outfit. Bill brushed my hair and put in my earrings for me, since raising my arms was uncomfortable, and he decided I needed a gold chain. I looked like I was going to a party at the outpa-tient ward for battered women. Bill called down for a rental car to be brought around. When the car had arrived in the underground garage, I had no idea. I didn't even know who had arranged for it. Bill drove. I didn't look out the window anymore. I was sick of Dallas.

When we got to the house on Green Valley Road, it looked as quiet as it had two nights ago. But after we'd been admitted, I found it was abuzz with vampires. We'd arrived in the midst of a welcome-home party for Farrell, who was standing in the living room with his arm around a handsome young man who might be all of eighteen. Farrell had a bottle of TrueBlood O negative in one hand, and his date had a Coke. The vampire looked almost as rosy as the boy.

Farrell had never actually seen me, so he was de-lighted to make my acquaintance. He was clad from head to toe in Western regalia, and as he bowed over my hand, I expected to hear spurs clink.

"You are so lovely," he said extravagantly, waving the bottle of synthetic blood, "that if I slept with women, you would receive my undivided attention for a week. I know you are self-conscious about your bruises, but they only set off your beauty."

I couldn't help laughing. Not only was I walking like I was about eighty, my face was black-and-blue on the left side.

"Bill Compton, you are one lucky vampire," Farrell told Bill.

"I am well aware of that," Bill said, smiling, though somewhat coolly.

"She is brave and beautiful!"

"Thanks, Farrell. Where's Stan?" I decided to break this stream of praise. Not only did it make Bill antsy, but Farrell's young companion was getting entirely too curious. My intention was to relate this story once again, and only once.

"He's in the dining room," the young vampire said, the one who'd brought poor Bethany into the dining room when we'd been here before. This must be Joseph Velasquez. He was maybe five foot eight, and his Hispanic ancestry gave him the toast-colored complexion and dark eyes of a don, while his vampire state gave him an unblinking stare and the instant willingness to do damage. He was scanning the room, waiting for trouble. I decided he was sort of the sergeant at arms of the nest. "He will be glad to see both of you."

I glanced around at all the vampires and the sprinkling of humans in the large rooms of the house. I didn't see Eric. I wondered if he'd gone back to Shreveport. "Where's Isabel?" I asked Bill, keeping my voice quiet.

"Isabel is being punished," he said, almost too softly to hear. He didn't want to talk about this any louder, and when Bill thought that was a wise idea, I knew I better shut up. "She brought a traitor into the nest, and she has to pay a price for that."

"But—"

"Shhh."

We came into the dining room to find it as crowded as

the living room. Stan was in the same chair, wearing virtually the same outfit he had been wearing last time I saw him. He stood up when we entered, and from the way he did this, I understood this was supposed to mark our status as important.

"Miss Stackhouse," he said formally, shaking my hand with great care. "Bill." Stan examined me with his eyes, their washed-out blue not missing a detail of my injuries. His glasses had been mended with Scotch tape. Stan was nothing if not thorough with his disguise. I thought I'd send him a pocket-protector for Christmas.

"Please tell me what happened to you yesterday, omitting nothing," Stan said.

This reminded me irresistibly of Archie Goodwin reporting to Nero Wolfe. "I'll bore Bill," I said, hoping to get out of this recitation.

"Bill will not mind being bored for a little."

There was no getting around this. I sighed, and began with Hugo picking me up from the Silent Shore Hotel. I tried to leave Barry's name out of my narrative, since I didn't know how he'd feel about being known by the vampires of Dallas. I just called him "a bellboy at the hotel." Of course, they could learn who he was if they tried.

When I got to the part where Gabe sent Hugo into Farrell's cell and then tried to rape me, my lips yanked up in a tight grin. My face felt so taut that I thought it might crack.

"Why does she do that?" Stan asked Bill, as though I weren't there.

"When she is tense . . ." Bill said.

"Oh." Stan looked at me even more thoughtfully. I reached up and began to pull my hair into a ponytail. Bill handed me an elastic band from his pocket, and with considerable discomfort, I held the hair in a tight hank so I could twist the band around it three times.

When I told Stan about the help the shapeshifters had given me, he leaned forward. He wanted to know more than I told, but I would not give any names away. He was intensely thoughtful after I told him about being dropped off at the hotel. I didn't know whether to include Eric or not; I left him out, completely. He was supposed to be from California. I amended my narrative to say I'd gone up to our room to wait for Bill.

And then I told him about Godfrey.

To my amazement, Stan could not seem to absorb Godfrey's death. He made me repeat the story. He swiveled in his chair to face the other way while I spoke. Behind his back, Bill gave me a reassuring caress. When Stan turned back to us, he was wiping his eyes with a red-stained handkerchief. So it was true that vampires could cry. And it was true that vampire tears were bloody.

I cried right along with him. For his centuries of molesting and killing children, Godfrey had deserved to die. I wondered how many humans were in jail for crimes Godfrey had committed. But Godfrey had helped me, and Godfrey had carried with him the most tremendous load of guilt and grief I'd ever encountered.

"What resolution and courage," Stan said admiringly. He hadn't been grieved at all, but lost in admiration. "It makes me weep." He said this in such a way that I knew it was meant to be a great tribute. "After Bill identified Godfrey the other night, I made some inquiries and found he had belonged to a nest in San Francisco. His nest mates will be grieved to hear of this. And of his betrayal of Farrell. But his courage in keeping his word, in fulfilling his plan!" It seemed to overwhelm Stan.

I just ached all over. I rummaged in my purse for a small bottle of Tylenol, and poured two out in my palm. At Stan's gesture, the young vampire brought me a glass of water, and I said, "Thank you," to his surprise.

"Thank you for your efforts," Stan said quite abruptly, as if he'd suddenly recalled his manners. "You have done the job we hired you to do, and more. Thanks to you we discovered and freed Farrell in time, and I'm sorry you sustained so much damage in the process."

That sounded mighty like a dismissal.

"Excuse me," I said, sliding forward in the chair. Bill made a sudden movement behind me, but I disregarded him.

Stan raised his light eyebrows at my temerity. "Yes? Your check will be mailed to your representative in Shreveport, as per our agreement. Please stay with us this evening as we celebrate Farrell's return."

"Our agreement was that if what I discovered resulted in a human being found at fault, that human would not be punished by the vampires but would be turned over to the police. For the court system to deal with. Where is Hugo?"

Stan's eyes slid from my face to focus on Bill's behind me. He seemed to be silently asking Bill why he couldn't control his human better.

"Hugo and Isabel are together," said Stan cryptically.

I *so* didn't want to know what that meant. But I was honor-bound to see this through. "So you are not going to honor your agreement?" I said, knowing that was a real challenge to Stan.

There should be an adage, proud as a vampire. They all are, and I'd pinked Stan in his pride. The implication that he was dishonorable enraged the vampire. I almost backed down, his face grew so scary. He really had nothing human left about him after a few seconds. His lips drew away from his teeth, his fangs extended, and his body hunched and seemed to elongate.

After a moment he stood, and with a curt little jerk of his hand, indicated I should follow him. Bill helped me up, and we trailed after Stan as he walked deeper into the house. There must have been six bedrooms in the place, and all the doors to them were closed. From behind one door came the unmistakable sounds of sex. To my relief, we passed that door by. We went up the stairs, which was quite uncomfortable for me. Stan never looked back and never slowed down. He went up the stairs at exactly the same pace at which he walked. He stopped at a door that looked like all the others. He unlocked it. He stood aside and gestured to me to go in.

That was something I didn't want to do—oh, so much. But I had to. I stepped forward and looked in.

Except for the dark blue wall-to-wall, the room was bare. Isabel was chained to the wall on one side of the room—with silver, of course. Hugo was on the other. He was chained, too. They were both awake, and they both looked at the doorway, naturally.

Isabel nodded as if we'd met in the mall, though she was naked. I saw that her wrists and ankles were padded to prevent the silver from burning her, though the chains would still keep her weak.

Hugo was naked, too. He could not take his eyes off Isabel. He barely glanced at me to see who I was before his gaze returned to her. I tried not to be embarrassed, because that seemed such a petty consideration; but I think it was the first time I'd seen another naked adult in my life, besides Bill.

Stan said, "She cannot feed off him, though she is hungry. He cannot have sex with her, though he is addicted. This is their punishment, for months. What would happen to Hugo in human courts?"

I considered. What had Hugo actually done that was indictable?

He'd deceived the vampires in that he'd been in the Dallas nest under false pretenses. That is, he actually loved Isabel, but he'd betrayed her compadres. Hmmm. No law about that.

"He bugged the dining room," I said. That was illegal. At least, I thought it was.

"How long in jail would he get for that?" Stan asked.

Good question. Not much, was my guess. A human jury might feel bugging a vampire hangout was even justified. I sighed, sufficient answer for Stan.

"What other time would Hugo serve?" he asked.

"He got me to the Fellowship under false pretenses . . . not illegal. He . . . well, he . . ."

"Exactly."

Hugo's infatuated gaze never shifted from Isabel.

Hugo had caused and abetted evil, just as surely as Godfrey had committed evil.

"How long will you keep them there?" I asked.

Stan shrugged. "Three or four months. We will feed Hugo, of course. Not Isabel."

"And then?"

"We'll unchain him first. He will get a day's head start."

Bill's hand clamped down on my wrist. He didn't want me to ask any more questions.

Isabel looked at me and nodded. This seemed fair to her, she was saying. "All right," I said, holding my palms forward in the "Stop" position. "All right." And I turned and made my way slowly and carefully down the stairs.

I had lost some integrity, but for the life of me, I couldn't figure out what I could do differently. The more I tried to think about it, the more confused I got. I am not used to thinking through moral issues. Things are bad to do, or they aren't.

Well, there was a gray area. That's where a few things fell, like sleeping with Bill though we weren't married or telling Arlene her dress looked good, when in fact it made her look like hell. Actually, I couldn't marry Bill. It wasn't legal. But then, he hadn't asked me.

My thoughts wandered in a dithery circle around the miserable couple in the upstairs bedroom. To my amazement, I felt much sorrier for Isabel than for Hugo. Hugo, after all, was guilty of active evil. Isabel was only guilty of negligence.

I had a lot of time to maunder on and on through similar dead-end thought patterns, since Bill was having a rip-roaring good time at the party. I'd only been to a mixed vampire and human party once or twice before, and it was a mixture that was still uneasy after two years of legally recognized vampirism. Open drinking—that is, bloodsucking—from humans was absolutely illegal, and I am here to tell you that in Dallas's vampire headquarters, that law was strictly observed. From time to time, I saw a couple vanish for a while upstairs, but all the humans seemed to come back in good health. I know, because I counted and watched.

Bill had mainstreamed for so many months that apparently it was a real treat for him to get together with other vampires. So he was deep in conversation with this vamp or that, reminiscing about Chicago in the twenties or discussing investment opportunities in various vampire holdings around the world. I was so shaky physically that I was content to sit on a soft couch and watch, sipping from time to time at my screwdriver. The bartender was a pleasant young man, and we talked bars for a little while. I should have been enjoying my break from waiting tables at Merlotte's, but I would gladly have dressed in my uniform and taken orders. I wasn't used to big changes in my routine.

Then a woman maybe a little younger than me plopped down on the couch beside me. Turned out she was dating the vampire who acted as sergeant at arms, Joseph Velasquez, who'd gone to the Fellowship Center with Bill the night before. Her name was Trudi Pfeiffer. Trudi had hair done in deep red spikes, a pierced nose and tongue, and macabre makeup, including black lipstick. She told me proudly its color was called Grave Rot. Her jeans were so low I wondered how she got up and down in them. Maybe she wore them so low-cut to show off her navel ring. Her knit top was cropped very short. The outfit I'd worn the night the maenad had gotten me paled in comparison. So, there was lots of Trudi to see.

When you talked to her, she wasn't as bizarre as her appearance led you to believe. Trudi was a college student. I discovered, through absolutely legitimate listening, that she believed herself to be waving the red flag at the bull, by dating Joseph. The bull was her parents, I gathered.

"They would even rather I dated someone *black*," she told me proudly.

I tried to look appropriately impressed. "They really hate the dead scene, huh?"

"Oh, do they ever." She nodded several times and waved her black fingernails extravagantly. She was drinking Dos Equis. "My mom always says, 'Can't you date someone *alive*?' " We both laughed.

"So, how are you and Bill?" She waggled her eyebrows up and down to indicate how significant the question was.

"You mean . . . ?"

"How's he in bed? Joseph is un-fucking-believable."

I can't say I was surprised, but I was dismayed. I cast around in my mind for a minute. "I'm glad for you," I finally said. If she'd been my good friend Arlene, I might have winked and smiled, but I wasn't about to discuss my sex life with a total stranger, and I really didn't want to know about her and Joseph.

Trudi lurched up to get another beer and remained in conversation with the bartender. I shut my eyes in relief and weariness, and felt the couch depress beside me. I cut my gaze to the right to see what new companion I had. Eric. Oh, great.

"How are you?" he asked.

"Better than I look." That wasn't true.

"You've seen Hugo and Isabel?"

"Yes." I looked at my hands folded in my lap.

"Appropriate, don't you think?"

I thought that Eric was trying to provoke me.

"In a way, yes," I said. "Assuming Stan sticks to his word."

"You didn't say that to him, I hope." But Eric looked only amused.

"No, I didn't. Not in so many words. You're all so damn proud."

He looked surprised. "Yes, I guess that's true."

"Did you just come to check up on me?"

"To Dallas?"

I nodded.

"Yes." He shrugged. He was wearing a knit shirt in a pretty tan and blue pattern, and the shrug made his shoulders look massive. "We are loaning you out for the first time. I wanted to see that things went smoothly without being here in my official capacity."

"Do you think Stan knows who you are?"

He looked interested in the idea. "It's not far-fetched," he said at last. "He would probably have done the same thing in my place."

"Do you think from now on, you could just let me stay at home, and leave me and Bill alone?" I asked.

"No. You are too useful," he said. "Besides, I'm hoping that the more you see me, the more I'll grow on you."

"Like a fungus?"

He laughed, but his eyes were fixed on me in a way that meant business. Oh, hell.

"You look especially luscious in that knit dress with nothing underneath," Eric said. "If you left Bill and came to me of your own free will, he would accept that."

"But I'm not going to do any such thing," I said, and then something caught at the edges of my consciousness.

Eric started to say something else to me, but I put my hand across his mouth. I moved my head from side to side, trying to get the best reception; that's the best way I can explain it.

"Help me up," I said.

Without a word, Eric stood and gently pulled me to my feet. I could feel my eyebrows draw together.

They were all around us. They circled the house.

Their brains were wound up to fever pitch. If Trudi hadn't been babbling earlier, I might have heard them as they crept up to circle the house.

"Eric," I said, trying to catch as many thoughts as I could, hearing a countdown, oh, God!

"Hit the floor!" I yelled at the top of my lungs.

Every vampire obeyed.

So when the Fellowship opened fire, it was the humans that died.

8

A YARD AWAY, TRUDI WAS CUT DOWN BY A SHOTGUN blast.

The dyed dark red of her hair turned another shade of red and her open eyes stared at me forever. Chuck, the bartender, was only wounded, since the structure of the bar itself offered him some protection.

Eric was lying on top of me. Given my sore condition, that was very painful, and I started to shove at him. Then I realized that if he were hit with bullets, he would most likely survive. But I wouldn't. So I accepted his shelter gratefully for the horrible minutes of the first wave of the attack, when rifles and shotguns and handguns were fired into the suburban mansion over and over.

Instinctively, I shut my eyes while the blasting lasted.

Glass shattered, vampires roared, humans screamed. The noise battered at me, just as the tidal wave of scores of brains at high gear washed over me. When it began to taper off, I looked up into Eric's eyes. Incredibly, he was excited. He smiled at me. "I knew I'd get on top of you somehow," he said.

"Are you trying to make me mad so I'll forget how scared I am?"

"No, I'm just opportunistic."

I wiggled, trying to get out from under him, and he said, "Oh, do that again. It felt great."

"Eric, that girl I was just talking to is about three feet away from us with part of her head missing."

"Sookie," he said, suddenly serious, "I've been dead for a few hundred years. I am used to it. But she is not quite gone. There is a spark. Do you want me to bring her over?"

I was shocked speechless. How could I make that decision?

And while I thought about it, he said, "She is gone."

While I stared up at him, the silence became complete. The only noise in the house was the sobbing of Farrell's wounded date, who was pressing both hands to his reddened thigh. From outside came the remote sounds of vehicles pulling out in a hurry up and down the quiet suburban street. The attack was over. I seemed to be having trouble breathing, and figuring out what I should do next. Surely there was something, some action, I should be taking?

This was as close to war as I would ever come.

The room was full of the survivors' screams and the vampires' howls of rage. Bits of stuffing from the couch and chairs floated in the air like snow. There was broken glass on everything and the heat of the night poured into the room. Several of the vampires were already up and giving chase, Joseph Velasquez among them, I noticed.

"No excuse to linger," Eric said with a mock sigh, and lifted off of me. He looked down at himself. "My shirts always get ruined when I am around you."

"Oh shit, Eric." I got to my knees with clumsy haste. "You're bleeding. You got hit. Bill! Bill!" My hair was slithering around my shoulders as I turned from side to side searching the room. The last time I'd noticed him he'd been talking to a black-haired vampire with a pronounced widow's peak. She'd looked something like Snow White to me. Now I half stood to search the floor, and I saw her sprawled close to a window. Something was protruding from her chest. The window had been hit by a shotgun blast, and some splinters had flown into the room. One of them had pierced her chest and killed her. Bill was not in sight, among the living or the dead.

Eric pulled off his sodden shirt and looked down at his shoulder. "The bullet is right inside the wound, Sookie," Eric said, through clenched teeth. "Suck it out."

"What?" I gaped at him.

"If you don't suck it out, it will heal inside my flesh. If you are so squeamish, go get a knife and cut."

"But I can't do that." My tiny party purse had a pocketknife inside, but I had no idea where I'd put it down, and I couldn't gather my thoughts to search.

He bared his teeth at me. "I took this bullet for you. You can get it out for me. You are no coward."

I forced myself to steady. I used his discarded shirt as a swab. The bleeding was slowing, and by peering into the torn flesh, I could just see the bullet. If I'd had long fingernails like Trudi, I'd have been able to get it out, but my fingers are short and blunt, and my nails are clipped close. I sighed in resignation.

The phrase "biting the bullet" took on a whole new meaning as I bent to Eric's shoulder.

Eric gave a long moan as I sucked, and I felt the bullet pop into my mouth. He'd been right. The rug could hardly be stained any worse than it already was, so though it made me feel like a real heathen, I spat the bullet onto the floor along with most of the blood in my mouth. But some of it, inevitably, I swallowed. His shoulder was already healing. "This room reeks of blood," he whispered.

"Well, there," I said, and looked up. "That was the grossest—"

"Your lips are bloody." He seized my face in both hands and kissed me.

It's hard not to respond when a master of the art of kissing is laying one on you. And I might have let myself enjoy it—well, enjoy it more—if I hadn't been so worried about Bill; because let's face it, brushes with death have that effect. You want to reaffirm the fact that you're alive. Though vampires actually aren't, it seems they are no more immune to that syndrome than humans, and Eric's libido was up because of the blood in the room.

But I was worried about Bill, and I was shocked by the violence, so after a long hot moment of forgetting the horror around me, I pulled away. Eric's lips were bloody now. He licked them slowly. "Go look for Bill," he said in a thick voice.

I glanced at his shoulder again, to see the hole had begun to close. I picked up the bullet off the carpet, tacky as it was with blood, and wrapped it in a scrap from Eric's shirt. It seemed like a good memento, at the time. I really don't know what I was thinking. There were still the injured and dead on the floor in the room, but most of those who were still alive had help from other humans or from two vampires who hadn't joined in the chase.

Sirens were sounding in the distance.

The beautiful front door was splintered and pitted. I stood to one side to open it, just in case there was a lone vigilante in the yard, but nothing happened. I peered around the doorframe.

"Bill?" I called. "Are you okay?"

Just then he sauntered back in the yard looking positively rosy.

"Bill," I said, feeling old and grim and gray. A dull horror, that really was just a deep disappointment, filled the pit of my stomach.

He stopped in his tracks.

"They fired at us and killed some of us," he said. His fangs gleamed, and he was shiny with excitement.

"You just killed somebody."

"To defend us."

"To get vengeance."

There was a clear difference between the two, in my mind, at that moment. He seemed nonplussed.

"You didn't even wait to see if I was okay," I said. Once a vampire, always a vampire. Tigers can't change their stripes. You can't teach an old dog new tricks. I heard every warning anyone had ever fed me, in the warm drawl of home.

I turned and went back into the house, walking obliviously through the bloodstains and chaos and mess as if I saw such things every day. Some of the things I saw I didn't even register I'd seen, until the next week when my brain would suddenly throw out a picture for my viewing: maybe a closeup of a shattered skull, or a spouting artery. What was important to me at the moment was that I find my purse. I found that purse in the second place I looked. While Bill fussed with the wounded so he wouldn't have to talk to me, I walked out of that house and got in that rental car and, despite my anxiety, I drove. Being at this house was worse than the fear of big-city traffic. I pulled away from the house right before the police got there.

After I'd driven a few blocks, I parked in front of a library and extricated the map from the glove compartment. Though it took twice as long as it should have, since my brain was so shell-shocked it was almost not functioning, I figured out how to get to the airport.

And that's where I went. I followed the signs that said RENTAL CARS and I parked the car and left the keys in it and walked away. I got a seat on the next flight to Shreveport, which was leaving within the hour. I thanked God I had my own credit card.

Since I'd never done it before, it took me a few minutes to figure out the pay phone. I was lucky enough to get hold of Jason, who said he'd meet me at the airport.

I was home in bed by early morning.

I didn't start crying until the next day.

9

W<small>E'D FOUGHT BEFORE, BILL AND I. I'D GOTTEN FED UP</small>
before, tired of the vampirey stuff I had to learn to accommodate, frightened of getting in deeper. Sometimes,
I just wanted to see humans for a while.

So for over three weeks, that was what I did. I didn't
call Bill; he didn't call me. I knew he was back from Dallas because he left my suitcase on my front porch. When
I unpacked it, I found a black velvet jeweler's box tucked
in the side pocket. I wish I'd had the strength to keep
from opening it, but I didn't. Inside was a pair of topaz
earrings, and a note that said, "To go with your brown
dress." Which meant the taupe knit thing I'd worn to the
vampires' headquarters. I stuck my tongue out at the box,
and drove over to his house that afternoon to leave it in

his mailbox. He'd finally gone out and bought me a present, and here I had to return it.

I didn't even try to "think things through." I figured my brain would clear up in a while, and then I would know what to do.

I did read the papers. The vampires of Dallas and their human friends were now martyrs, which probably suited Stan down to the ground. The Dallas Midnight Massacre was being touted in all the newsmagazines as the perfect example of a hate crime. Legislatures were being pressured to pass all kinds of laws that would never make it onto the books, but it made people feel better to think they might; laws that would provide vampire-owned buildings with federal protection, laws that would permit vampires to hold certain elected positions (though no one yet suggested a vampire could run for the U.S. Senate or serve as a representative). There was even a motion in the Texas legislature to appoint a vampire as legal executioner of the state. After all, a Senator Garza was quoted as saying, "Death by vampire bite is at least supposed to be painless, and the vampire receives nutrition from it."

I had news for Senator Garza. Vampire bites were only pleasant by the will of the vampire. If the vampire didn't glamour you first, a serious vampire bite (as opposed to a love nip) hurt like hell.

I wondered if Senator Garza was related to Luna, but Sam told me that "Garza" was as common among Americans of Mexican descent as "Smith" was among Americans of English stock.

Sam didn't ask why I wanted to know. That made me feel a little forlorn, because I was used to feeling important to Sam. But he was preoccupied these days, on the job and off. Arlene said she thought he was dating someone, which was a first, as far as any of us could remember. Whoever she was, none of us got to see her, which was strange in and of itself. I tried to tell him about the shapeshifters of Dallas, but he just smiled and found an excuse to go do something else.

My brother, Jason, dropped by the house for lunch one day. It wasn't like it had been when my grandmother was alive. Gran would have a huge meal on the table at lunchtime, and then we'd just eat sandwiches at night. Jason had come by pretty frequently then; Gran had been an excellent cook. I managed to serve him meatloaf sandwiches and potato salad (though I didn't tell him it was from the store), and I had some peach tea fixed, which was lucky.

"What's with you and Bill?" he asked bluntly, when he was through. He'd been real good about not asking on the drive back from the airport.

"I got mad at him," I said.

"Why?"

"He broke a promise to me," I said. Jason was trying hard to act like a big brother, and I should try to accept his concern instead of getting mad. It occurred to me, not for the first time, that possibly I had a pretty hot temper. Under some circumstances. I locked my sixth sense down firmly, so I would only hear what Jason was actually saying.

"He's been seen over in Monroe."

I took a deep breath. "With someone else?"

"Yes."

"Who?"

"You're not going to believe this. Portia Bellefleur."

I couldn't have been more surprised if Jason had told me Bill had been dating Hillary Clinton (though Bill *was* a Democrat). I stared at my brother as if he'd suddenly announced he was Satan. The only things Portia Belle-fleur and I had in common were a birthplace, female organs, and long hair. "Well," I said blankly. "I don't know whether to pitch a fit or laugh. What do you make of that?"

Because if anyone knew about man-woman stuff, it was Jason. At least, he knew about it from the man's point of view.

"She's your opposite," he said, with undue thoughtfulness. "In every way that I can think of. She's real educated, she comes from an, I guess you'd call it, aristocratic background, and she's a lawyer. Plus, her brother's a cop. And they go to symphonies and shit."

Tears prickled at my eyes. I would have gone to a symphony with Bill, if he'd ever asked me.

"On the other hand, you're smart, you're pretty, and you're willing to put up with his little ways." I wasn't exactly sure what Jason meant by that, and thought it better not to ask. "But we sure ain't aristocracy. You work in a bar, and your brother works on a road crew." Jason smiled at me lopsidedly.

"We've been here as long as the Bellefleurs," I said, trying not to sound sullen.

"I know that, and you know that. And Bill sure knows that, because he was alive then." True enough.

"What's happening about the case against Andy?" I asked.

"No charges brought against him yet, but the rumors

are flying around town thick and fast about this sex club thing. Lafayette was so pleased to have been asked; evidently he mentioned it to quite a few people. They say that since the first rule of the club is Keep Silent, Lafayette got whacked for his enthusiasm."

"What do you think?"

"I think if anyone was forming a sex club around Bon Temps, they woulda called me," he said, dead serious.

"You're right," I said, struck again by how sensible Jason could be. "You'd be number one on the list." Why hadn't I thought of that before? Not only did Jason have a reputation as a guy who'd heated up many a bed, he was both very attractive and unmarried.

"The only thing I can think of," I said slowly, "Lafayette was gay, as you well know."

"And?"

"And maybe this club, if it exists, only accepts people who are all right with that."

"You might have a point there," Jason said.

"Yes, Mr. Homophobe."

Jason smiled and shrugged. "Everybody's got a weak point," he said. "Plus, as you know, I've been going out with Liz pretty steady. I think anyone with a brain would see Liz ain't about to share a napkin, much less a boyfriend."

He was right. Liz's family notoriously took "Neither a borrower nor a lender be" to a complete extreme.

"You are a piece of work, brother," I said, focusing on his shortcomings, rather than those of Liz's folks. "There are so many worse things to be than gay."

"Such as?"

"Thief, traitor, murderer, rapist . . ."

"Okay, okay, I get the idea."

"I hope you do," I said. Our differences grieved me. But I loved Jason anyway; he was all I had left.

I saw Bill out with Portia that same night. I caught a glimpse of them together in Bill's car, driving down Claiborne Street. Portia had her head turned to Bill, talking; he was looking straight ahead, expressionless, as far as I could tell. They didn't see me. I was coming from the automated teller at the bank, on my way to work.

Hearing of and seeing directly are two very different things. I felt an overwhelming surge of rage; and I understood how Bill had felt, when he'd seen his friends dying. I wanted to kill someone. I just wasn't sure who I wanted to kill.

Andy was in the bar that evening, sitting in Arlene's section. I was glad, because Andy looked bad. He was not clean-shaven, and his clothes were rumpled. He came up to me as he was leaving, and I could smell the booze. "Take him back," he said. His voice was thick with anger. "Take the damn vampire back so he'll leave my sister alone."

I didn't know what to say to Andy Bellefleur. I just stared at him until he stumbled out of the bar. It crossed my mind that people wouldn't be as surprised to hear of a dead body in his car now as they had been a few weeks ago.

The next night I had off, and the temperature dropped. It was a Friday, and suddenly I was tired of being alone. I decided to go to the high school football game. This is a townwide pastime in Bon Temps, and the games are discussed thoroughly on Monday morning in every store in town. The film of the game is shown twice on a local-access channel, and boys who show promise with pigskin are minor royalty, more's the pity.

You don't show up at the game all disheveled.

I pulled my hair back from my forehead in an elastic band and used my curling iron on the rest, so I had thick curls hanging around my shoulders. My bruises were gone. I put on complete makeup, down to the lip liner. I put on black knit slacks and a black and red sweater. I wore my black leather boots and my gold hoop earrings, and I pinned a red and black bow to hide the elastic band in my hair. (Guess what our school colors are.)

"Pretty good," I said, viewing the result in my mirror. "Pretty *damn* good." I gathered up my black jacket and my purse, and drove into town.

The stands were full of people I knew. A dozen voices called to me, a dozen people told me how cute I looked, and the problem was . . . I was miserable. As soon as I realized this, I pasted a smile on my face and searched for someone to sit with.

"Sookie! Sookie!" Tara Thornton, one of my few good high school friends, was calling me from high up in the stands. She made a frantic beckoning gesture, and I smiled back and began to hike up, speaking to more people along the way. Mike Spencer, the funeral home director, was there, in his favorite Western regalia, and my grandmother's good friend Maxine Fortenberry, and her son, Hoyt, who was a buddy of Jason's. I saw Sid Matt Lancaster, the ancient lawyer, bundled up beside his wife.

Tara was sitting with her fiancé, Benedict Tallie, who

was inevitably and regrettably called "Eggs." With them was Benedict's best friend, JB du Rone. When I saw JB, my spirits began to rise, and so did my repressed libido. JB could have been on the cover of a romance novel, he was so lovely. Unfortunately, he didn't have a brain in his head, as I'd discovered on our handful of dates. I'd often thought I'd hardly have to put up any mental shield to be with JB, because he had no thoughts to read.

"Hey, how y'all doing?"

"We're great!" Tara said, with her party-girl face on. "How about you? I haven't seen you in a coon's age!" Her dark hair was cut in a short pageboy, and her lipstick could have lit a fire, it was so hot. She was wearing off-white and black with a red scarf to show her team spirit, and she and Eggs were sharing a drink in one of the paper cups sold in the stadium. It was spiked; I could smell the bourbon from where I stood. "Move over, JB, and let me sit with you," I said with an answering smile.

"Sure, Sookie," he said, looking very happy to see me. That was one of JB's charms. The others included white perfect teeth, an absolutely straight nose, a face so masculine yet so handsome that it made you want to reach out and stroke his cheeks, and a broad chest and trim waist. Maybe not quite as trim as it used to be, but then, JB was human, and that was a Good Thing. I settled in between Eggs and JB, and Eggs turned to me with a sloppy smile.

"Want a drink, Sookie?"

I am kind of spare on drinking, since I see its results every day. "No, thank you," I said. "How you been doing, Eggs?"

"Good," he said, after considering. He'd had more to drink than Tara. He'd had too much to drink.

We talked about mutual friends and acquaintances until the kickoff, after which the game was the sole topic of conversation. The Game, broadly, because every game for the past fifty years lay in the collective memory of Bon Temps, and this game was compared to all other games, these players to all others. I could actually enjoy this occasion a little, since I had developed my mental shielding to such an extent. I could pretend people were exactly what they said, since I was absolutely not listening in.

JB snuggled closer and closer, after a shower of compliments on my hair and my figure. JB's mother had taught him early on that appreciated women are happy women, and it was a simple philosophy that had kept JB's head above water for some time.

"You remember that doctor at that hospital, Sookie?" he asked me suddenly, during the second quarter.

"Yes. Dr. Sonntag. Widow." She'd been young to be a widow, and younger to be a doctor. I'd introduced her to JB.

"We dated for a while. Me and a doctor," he said wonderingly.

"Hey, that's great." I'd hoped as much. It had seemed to me that Dr. Sonntag could sure use what JB had to offer, and JB needed . . . well, he needed someone to take care of him.

"But then she got rotated back to Baton Rouge," he told me. He looked a little stricken. "I guess I miss her." A health care system had bought our little hospital, and the emergency room doctors were brought in for four months at a stretch. His arm tightened around my shoulders. "But it's awful good to see you," he reassured me.

Bless his heart. "JB, you could go to Baton Rouge to see her," I suggested. "Why don't you?"

"She's a doctor. She doesn't have much time off."

"She'd make time off for you."

"Do you think so?"

"Unless she's an absolute idiot," I told him.

"I might do that. I did talk to her on the phone the other night. She did say she wished I was there."

"That was a pretty big hint, JB."

"You think?"

"I sure do."

He looked perkier. "Then I'm fixing to drive to Baton Rouge tomorrow," he said again. He kissed my cheek. "You make me feel good, Sookie."

"Well, JB, right back at you." I gave him a peck on the lips, just a quick one.

Then I saw Bill staring a hole in me.

He and Portia were in the next section of seats, close to the bottom. He had twisted around and was looking up at me.

If I'd planned it, it couldn't have worked out better. This was a magnificent screw-him moment.

And it was ruined.

I just wanted him.

I turned my eyes away and smiled at JB, and all the time what I wanted was to meet with Bill under the stands and have sex with him right then and there. I wanted him to pull down my pants and get behind me. I wanted him to make me moan.

I was so shocked at myself I didn't know what to do. I could feel my face turning a dull red. I could not even pretend to smile.

After a minute, I could appreciate that this was almost funny. I had been brought up as conventionally as possible, given my unusual disability. Naturally, I'd learned the facts of life pretty early since I could read minds (and, as a child, had no control over what I absorbed). And I'd always thought the idea of sex was pretty interesting, though the same disability that had led to me learning so much about it theoretically had kept me from putting that theory into practice. After all, it's hard to get really involved in sex when you know your partner is wishing you were Tara Thornton instead (for example), or when he's hoping you remembered to bring a condom, or when he's criticizing your body parts. For successful sex, you have to keep your concentration fixed on what your partner's *doing*, so you can't get distracted by what he's *thinking*.

With Bill, I couldn't hear a single thing. And he was so experienced, so smooth, so absolutely dedicated to getting it right. It appeared I was as much a junkie as Hugo.

I sat through the rest of the game, smiling and nodding when it seemed indicated, trying not to look down and to my left, and finding after the halftime show was over that I hadn't heard a single song the band had played. Nor had I noticed Tara's cousin's twirling solo. As the crowd moved slowly to the parking lot after the Bon Temps Hawks had won, 28–18, I agreed to drive JB home. Eggs had sobered some by then, so I was pretty sure he and Tara would be okay; but I was relieved to see Tara take the wheel.

JB lived close to downtown in half a duplex. He asked me very sweetly to come in, but I told him I had to get home. I gave him a big hug, and I advised him to call Dr. Sonntag. I still didn't know her first name.

He said he would, but then, with JB, you couldn't really tell.

Then I had to stop and get gas at the only late-night gas station, where I had a long conversation with Arlene's cousin Derrick (who was brave enough to take the night shift), so I was a little later getting home than I had planned.

As I unlocked the front door, Bill came out of the darkness. Without a word, he grabbed my arm and turned me to him, and then he kissed me. In a minute we were pressed against the door with his body moving rhythmically against mine. I reached one hand behind myself to fumble with the lock, and the key finally turned. We stumbled into the house, and he turned me to face the couch. I gripped it with my hands and, just as I'd imagined, he pulled down my pants, and then he was in me.

I made a hoarse noise I'd never heard come from my throat before. Bill was making noises equally as primitive. I didn't think I could form a word. His hands were under my sweater, and my bra was in two pieces. He was relentless. I almost collapsed after the first time I came. "No," he growled when I was flagging, and he kept pounding. Then he increased the pace until I was almost sobbing, and then my sweater tore, and his teeth found my shoulder. He made a deep, awful sound, and then, after long seconds, it was over.

I was panting as if I'd run a mile, and he was shivering, too. Without bothering to refasten his clothing, he turned me around to face him, and he bent his head to my shoulder again to lick the little wound. When it had stopped bleeding and begun healing, he took off everything I had on, very slowly. He cleaned me below; he kissed me above.

"You smell like him" was the only thing he said. He proceeded to erase that smell and replace it with his own.

Then we were in the bedroom, and I had a moment to be glad I'd changed the sheets that morning before he bent his mouth to mine again.

If I'd had doubts up until then, I had them no longer. He was not sleeping with Portia Bellefleur. I didn't know what he was up to, but he did not have a true relationship with her. He slid his arms underneath me and held me to him as tightly as possible; he nuzzled my neck, kneaded my hips, ran his fingers down my thighs, and kissed the backs of my knees. He bathed in me. "Spread your legs for me, Sookie," he whispered, in his cold dark voice, and I did. He was ready again, and he was rough with it, as if he were trying to prove something.

"Be sweet," I said, the first time I had spoken.

"I can't. It's been too long, next time I'll be sweet, I swear," he said, running his tongue down the line of my jaw. His fangs grazed my neck. Fangs, tongue, mouth, fingers, manhood; it was like being made love to by the Tasmanian Devil. He was everywhere, and everywhere in a hurry.

When he collapsed on top of me, I was exhausted. He shifted to lie by my side, one leg draped over mine, one arm across my chest. He might as well have gotten out a branding iron and had done with it, but it wouldn't have been as much fun for me.

"Are you okay?" he mumbled.

"Except for having run into a brick wall a few times," I said indistinctly.

We both drifted off to sleep for a little, though Bill woke first, as he always did at night. "Sookie," he said quietly. "Darling. Wake up."

"Oo," I said, slowly coming to consciousness. For the first time in weeks, I woke with the hazy conviction that all was right with the world. With slow dismay, I realized that things were far from right. I opened my eyes. Bill's were right above me.

"We have to talk," he said, stroking the hair back from my face.

"So talk." I was awake now. What I was regretting was not the sex, but having to discuss the issues between us.

"I got carried away in Dallas," he said immediately. "Vampires do, when the chance to hunt presents itself so obviously. We were attacked. We have the right to hunt down those who want to kill us."

"That's returning to days of lawlessness," I said.

"But vampires hunt, Sookie. It is our nature," he said very seriously. "Like leopards; like wolves. We are not human. We can pretend to be, when we're trying to live with people . . . in your society. We can sometimes remember what it was like to be among you, one of you. But we are not the same race. We are no longer of the same clay."

I thought this over. He'd told me this, over and over, in different words, since we'd begun seeing each other.

Or maybe, he'd been seeing me, but I hadn't been seeing him: clearly, truly. No matter how often I thought I'd made my peace with his otherness, I realized that I still expected him to react as he would if he were JB du Rone, or Jason, or my church pastor.

"I think I'm finally getting this," I said. "But you got to realize, sometimes I'm not going to like that difference. Sometimes I have to get away and cool down. I'm really going to try. I really love you." Having done my best to promise to meet him halfway, I was reminded of my own grievance. I grabbed his hair and rolled him over so I was looking down at him. I looked right in his eyes.

"Now, you tell me what you're doing with Portia."

Bill's big hands rested on my hips as he explained.

"She came to me after I got back from Dallas, the first night. She had read about what happened there, wondered if I knew anyone who'd been there that day. When I said that I had been there myself—I didn't mention you—Portia said she had information that some of the arms used in the attack had come from a place in Bon Temps, Sheridan's Sport Shop. I asked her how she had heard this; she said as a lawyer, she couldn't say. I asked her why she was so concerned, if there wasn't anything further she'd tell me about it; she said she was a good citizen and hated to see other citizens persecuted. I asked her why she came to me; she said I was the only vampire she knew."

I believed that like I believed Portia was a secret belly dancer.

I narrowed my eyes as I worked this through. "Portia doesn't care one damn thing about vampire rights," I said. "She might want to get in your pants, but she doesn't care about vampire legal issues."

" 'Get in my pants'? What a turn of phrase you have."

"Oh, you've heard that before," I said, a little abashed.

He shook his head, amusement sparkling in his face.

"Get in my pants," he repeated, sounding it out slowly. "I would be in your pants, if you had any on." He rubbed his hands up and down to demonstrate.

"Cut that out," I said. "I'm trying to think."

His hands were pressing my hips, then releasing, moving me back and forth on him. I began to have difficulty forming thoughts.

"Stop, Bill," I said. "Listen, I think Portia wants to be seen with you so she might be asked to join that supposed sex club here in Bon Temps."

"Sex club?" Bill said with interest, not stopping in the least.

"Yes, didn't I tell you . . . oh, Bill, no . . . Bill, I'm still worn out from last . . . Oh. Oh, God." His hands had gripped me with their great strength, and moved me purposefully, right onto his stiffness. He began rocking me again, back and forth. "Oh," I said, lost in the moment. I began to see colors floating in front of my eyes, and then I was being rocked so fast I couldn't keep track of my motion. The end came at the same time for both of us, and we clung together panting for several minutes.

"We should never separate again," Bill said.

"I don't know, this makes it almost worth it."

A little aftershock rippled his body. "No," he said. "This is wonderful, but I would rather just leave town for a few days, than fight with you again." He opened his eyes wide. "Did you really suck a bullet from Eric's shoulder?"

"Yeah, he said I had to get it out before his flesh closed over it."

"Did he tell you he had a pocketknife in his pocket?"

I was taken aback. "No. Did he? Why would he do that?"

Bill raised his eyebrows, as if I had said something quite ridiculous.

"Guess," he said.

"So I would suck on his shoulder? You can't mean that."

Bill just maintained the skeptical look.

"Oh, Bill. I fell for it. Wait a minute—he got shot! That bullet could have hit me, but instead it hit him. He was guarding me."

"How?"

"Well, by lying on top of me . . ."

"I rest my case." There was nothing old-fashioned about Bill at the moment. On the other hand, there was a pretty old-fashioned look on his face.

"But, Bill . . . you mean he's that devious?"

Again with the raised eyebrows.

"Lying on top of me is not such a big treat," I protested, "that someone should take a bullet for it. Geez. That's nuts!"

"It got some of his blood in you."

"Only a drop or two. I spit the rest out," I said.

"A drop or two is enough when you are as old as Eric is."

"Enough for what?"

"He will know some things about you, now."

"What, like my dress size?"

Bill smiled, not always a relaxing sight. "No, like how you are feeling. Angry, horny, loving."

I shrugged. "Won't do him any good."

"Probably it is not too important, but be careful from now on," Bill warned me. He seemed quite serious.

"I still can't believe someone would put themselves in a position to take a bullet for me just in the hopes I'd ingest a drop of blood getting the bullet out. That's ridiculous. You know, it seems like to me you introduced this subject so I'd quit bugging you about Portia, but I'm not going to. I think Portia believes if she's dating you, someone will ask her to go to this sex club, since if she's willing to ball a vampire, she's willing to do anything. They *think*," I said hastily after looking at Bill's face. "So Portia figures she'll go, she'll learn stuff, she'll find out who actually killed Lafayette, Andy'll be off the hook."

"That's a complicated plot."

"Can you refute it?" I was proud to use *refute*, which had been on my Word of the Day calendar.

"As a matter of fact, I can't." He became immobile. His eyes were fixed and unblinking, and his hands relaxed. Since Bill doesn't breathe, he was absolutely still.

Finally he blinked. "It would have been better if she had told me the truth to begin with."

"You better not have had sex with her," I said, finally admitting to myself that the bare possibility had made me nearly blind with jealousy.

"I wondered when you were going to ask me," he said calmly. "As if I would ever bed a Bellefleur. No, she has not the slightest desire to have sex with me. She even has a hard time pretending she wants to at some later date. Portia is not much of an actress. Most of the time we are together, she takes me on wild-goose chases to find this cache of arms the Fellowship has stowed here, saying all the Fellowship sympathizers are hiding them."

"So why'd you go along with any of this?"

"There's something about her that's honorable. And I wanted to see if you would be jealous."

"Oh, I see. Well, what do you think?"

"I think," he said, "I had better never see you within a yard of that handsome moron again."

"JB? I'm like his sister," I said.

"You forget, you've had my blood, and I can tell what you are feeling," Bill said. "I don't think you feel exactly like a sister to him."

"That would explain why I'm here in bed with you, right?"

"You love me."

I laughed, up against his throat.

"It's close to dawn," he said. "I have to go."

"Okay, baby." I smiled up at him as he gathered up his clothes. "Hey, you owe me a sweater and a bra. Two bras. Gabe tore one, so that was a work-related clothes injury. And you tore one last night, plus my sweater."

"That's why I bought a women's clothing store," he said smoothly. "So I could rip if the spirit moves me."

I laughed and lay back down. I could sleep for a couple more hours. I was still smiling when he let himself out of my house, and I woke up in the middle of the morning with a lightness in my heart that hadn't been there for a long time. (Well, it felt like a long time.) I walked, somewhat gingerly, into the bathroom to soak in a tubful of hot water. When I began to wash, I felt something in my earlobes. I stood up in the tub and looked over at the mirror above the sink. He'd put the topaz earrings in while I was asleep.

Mr. Last Word.

* * *

Since our reunion had been secret, it was I who got invited to the club first. It had never occurred to me that that might happen; but after it did, I realized that if Portia had figured she might be invited after going with a vampire, I was even primer meat.

To my surprise and disgust, the one to broach the subject was Mike Spencer. Mike was the funeral home director and the coroner in Bon Temps, and we had not always had a completely cordial relationship. However, I'd known him all my life and was used to offering him respect, a hard habit to break. Mike was wearing his funeral home duds when he came in to Merlotte's that evening, because he'd come from Mrs. Cassidy's visitation. A dark suit, white shirt, subdued striped tie, and polished wingtips changed Mike Spencer from the guy who really preferred bolo ties and pointy-toed cowboy boots.

Since Mike was at least twenty years older than me, I'd always related to him as an elder, and it shocked me silly when he approached me. He was sitting by himself, which was unusual enough to be noteworthy. I brought him a hamburger and a beer. As he paid me, he said casually, "Sookie, some of us are getting together at Jan Fowler's lake house tomorrow night and we wondered if we could get you to come."

I am fortunate I have a well-schooled face. I felt as if a pit had opened beneath my feet, and I was actually a little nauseated. I understood immediately, but I couldn't quite believe it. I opened my mind to him, while my mouth was saying, "You said 'some of us'? Who would that be, Mr. Spencer?"

"Why don't you call me Mike, Sookie?" I nodded, looking inside his head all the while. Oh, geez Louise. Ick. "Well, some of your friends will be there. Eggs and Portia and Tara. The Hardaways."

Tara and Eggs . . . that really shocked me.

"So, what goes on at these parties? Is this just a drinking-and-dancing type thing?" This was not an unreasonable question. No matter how many people knew I was supposed to be able to read minds, they almost never believed it, no matter how much evidence to the contrary they'd witnessed. Mike simply could not believe that I could receive the images and concepts floating in his mind.

"Well, we get a little wild. We thought since you'd broken up with your boyfriend, that you might want to come let your hair down a little."

"Maybe I'll come," I said, without enthusiasm. It wouldn't do to look eager. "When?"

"Oh, ten o'clock tomorrow night."

"Thanks for the invite," I said, as if remembering my manners, and then sauntered off with my tip. I thought furiously, in the odd moments I had to myself during the rest of my shift.

What good could my going serve? Could I really learn anything that would solve the mystery of Lafayette's death? I didn't like Andy Bellefleur much, and now I liked Portia even less, but it wasn't fair that Andy might be prosecuted, his reputation ruined, for something that wasn't his fault. On the other hand, it stood to reason that no one present at a party at the lake house would trust me with any deep dark secrets until I'd become a regular, and I just couldn't stomach that. I wasn't even sure I could get through one gathering. The last thing in the world I wanted to see was my friends and my neighbors "letting their hair down." I didn't want to see them let down their hair, or anything else.

"What's the matter, Sookie?" Sam asked, so close to me that I jumped.

I looked at him, wishing that I could ask what he thought. Sam was strong and wiry, and he was clever, too. The bookkeeping, the ordering, the maintenance and planning, he never seemed to be taxed with any of it. Sam was a self-sufficient man, and I liked and trusted him.

"I'm just in a little quandary," I said. "What's up with you, Sam?"

"I got an interesting phone call last night, Sookie."

"Who from?"

"A squeaky woman in Dallas."

"Really?" I found myself smiling, really, not the grin I used to cover my nerves. "Would that be a lady of Mexican descent?"

"I believe so. She spoke of you."

"She's feisty," I said.

"She's got a lot of friends."

"Kind of friends you'd want to have?"

"I already have some good friends," Sam said, squeezing my hand briefly. "But it's always nice to know people who share your interests."

"So, are you driving over to Dallas?"

"I just might. In the meantime, she's put me in touch with some people in Ruston who also . . ."

Change their appearance when the moon is full, I finished mentally.

"How did she trace you? I didn't give her your name, on purpose, because I didn't know if you'd want me to."

"She traced you," Sam said. "And she found out who your boss was through local . . . people."

"How come you had never hooked up with them on your own?"

"Until you told me about the maenad," Sam said, "I never realized that there were so many more things I had to learn."

"Sam, you haven't been hanging around with her?"

"I've spent a few evenings in the woods with her, yes. As Sam, and in my other skin."

"But she's so evil," I blurted.

Sam's back stiffened. "She's a supernatural creature like me," he said evenly. "She's neither evil nor good, she just is."

"Oh, bullshit." I couldn't believe I was hearing this from Sam. "If she's feeding you this line, then she wants something from you." I remembered how beautiful the maenad had been, if you didn't mind bloodstains. And Sam, as a shapeshifter, wouldn't. "Oh," I said, comprehension sweeping me. Not that I could read Sam's mind clearly, since he was a supernatural creature, but I could get a lock on his emotional state, which was—embarrassed, horny, resentful, and horny.

"Oh," I said again, somewhat stiffly. "Excuse me, Sam. I didn't mean to speak ill of someone you . . . you, ah . . ." I could hardly say, "are screwing," however apropos it might be. "You're spending time with," I finished lamely. "I'm sure she's lovely once you get to know her. Of course, the fact that she cut my back to bloody ribbons may have something to do with my prejudice against her. I'll try to be more open-minded." And I stalked off to take an order, leaving Sam openmouthed behind me.

I left a message on Bill's answering machine. I didn't know what Bill intended to do about Portia, and I guessed there was a possibility someone else would be there when he played his messages, so I said, "Bill, I got invited to that party tomorrow night. Let me know if you think I should go." I didn't identify myself, since he'd know my voice. Possibly, Portia had left an identical message, an idea that just made me furious.

When I drove home that night, I half hoped Bill would be waiting to ambush me again in an erotic way, but the house and yard were silent. I perked up when I noticed the light on my answering machine was blinking.

"Sookie," said Bill's smooth voice, "stay out of the woods. The maenad was dissatisfied with our tribute. Eric will be in Bon Temps tomorrow night to negotiate with her, and he may call you. The—other people—of Dallas, the ones who helped you, are asking for outrageous recompense from the vampires of Dallas, so I am going over there on Anubis to meet with them, with Stan. You know where I'll be staying."

Yikes. Bill wouldn't be in Bon Temps to help me, and he was out of my reach. Or was he? It was one in the morning. I called the number I'd put in my address book, for the Silent Shore. Bill had not yet checked in, though his coffin (which the concierge referred to as his "baggage") had been put in his room. I left a message, which I had to phrase so guardedly that it might be incomprehensible.

I was really tired, since I hadn't gotten much sleep the night before, but I had no intention of going to the next night's party alone. I sighed deeply, and called Fangtasia, the vampire bar in Shreveport.

"You've reached Fangtasia, where the undead live again every night," said a recording of Pam's voice. Pam was a co-owner. "For bar hours, press one. To make a party reservation, press two. To talk to a live person or a dead vampire, press three. Or, if you were intending to leave a humorous prank message on our answering machine, know this: we will find you."

I pressed three.

"Fangtasia," Pam said, as if she were bored more completely than anyone had ever been bored.

"Hi," I said, weighing in on the perky side to counteract the ennui. "This is Sookie, Pam. Is Eric around?"

"He is enthralling the vermin," Pam said. I took that to mean Eric was sprawling in a chair on the main floor of the bar, looking gorgeous and dangerous. Bill had told me that some vampires were under contract to Fangtasia, to put in one or two appearances a week of a stated duration, so the tourists would keep coming. Eric, as an owner, was there almost every night. There was another bar where vampires went of their own accord, a bar a tourist would never enter. I'd never been in it, because frankly, I see enough of bars while I'm at work.

"Could you take him the phone, please, ma'am?"

"Oh, all right," she said grudgingly. "I hear you had quite a time in Dallas," she said as she walked. Not that I could hear her steps, but the noise in the background ebbed and flowed.

"Unforgettable."

"What did you think of Stan Davis?"

Hmmm. "He's one of a kind."

"I like that nerdy, geeky look myself."

I was glad she wasn't there to see the astonished look I gave the telephone. I'd never realized Pam liked guys, too. "He certainly didn't seem to be dating anyone," I said, I hoped casually.

"Ah. Maybe I'll take a vacation to Dallas soon."

It was also news to me that vampires were interested in each other. I'd never actually seen two vampires together.

"I am here," Eric said.

"And I am here." I was a little amused at Eric's phone answering technique.

"Sookie, my little bullet-sucker," he said, sounding fond and warm.

"Eric, my big bullshitter."

"You want something, my darling?"

"I'm not your darling, and you know it, for one thing. For another—Bill said you were coming over here tomorrow night?"

"Yes, to tromp up in the woods looking for the maenad. She finds our offerings of vintage wine and a young bull inadequate."

"You took her a live bull?" I was momentarily sidetracked by the vision of Eric herding a cow into a trailer and driving it to the shoulder of the interstate and shooing it into the trees.

"Yes, indeed we did. Pam and Indira and I."

"Was it fun?"

"Yes," he said, sounding faintly surprised. "It had been several centuries since I dealt with livestock. Pam is a city girl. Indira had too much awe of the bull to be a lot of help. But if you like, the next time I have to transport animals I will give you a call, and you can go along."

"Thanks, that would be lovely," I said, feeling pretty confident that was a call I'd never get. "The reason I called you is that I need you to go to a party with me tomorrow night."

A long silence.

"Bill is no longer your bedmate? The differences you developed in Dallas are permanent?"

"What I should have said is, 'I need a bodyguard for tomorrow night.' Bill's in Dallas." I was smacking myself on the forehead with the heel of my hand. "See, there's a long explanation, but the situation is that I need to go to a party tomorrow night that's really just a . . . well, it's a . . . kind of orgy thing? And I need someone with me in case . . . just in case."

"That's fascinating," Eric said, sounding fascinated. "And since I'm going to be in the neighborhood, you thought I might do as an escort? To an orgy?"

"You can look almost human," I said.

"This is a human orgy? One that excludes vampires?"

"It's a human orgy that doesn't know a vampire is coming."

"So, the more human I look, the less frightening I'll be?"

"Yes, I need to read their thoughts. Pick their brains. And if I get them thinking about a certain thing, and pick their brains, then we can get out of there." I'd just had a great idea about how to get them to think about Lafayette. Telling Eric was going to be the problem.

"So you want me to go to a human orgy, where I will

not be welcome, and you want us to leave before I get to enjoy myself?"

"Yes," I said, almost squeaking in my anxiety. In for a penny, in for a pound. "And . . . do you think you could pretend to be gay?"

There was a long silence. "What time do I need to be there?" Eric asked softly.

"Um. Nine thirty? So I can brief you?"

"Nine thirty at your house."

"I am carrying the phone back," Pam informed me. "What did you say to Eric? He is shaking his head back and forth with his eyes shut."

"Is he laughing, even a little bit?"

"Not that I can tell," Pam said.

10

Bill DIDN'T CALL BACK THAT NIGHT, AND I LEFT FOR
work before sunset the next day. He'd left a message on
the answering machine when I came home to dress for
the "party."

"Sookie, I had a hard time making out what the situation was, from your very guarded message," he said. His
usually calm voice was definitely on the unhappy side.
Miffed. "If you are going to this party, don't go alone,
whatever you do. It isn't worth it. Get your brother or
Sam to go with you."

Well, I'd gotten someone even stronger to go with me,
so I should be feeling pretty virtuous. Somehow, I didn't
think that my having Eric with me would reassure Bill.

"Stan Davis and Joseph Velasquez send their regards, and Barry the bellhop."

I smiled. I was sitting cross-legged on my bed wearing only an old chenille bathrobe, giving my hair a brushing while I listened to my messages.

"I haven't forgotten Friday night," Bill said, in the voice that always made me shiver. "I will never forget."

"So what happened Friday night?" Eric asked.

I shrieked. Once I could feel my heart was going to stay in my chest cavity, I scrambled off the bed and strode over to him with my fists balled.

"You are old enough to know you don't come in someone's house without knocking on the door and having it answered. Besides, when did I ever invite you inside?" I had to have extended the invitation, or else Eric couldn't have crossed the threshold.

"When I stopped by last month to see Bill. I did knock," Eric said, trying his best to look wounded. "You didn't answer, and I thought I heard voices, so I came in. I even called your name."

"You may have whispered my name." I was still furious. "But you acted bad, and you know it!"

"What are you wearing to the party?" Eric asked, effectively changing the subject. "If this is to be an orgy, what does a good girl like you wear?"

"I just don't know," I said, deflated by the reminder. "I'm sure I'm supposed to look like the kind of girl who goes to orgies, but I've never been to one and I have no idea how to start out, though I have a pretty clear idea of how I'm supposed to end up."

"I have been to orgies," he offered.

"Why does that not surprise me? What do you wear?"

"The last time I wore an animal hide; but this time I settled for this." Eric had been wearing a long trench coat. Now he threw it off dramatically, and I could only stand and stare. Normally, Eric was a blue-jeans-and-T-shirt kind of guy. Tonight, he wore a pink tank top and Lycra leggings. I don't know where he got them; I didn't know any company made Lycra leggings in Men's Xtra-Large Tall. They were pink and aqua, like the swirls down the sides of Jason's truck.

"Wow," I said, since it was all I could think of to say. "Wow. That's some outfit." When you've got a big guy wearing Lycra, it doesn't leave a whole lot to the imagination. I resisted the temptation to ask Eric to turn around.

"I don't believe I could be convincing as a queen," Eric said, "but I decided this sent such a mixed signal, almost anything was possible." He fluttered his eyelashes at me. Eric was definitely enjoying this.

"Oh, yes," I said, trying to find somewhere else to look.

"Shall I go through your drawers and find something for you to wear?" Eric suggested. He had actually opened the top drawer of my bureau before I said, "No, no! I'll find something!" But I couldn't find anything more informally sexy than shorts and a tee shirt. However, the shorts were some I had left over from my junior high days, and they encased me "like a caterpillar embraces a butterfly," Eric said poetically.

"More like Daisy Dukes," I muttered, wondering if the lace pattern of my bikini underwear would be imprinted on my butt for the rest of my life. I wore a matching steel blue bra with a dipping white tank top that exposed a lot of the decoration on the bra. This was one of my replacement bras, and Bill hadn't even gotten to see it yet, so I

sure hoped nothing happened to it. My tan was still holding up, and I wore my hair loose.

"Hey, our hair's the same color," I said, eyeing us side
by side in the mirror.

"Sure is, girlfriend." Eric grinned at me. "But are you
blond all the way down?"

"Don't you wish you knew?"

"Yes," he said simply.

"Well, you'll just have to wonder."

"I am," he said. "Blond everywhere."

"I could tell as much from your chest hair."

He raised my arm to check my armpit. "You silly
women, shaving your body hair," he said, dropping my
arm.

I opened my mouth to say something else on the topic,
suddenly realized that would lead to disaster, and said instead, "We need to go."

"Aren't you going to wear perfume?" He was sniffing
all the bottles on top of my dressing table. "Oh, wear
this!" He tossed me a bottle and I caught it without thinking. His eyebrows flew up. "You have had more vampire
blood than I thought, Miss Sookie."

"Obsession," I said, looking at the bottle. "Oh, okay."
Carefully not responding to his observation, I dabbed a
little bit of Obsession between my breasts and behind my
knees. I figured that way I was covered from head to toe.

"What is our agenda, Sookie?" Eric asked, eyeing this
procedure with interest.

"What we're going to do is go to this stupid so-called
sex party and do as little as possible in that line while I
gather information from the minds of the people there."

"Pertaining to?"

"Pertaining to the murder of Lafayette Reynold, the cook at Merlotte's Bar."

"And why are we doing this?"

"Because I liked Lafayette. And to clear Andy Belle-fleur of the suspicion that he murdered Lafayette."

"Bill knows you are trying to save a Bellefleur?"

"Why do you ask that?"

"You know Bill hates the Bellefleurs," Eric said, as if that were the best-known fact in Louisiana.

"No," I said. "No, I didn't know that at all." I sat down on the chair by my bed, my eyes fixed on Eric's face. "Why?"

"You'll have to ask Bill that, Sookie. And this is the only reason we're going? You're not cleverly using this as an excuse to make out with me?"

"I'm not that clever, Eric."

"I think you deceive yourself, Sookie," Eric said with a brilliant smile.

I remembered he could now sense my moods, according to Bill. I wondered what Eric knew about me that I didn't know.

"Listen, Eric," I began, as we went out the door and across the porch. Then I had to stop and cast around in my mind for how to say what I wanted to say.

He waited. The evening had been cloudy, and the woods felt closer around the house. I knew the night just seemed oppressive because I was going to go to an event personally distasteful to me. I was going to learn things about people that I didn't know and didn't want to know. It seemed stupid to be seeking the kind of information that I'd spent my life learning how to block out. But I felt a sort of public service obligation to Andy Bellefleur to discover the truth; and I respected Portia, in an odd way, for her willingness to subject herself to something unpleasant in order to save her brother. How Portia could feel a genuine distaste for Bill was simply incomprehensible to me, but if Bill said she was frightened of him, it was true. This coming evening, the idea of seeing the true secret face of people I'd known forever was just as frightening to me.

"Don't let anything happen to me, okay?" I said to Eric directly. "I have no intention of getting intimate with any of those people. I guess I'm scared that something will happen, someone will go too far. Even for the sake of Lafayette's murder being avenged, I won't willingly have sex with any of those people." That was my real fear, one I hadn't admitted to myself until this moment: that some cog would slip, some safeguard fail, and I would be a victim. When I'd been a child, something had happened to me, something that I could neither prevent nor control, something incredibly vile. I would almost rather die than be subjected to abuse like that again. That was why I'd fought so hard against Gabe and been so relieved when Godfrey had killed him.

"You trust me?" Eric sounded surprised.

"Yes."

"That's . . . crazy, Sookie."

"I don't think so." Where that surety had come from, I didn't know, but it was there. I pulled on a thigh-length heavy sweater I had brought out with me.

Shaking his blond head, his trench coat drawn close around him, Eric opened the door to his red Corvette. I would be arriving at the orgy in style.

I gave Eric directions to Mimosa Lake, and I filled

him in as much as I could on the background of this series of events as we drove (flew) down the narrow two-
lane. Eric drove with great zest and élan—and the
recklessness of someone extremely hard to kill.

"Remember, I'm mortal," I said, after going around a
curve at a speed that made me wish my fingernails were
long enough to bite.

"I think about that often," Eric said, his eyes fixed on
the road ahead of him.

I didn't know what to make of that, so I let my mind
drift to relaxing things. Bill's hot tub. The nice check I
would get from Eric when the check from the Dallas
vampires cleared. The fact that Jason had dated the same
woman several months in a row, which might mean he
was serious about her, or might mean he'd run through all
the available women (and a few who shouldn't have
been) in Renard Parish. That it was a beautiful, cool night
and I was riding in a wonderful car.

"You are happy," Eric said.

"Yes. I am."

"You will be safe."

"Thanks. I know I will."

I pointed to the little sign marked FOWLER that indicated a driveway almost hidden by a stand of myrtle and
hawthorn. We turned down a short, rutted gravel driveway
lined with trees. It canted sharply downhill. Eric frowned
as the Corvette lurched along the deep ruts. By the time
the drive leveled out into the clearing where the cabin
stood, the slope was enough to render the roof a little below the height of the road around the lake. There were
four cars parked on the beaten dirt in front of the cabin.
The windows were open to admit the sharp cool of the

evening, but the shades were drawn. I could hear voices drifting out, though I couldn't make out words. I was suddenly, deeply reluctant to enter Jan Fowler's cabin.

"I could be bisexual?" Eric asked. It didn't seem to bother him; he seemed, if anything, amused. We stood by Eric's car, facing each other, my hands stuffed in the sweater pockets.

"Okay." I shrugged. Who cared? This was make believe. I caught a movement out of the corner of my eye. Someone was watching us through a partially raised shade. "We're being watched."

"Then I'll act friendly."

We were out of the car by that time. Eric bent, and without yanking me to him, set his mouth on mine. He didn't grab me, so I felt fairly relaxed. I'd known that at the very minimum I'd have to kiss other people. So I set my mind to it.

Maybe I had natural talent, which had been nurtured by a great teacher. Bill had pronounced me an excellent kisser, and I wanted to do him proud.

Judging from the state of Eric's Lycra, I succeeded.

"Ready to go in?" I asked, doing my best to keep my eyes above his chest.

"Not really," Eric said. "But I suppose we have to. At least I look in the mood."

Though it was dismaying to think that this was the second time I had kissed Eric and that I had enjoyed it more than I should, I could feel a smile twitch the corners of my mouth as we crossed the bumpy ground of the clearing. We went up the steps to a large wooden deck, strewn with the usual aluminum folding chairs and a large gas grill. The screen door screeched as Eric pulled it open, and I knocked lightly on the inner door. "Who is it?" Jan's voice said.

"It's Sookie and a friend," I answered.

"Oh, goodie! Come on in!" she called.

When I pushed open the door, all the faces in the room were turned toward us. The welcoming smiles turned to startled looks as Eric came in behind me.

Eric stepped to my side, his coat over his arm, and I almost hooted at the variety of expressions. After the shock of realizing Eric was vampire, which everyone in the room did after a minute or so, eyes flickered up and down the length of Eric's body, taking in the panorama.

"Hey, Sookie, who's your friend?" Jan Fowler, a multiple divorcée in her thirties, was wearing what looked like a lace slip. Jan's hair was streaked and professionally tousled, and her makeup would have seemed in place on stage, though for a cabin by Mimosa Lake the effect was a bit much. But as hostess, I guess she felt she could wear what she wanted to her own orgy. I slid out of my sweater and endured the embarrassment of receiving the same scrutiny Eric had been given.

"This is Eric," I said. "I hope you don't mind me bringing a friend?"

"Oh, the more the merrier," she said with undoubted sincerity. Her eyes never rose to Eric's face. "Eric, what can I get you to drink?"

"Blood?" Eric asked hopefully.

"Yeah, I think I've got some O here," she said, unable to tear her gaze away from the Lycra. "Sometimes we . . . pretend." She raised her eyebrows significantly, and kind of leered at Eric.

"No need to pretend anymore," he said, giving her

back look for look. On his way to join her at the refrigerator, he managed to stroke Eggs's shoulder, and Eggs's
face lit up.

Oh. Well, I'd known I'd learn some things. Tara, beside him, was sulking, her dark brows drawn down over
dark eyes. Tara was wearing a bra and panties of shrieking red, and she looked pretty good. Her toenails and fingernails were painted so they matched, and so did her
lipstick. She'd come prepared. I met her eyes, and she
looked away. It didn't take a mind reader to recognize
shame.

Mike Spencer and Cleo Hardaway were on a dilapi-
dated couch against the left-hand wall. The whole cot-
tage, basically one large room with a sink and stove
against the right-hand wall and a walled-in bathroom in
the far corner, was furnished in castoffs, because in Bon
Temps that was what you did with your old furniture.
However, most lake cabins would not have featured such
a thick, soft rug and such a lot of pillows tossed around at
random, and there would not have been such thick shades
drawn at all the windows. Plus, the knickknacks strewn
around on that soft rug were simply nasty. I didn't even
know what some of them were.

But I pasted a cheerful smile on my face, and hugged
Cleo Hardaway, as I usually did when I saw her. Granted,
she had always been wearing more clothes when she ran
the high school cafeteria. But panties were more than
Mike was wearing, which was not a stitch.

Well, I'd known it would be bad, but I guess you just
can't prepare yourself for some sights. Cleo's huge milk-
chocolate brown boobs were glistening with some kind

of oil, and Mike's private parts were equally shiny. I didn't even want to think about that.

Mike tried to grab my hand, probably to assist with the oil, but I slithered away and edged over to Eggs and Tara.

"I sure never thought you'd come," Tara said. She was smiling, too, but not real happily. In fact, she looked pretty damn miserable. Maybe the fact that Tom Hardaway was kneeling in front of her smooching up the inside of her leg had something to do with that. Maybe it was Eggs's obvious interest in Eric. I tried to meet Tara's eyes, but I felt sick.

I'd only been here five minutes, but I was willing to bet this was the longest five minutes of my life.

"Do you do this real often?" I asked Tara, absurdly. Eggs, his eyes on Eric's bottom while Eric stood talking at the refrigerator with Jan, began fumbling with the button on my shorts. Eggs had been drinking again. I could smell it. His eyes were glassy and his jaw was slack. "Your friend is really big," he said, as if his mouth were watering, and maybe it was.

"Lots bigger than Lafayette," I whispered, and his gaze jerked up to meet mine. "I figured he'd be welcome."

"Oh, yes," Eggs said, deciding not to confront my statement. "Yes, Eric's . . . very large. It's good to have some diversity."

"This is as rainbow as Bon Temps gets," I said, trying hard not to sound perky. I endured Eggs's continued struggle with the button. This had been a big mistake. Eggs was just thinking about Eric's butt. And other things about Eric.

Speaking of the devil, he snugged up behind me and

ran his arms around me, pulling me to him and removing me from Eggs's clumsy fingers. I leaned back into Eric, really glad he was there. I realized that was because I *expected* Eric to misbehave. But seeing people you'd known all your life act like this, well, it was deeply disgusting. I wasn't too sure I could keep my face from showing this, so I wiggled against Eric, and when he made a happy sound, I turned in his arms to face him. I put my arms up around his neck and raised my face. He happily complied with my silent suggestion. With my face concealed, my mind was free to roam. I opened myself up mentally, just as Eric parted my lips with his tongue, so I felt completely unguarded. There were some strong "senders" in that room, and I no longer felt like myself, but like a pipeline for other people's overwhelming needs.

I could taste the flavor of Eggs's thoughts. He was remembering Lafayette, thin brown body, talented fingers, and heavily made-up eyes. He was remembering Lafayette's whispered suggestions. Then he was choking those happy memories off with more unpleasant ones: Lafayette protesting violently, shrilly . . .

"Sookie," Eric said in my ear, so low that I don't think another person in the room could've heard him. "Sookie, relax. I have you."

I made my hand stroke his neck. I found that someone else was behind Eric, sort of making out with him from behind.

Jan's hand reached around Eric and began rubbing my rear. Since she was touching me, her thoughts were absolutely clear; she was an exceptional "sender." I flicked through her mind like the pages of a book, and read nothing of interest. She was only thinking of Eric's anatomy, and worrying about her own fascination with Cleo's chest. Nothing there for me.

I reached in another direction, wormed into the head of Mike Spencer, found the nasty tangle I'd expected, found that as he rolled Cleo's breasts in his hands he was seeing other brown flesh, limp and lifeless. His own flesh rose as he remembered this. Through his memories I saw Jan asleep on the lumpy couch, Lafayette's protest that if they didn't stop hurting him he would tell everyone what he'd done and with whom, and then Mike's fists descending, Tom Hardaway kneeling on the thin dark chest . . .

I had to get out of here. I couldn't bear it, even if I hadn't just learned what I needed to know. I didn't see how Portia could have endured it, either, especially since she would have had to stay to learn anything, not having the "gift" I had.

I felt Jan's hand massaging my ass. This was the most joyless excuse for sex I had ever seen: sex separated from mind and spirit, from love or affection. Even simple liking.

According to my four-times-married friend Arlene, men had no problem with this. Evidently, some women didn't, either.

"I have to get out," I breathed into Eric's mouth. I knew he could hear me.

"Go along with me," he replied, and it was almost as if I was hearing him in my head.

He lifted me and slung me over his shoulder. My hair trailed down almost to the middle of his thigh.

"We're going outside for a minute," he told Jan, and I heard a big smacking noise. He'd given her a kiss.

"Can I come, too?" she asked, in a breathless Marlene Dietrich voice. It was lucky my face wasn't showing.

"Give us a minute. Sookie is still a little shy," Eric said in a voice as full of promise as a tub of a new flavor of ice cream.

"Warm her up good," Mike Spencer said in a muffled voice. "We all want to see our Sookie fired up."

"She will be hot," Eric promised.

"Hot damn," said Tom Hardaway, from between Tara's legs.

Then, bless Eric, we were out the door and he laid me out on the hood of the Corvette. He lay on top of me, but most of his weight was supported by his hands resting on the hood on either side of my shoulders.

He was looking down at me, his face clamped down like a ship's deck during a storm. His fangs were out. His eyes were wide. Since the whites were so purely white, I could see them. It was too dark to see the blue of his eyes, even if I'd wanted to.

I didn't want. "That was . . ." I began, and had to stop. I took a deep breath. "You can call me a Goody Two-shoes if you want to, and I wouldn't blame you, after all this was my idea. But you know what I think? I think that's awful. Do men really like that? Do women, for that matter? Is it fun to have sex with someone you don't even like?"

"Do you like me, Sookie?" Eric asked. He rested more heavily on me and moved a little.

Uh-oh. "Eric, remember why we're here?"

"They're watching."

"Even if they are, remember?"

"Yes, I remember."

"So we need to go."

"Do you have any evidence? Do you know what you wanted to find out?"

"I don't have any more evidence than I had before tonight, not evidence you can hand out in court." I made myself put my arms around his ribs. "But I know who did it. It was Mike, Tom, and maybe Cleo."

"This is interesting," Eric said, with a complete lack of sincerity. His tongue flicked into my ear. I happen to particularly like that, and I could feel my breathing speed up. Maybe I wasn't as immune to uninvolved sex as I'd thought. But then, I liked Eric, when I wasn't afraid of him.

"No, I just hate this," I said, reaching some inner conclusion. "I don't like any part of this." I shoved Eric hard, though it didn't make a bit of difference. "Eric, you listen to me. I've done everything for Lafayette and Andy Bellefleur I can, though it's precious little. He'll just have to go from here on the little snatches I caught. He's a cop. He can find court evidence. I'm not selfless enough to go any further with this."

"Sookie," Eric said. I didn't think he'd heard a word. "Yield to me."

Well, that was pretty direct.

"No," I said, in the most definite voice I could summon. "No."

"I will protect you from Bill."

"You're the one that's gonna need protection!" When I reflected on that sentence, I was not proud of it.

"You think Bill is stronger than me?"

"I am not having this conversation." Then I proceeded to have it. "Eric, I appreciate your offering to help me, and I appreciate your willingness to come to an awful place like this."

"Believe me, Sookie, this little gathering of trash is nothing, nothing, compared to some of the places I have been."

And I believed him utterly. "Okay, but it's awful to me. Now, I realize that I should've known this would, ah, rouse your expectations, but you know I did not come out here tonight to have sex with anyone. Bill is my boyfriend." Though the words *boyfriend* and *Bill* sounded ludicrous in the same sentence, "boyfriend" was Bill's function in my world, anyway.

"I am glad to hear it," said a cool, familiar voice. "This scene would make me wonder, otherwise."

Oh, great.

Eric rose up off of me, and I scrambled off the hood of the car and stumbled in the direction of Bill's voice.

"Sookie," he said, when I drew near, "it's getting to where I just can't let you go anywhere alone."

As far as I could tell in the poor lighting, he didn't look very glad to see me. But I couldn't blame him for that. "I sure made a big mistake," I said, from the bottom of my heart. I hugged him.

"You smell like Eric," he said into my hair. Well, hell, I was forever smelling like other men to Bill. I felt a flood of misery and shame, and I realized things were about to happen.

But what happened was not what I expected.

Andy Bellefleur stepped out of the bushes with a gun

in his hand. His clothes looked torn and stained, and the gun looked huge.

"Sookie, step away from the vampire," he said.

"No." I wrapped myself around Bill. I didn't know if I was protecting him or he was protecting me. But if Andy wanted us separated, I wanted us joined.

There was a sudden surge of voices on the porch of the cabin. Someone clearly had been looking out of the window—I had kind of wondered if Eric had made that up—because, though no voices had been raised, the showdown in the clearing had attracted the attention of the revelers inside. While Eric and I had been in the yard, the orgy had progressed. Tom Hardaway was naked, and Jan, too. Eggs Tallie looked drunker.

"You smell like Eric," Bill repeated, in a hissing voice.

I reared back from him, completely forgetting about Andy and his gun. And I lost my temper.

This is a rare thing, but not as rare as it used to be. It was kind of exhilarating. "Yeah, uh-huh, and I can't even tell what you smell like! For all I know you've been with six women! Hardly fair, is it?"

Bill gaped at me, stunned. Behind me, Eric started laughing. The crowd on the sundeck was silently enthralled. Andy didn't think we should all be ignoring the man with the gun.

"Stand together in a group," he bellowed. Andy had had a lot to drink.

Eric shrugged. "Have you ever dealt with vampires, Bellefleur?" he asked.

"No," Andy said. "But I can shoot you dead. I have silver bullets."

"That's—" I started to say, but Bill's hand covered my mouth. Silver bullets were only definitely fatal to were-wolves, but vampires also had a terrible reaction to silver, and a vampire hit in a vital place would certainly suffer.

Eric raised an eyebrow and sauntered over to the or-giasts on the deck. Bill took my hand, and we joined them. For once, I would have loved to know what Bill was thinking.

"Which one of you was it, or was it all of you?" Andy bellowed.

We all kept silent. I was standing by Tara, who was shivering in her red underwear. Tara was scared, no big surprise. I wondered if knowing Andy's thoughts would help any, and I began to focus on him. Drunks don't make for good reading, I can tell you, because they only think about stupid stuff, and their ideas are quite unreliable. Their memories are shaky, too. Andy didn't have too many thoughts at the moment. He didn't like anyone in the clearing, not even himself, and he was determined to get the truth out of someone.

"Sookie, come here," he yelled.

"No," Bill said very definitely.

"I have to have her right here beside me in thirty sec-onds, or I shoot—her!" Andy said, pointing his gun right at me.

"You will not live thirty seconds after, if you do," Bill said.

I believed him. Evidently Andy did, too.

"I don't care," Andy said. "She's not much loss to the world."

Well, that made me mad all over again. My temper had begun to die down, but that made it flare up in a big way.

I yanked free from Bill's hand and stomped down the steps to the yard. I wasn't so blind with anger that I ignored the gun, though I was sorely tempted to grab Andy by his balls and squeeze. He'd still shoot me, but he'd hurt, too. However, that was as self-defeating as drinking was. Would the moment of satisfaction be worth it?

"Now, Sookie, you read the minds of those people and you tell me which one did it," Andy ordered. He gripped the back of my neck with his big hands, like I was an untrained puppy, and swiveled me around to face the deck.

"What the hell do you think I was doing here, you stupid shit? Do you think this is the way I like to spend my time, with assholes like these?"

Andy shook me by my neck. I am very strong, and there was a good chance that I could break free from him and grab the gun, but it was not close enough to a sure thing to make me comfortable. I decided to wait for a minute. Bill was trying to tell me something with his face, but I wasn't sure what it was. Eric was trying to cop a feel from Tara. Or Eggs. It was hard to tell.

A dog whined at the edge of the woods. I rolled my eyes in that direction, unable to turn my head. Well, great. Just great.

"That's my collie," I told Andy. "Dean, remember?" I could have used some human-shaped help, but since Sam had arrived on the scene in his collie persona, he'd have to stay that way or risk exposure.

"Yeah. What's your dog doing out here?"

"I don't know. Don't shoot him, okay?"

"I'd never shoot a dog," he said, sounding genuinely shocked.

"Oh, but me, it's okay," I said bitterly.

The collie padded over to where we were standing. I wondered what was on Sam's mind. I wondered if he retained much human thinking while he was in his favorite form. I rolled my eyes toward the gun, and Sam/Dean's eyes followed mine, but how much comprehension was in there, I just couldn't estimate.

The collie began to growl. His teeth were bared and he was glaring at the gun.

"Back up, dog," Andy said, annoyed.

If I could just hold Andy still for a minute, the vampires could get him. I tried to work out all the moves in my mind. I'd have to grab his gun hand with both of my hands and force it up. But with Andy holding me out from him like this, that wasn't going to be easy.

"No, sweetheart," Bill said.

My eyes flashed over to him. I was considerably startled. Bill's eyes moved from my face to behind Andy. I could take a hint.

"Oh, who is being held like a little cub?" inquired a voice behind Andy.

Oh, this was just *peachy*.

"It is my messenger!" The maenad sauntered around Andy in a wide circle and came to stand to his right, a few feet before him. She was not between Andy and the group on the deck. She was clean tonight, and wearing nothing at all. I guessed she and Sam had been out in the woods making whoopee, before they heard the crowd. Her black hair fell in a tangled mass all the way to her hips. She didn't seem cold. The rest of us (except the vampires) were definitely feeling the nip in the air. We'd come dressed for an orgy, not an outdoors party.

"Hello, messenger," the maenad said to me. "I forgot to introduce myself last time, my canine friend reminds me. I am Callisto."

"Miss Callisto," I said, since I had no idea what to call her. I would have nodded, but Andy had hold of my neck. It was sure beginning to hurt.

"Who is this stalwart brave gripping you?" Callisto moved a little closer.

I had no idea what Andy looked like, but everyone on the deck was enthralled and terrified, Eric and Bill excepted. They were easing back, away from the humans. This wasn't good.

"This is Andy Bellefleur," I croaked. "He has a problem."

I could tell from the way my skin crawled that the maenad had eased forward a little.

"You have never seen anything like me, have you?" she said to Andy.

"No," Andy admitted. He sounded dazed.

"Am I beautiful?"

"Yes," he said, without hesitation.

"Do I deserve tribute?"

"Yes," he said.

"I love drunkenness, and you are very drunk," Callisto said happily. "I love pleasures of the flesh, and these people are full of lust. This is my kind of place."

"Oh, good," Andy said uncertainly. "But one of these people is a murderer, and I need to know which."

"Not just one," I muttered. Reminded I was on the end of his arm, Andy shook me again. I was getting really tired of this.

The maenad had gotten close enough now to touch

me. She gently stroked my face, and I smelled earth and wine on her fingers.

"You are not drunk," she observed.

"No, ma'am."

"And you have not had the pleasures of the flesh this evening."

"Oh, just give me time," I said.

She laughed. It was a high, whooping laugh. It went on and on.

Andy's grip loosened, as he grew more and more disconcerted by the maenad's nearness. I don't know what the people on the deck thought they saw. But Andy knew he was seeing a creature of the night. He let go of me, quite suddenly.

"Come on up here, new girl," called Mike Spencer. "Let's have a look at you."

I was on a heap on the ground by Dean, who was licking my face enthusiastically. From that point of view, I could see the maenad's arm snake around Andy's waist. Andy transferred his gun to his left hand so he could return the compliment.

"Now, what did you want to know?" she asked Andy. Her voice was calm and reasonable. She idly waved the long wand with the tuft on the end. It was called a thyrsis; I'd looked *maenad* up in the encyclopedia. Now I could die educated.

"One of those people killed a man named Lafayette, and I want to know which one," Andy said with the belligerence of a drunk.

"Of course you do, my darling," the maenad crooned. "Shall I find out for you?"

"Please," he begged.

"All right." She scanned the people, and crooked her finger at Eggs. Tara held on to his arm to try to keep him with her, but he lurched down the steps and over to the maenad, grinning foolishly all the while.

"Are you a girl?" Eggs asked.

"Not by any stretch of the imagination," Callisto said. "You have had a lot of wine." She touched him with the thyrsis.

"Oh, yeah," he agreed. He wasn't smiling anymore. He looked into Callisto's eyes, and he shivered and shook. Her eyes were glowing. I looked at Bill, and saw he had his own eyes focused on the ground. Eric was looking at the hood of his car. Ignored by everyone, I began to crawl toward Bill.

This was a fine kettle of fish.

The dog paced beside me, nosing me anxiously. I felt he wanted me to move faster. I reached Bill's legs and gripped them. I felt his hand on my hair. I was scared to make the large movement of rising to my feet.

Callisto wrapped her thin arms around Eggs and began to whisper to him. He nodded and whispered back. She kissed him, and he went rigid. When she left him to glide over to the deck, he stood absolutely still, staring into the woods.

She stopped by Eric, who was closer to the deck than we were. She looked him up and down, and smiled that terrifying smile again. Eric looked at her chest fixedly, careful not to meet her eyes. "Lovely," she said, "just lovely. But not for me, you beautiful piece of dead meat."

Then she was up amongst the people on the deck. She

took a deep breath, inhaling the scents of drinking and sex. She sniffed as if she were following a trail, and then she swung to face Mike Spencer. His middle-aged body did not fare well in the chilly air, but Callisto seemed delighted with him.

"Oh," she said as happily as though she'd just gotten a present, "you're so proud! Are you a king? Are you a great soldier?"

"No," Mike said. "I own a funeral home." He didn't sound too sure. "What are you, lady?"

"Have you ever seen anything like me before?"

"No," he said, and all the others shook their heads.

"You don't remember my first visit?"

"No, ma'am."

"But you've made me an offering before."

"I have? An offering?"

"Oh, yes, when you killed the little black man. The pretty one. He was a lesser child of mine, and a fitting tribute for me. I thank you for leaving him outside the drinking place; bars are my particular delight. Could you not find me in the woods?"

"Lady, we didn't make no offering," Tom Hardaway said, his dark skin all over goose pimples and his penis gone south.

"I saw you," she said.

Everything fell silent then. The woods around the lake, always full of little noises and tiny movements, became still. I very carefully rose to my feet beside Bill.

"I love the violence of sex, I love the reek of drink," she said dreamily. "I can run from miles away to be there for the end."

The fear pouring out of their heads began to fill mine

up, and run out. I covered my face with my hands. I threw up the strongest shields I could fashion, but I could still barely contain the terror. My back arched, and I bit my tongue to keep from making a sound. I could feel the movement as Bill turned to me, and then Eric was by his side and they were both mashing me between them. There is not a thing erotic about being pressed between two vampires under those circumstances. Their own urgent desire for my silence fed the fear, because what would frighten vampires? The dog pressed against our legs as if he offered us protection.

"You hit him during sex," the maenad said to Tom. "You hit him, because you are proud, and his subservience disgusted and excited you." She stretched her bony hand to caress Tom's dark face. I could see the whites of his eyes. "And you"—she patted Mike with her other hand—"you beat him, too, because you were seized with the madness. Then he threatened to tell." Her hand left Tom and rubbed his wife, Cleo. Cleo had thrown on a sweater before she went out, but it wasn't buttoned.

Since she had avoided notice, Tara began backing up. She was the only one who wasn't paralyzed by fear. I could feel the tiny spark of hope in her, the desire to survive. Tara crouched under a wrought-iron table on the deck, made herself into a little ball, and squeezed her eyes shut. She was making a lot of promises to God about her future behavior, if he'd get her out of this. That poured into my mind, too. The reek of fear from the others built to a peak, and I could feel my body go into tremors as they broadcast so heavily that it broke through all my barriers. I had nothing left of myself. I was only fear. Eric and Bill locked arms with each other, to hold me upright and immobile between them.

Jan, in her nudity, was completely ignored by the maenad. I can only suppose that there was nothing in Jan that appealed to the creature; Jan was not proud, she was pathetic, and she hadn't had a drink that night. She embraced sex out of other needs than the need for its loss of self—needs that had nothing to do with leaving one's mind and body for a moment of wonderful madness. Trying, as always, to be the center of the group, Jan reached out with a would-be flirty smile and took the maenad's hand. Suddenly she began to convulse, and the noises coming from her throat were horrible. Foam came from her mouth, and her eyes rolled up. She collapsed to the deck, and I could hear her heels drumming the wood.

Then the silence resumed. But something was brewing a few yards away in the little group on the deck: something terrible and fine, something pure and horrible. Their fear was subsiding, and my body began to calm again. The awful pressure eased in my head. But as it ebbed, a new force began to build, and it was indescribably beautiful and absolutely evil.

It was pure madness, it was mindless madness. From the maenad poured the berserker rage, the lust of pillage, the hubris of pride. I was overwhelmed when the people on the deck were overwhelmed, I jerked and thrashed as the insanity rolled off Callisto and into their brains, and only Eric's hand across my mouth kept me from screaming as they did. I bit him and tasted his blood, and heard him grunt at the pain.

It went on and on and on, the screaming, and then

there were awful wet sounds. The dog, pressed against our legs, whimpered.

Suddenly, it was over.

I felt like a dancing puppet whose strings have suddenly been severed. I went limp. Bill laid me down on Eric's car hood again. I opened my eyes. The maenad looked down at me. She was smiling again, and she was drenched in blood. It was like someone had poured a bucket of red paint over her head; her hair was drenched, as was every bit of her bare body, and she reeked of the copper smell, enough to set your teeth on edge.

"You were close," she said to me, her voice as sweet and high as a flute. She moved a little more deliberately, as if she'd eaten a heavy meal. "You were very close. Maybe as close as you'll ever come, maybe not. I've never seen anyone maddened by the insanity of others. An entertaining thought."

"Entertaining for you, maybe," I gasped. The dog bit my leg to bring me to myself. She looked down at him.

"My dear Sam," she murmured. "Darling, I must leave you."

The dog looked up at her with intelligent eyes.

"We've had some good nights running through the woods," she said, and stroked his head. "Catching little rabbits, little coons."

The dog wagged his tail.

"Doing other things."

The dog grinned and panted.

"But it's time for me to go, darling. The world is full of woods and people that need to learn their lesson. I must be paid tribute. They mustn't forget me. I'm owed," she said, in her sated voice, "owed the madness and death." She began to drift to the edge of the woods.

"After all," she said over her shoulder, "it can't always be hunting season."

11

Even if I'd wanted to, I couldn't have walked over to see what was on the deck. Bill and Eric seemed subdued, and when vampires seem subdued, it means you don't really want to go investigate.

"We'll have to burn the cabin," Eric said from a few yards away. "I wish Callisto had taken care of her own mess."

"She never has," Bill said, "that I have heard. It is the madness. What does true madness care about discovery?"

"Oh, I don't know," Eric said carelessly. He sounded as if he was lifting something. There was a heavy thud. "I have seen a few people who were definitely mad and quite crafty with it."

"That's true," Bill said. "Shouldn't we leave a couple of them on the porch?"

"How can you tell?"

"That's true, too. It's a rare night I can agree with you this much."

"She called me and asked me to help." Eric was responding to the subtext rather than the statement.

"Then, all right. But you remember our agreement."

"How can I forget?"

"You know Sookie can hear us."

"Quite all right with me," Eric said, and laughed. I stared up at the night and wondered, not too curiously, what the hell they were talking about. It's not like I was Russia, to be parceled out to the strongest dictator. Sam was resting beside me, back in his human form, and stark naked. At the moment, I could not have cared less. The cold didn't bother Sam since he was a shapeshifter.

"Whoops, here's a live one," Eric called.

"Tara," Sam called.

Tara scrambled down the steps of the deck and over to us. She flung her arms around me and began sobbing. With tremendous weariness, I held her and let her boo-hoo. I was still in my Daisy Duke outfit, and she was in her fire-engine lingerie. We were like big white water lilies in a cold pond, we two. I made myself straighten up and hold Tara.

"Would there be a blanket in that cabin, you think?" I asked Sam. He trotted over to the steps, and I noticed the effect was interesting from behind. After a minute, he trotted back—wow, this view was even more arresting—and wrapped a blanket around the two of us.

"I must be gonna live," I muttered.

"Why do you say that?" Sam was curious. He didn't seem unduly surprised by the events of the night.

I could hardly tell him it was because I'd watched him bounce around, so I said, "How are Eggs and Andy?"

"Sounds like a radio show," Tara said suddenly, and giggled. I didn't like the sound of it.

"They're still standing where she left them," Sam reported. "Still staring."

"I'm—still—staring," Tara sang, to the tune of Elton's "I'm Still Standing."

Eric laughed.

He and Bill were just about to start the fire. They strolled over to us for a last-minute check.

"What car did you come in?" Bill asked Tara.

"Ooo, a vampire," she said. "You're Sookie's honey, aren't you? Why were you at the game the other night with a dog like Portia Bellefleur?"

"She's kind, too," Eric said. He looked down at Tara with a sort of beneficent but disappointed smile, like a dog breeder regarding a cute, but inferior, puppy.

"What car did you come in?" Bill asked again. "If there is a sensible side to you, I want to see it now."

"I came in the white Camaro," she said, quite soberly. "I'll drive it home. Or maybe I better not. Sam?"

"Sure, I'll drive you home. Bill, you need my help here?"

"I think Eric and I can cope. Can you take the skinny one?"

"Eggs? I'll see."

Tara gave me a kiss on the cheek and began picking

her way across the yard to her car. "I left the keys in it," she called.

"What about your purse?" The police would surely wonder if they found Tara's purse in a cabin with a lot of bodies.

"Oh . . . it's in there."

I looked at Bill silently, and he went in to fetch the purse. He returned with a big shoulder bag, large enough to contain not only makeup and everyday items but also a change of clothing.

"This is yours?"

"Yes, thanks," Tara said, taking the bag from him as if she were afraid his fingers might touch hers. She hadn't been so picky earlier in the evening, I thought.

Eric was carrying Eggs to her car. "He will not remember any of this," Eric told Tara as Sam opened the door of the Camaro and flipped the front seat forward so Eric could lay Eggs down on the backseat.

"I wish I could say the same." Her face seemed to sag on its bones under the weight of the knowledge of what had happened this night. "I wish I'd never seen that thing, whatever she is. I wish I'd never come here, to start with. I hated doing this. I just thought Eggs was worth it." She gave a look to the inert form in the backseat of her car. "He's not. No one is."

"I can remove your memory, too." Eric made the offer offhandedly.

"No," she said. "I need to remember some of this, and it's worth carrying the burden of the rest." Tara sounded twenty years older. Sometimes we can grow up all in a minute; I'd done that when I was about seven and my parents died. Tara had done that this night.

"But they're all dead, all but me and Eggs and Andy. Aren't you afraid we'll talk? Are you gonna come after us?"

Eric and Bill exchanged glances. Eric moved a little closer to Tara. "Look, Tara," he began, in a very reasonable voice, and she made the mistake of glancing up. Then, once her gaze was fixed, Eric began to erase the memory of the night. I was just too tired to protest, as if that would do any good. If Tara could even raise the question, she shouldn't be burdened with the knowledge. I hoped she wouldn't repeat her mistakes, having been separated from the knowledge of what they had cost her; but she couldn't be allowed to tell tales.

Tara and Eggs, driven by Sam (who had borrowed Eggs's pants), were on their way back to town when Bill began arranging a natural-looking fire to consume the cabin. Eric was apparently counting bones up on the deck, to make sure the bodies there were complete enough to reassure the investigators. He went across the yard to check on Andy.

"Why does Bill hate the Bellefleurs so much?" I asked him again.

"Oh, that's an old story," Eric said. "Back from before Bill had even changed over." He seemed satisfied by Andy's condition and went back to work.

I heard a car approaching, and Bill and Eric both appeared in the yard instantly. I could hear a faint crackle from the far side of the cabin. "We can't start the fire from more than one place, or they may be able to tell it wasn't natural," Bill said to Eric. "I hate these strides in police science."

"If we hadn't decided to go public, they'd have to blame it on one of them," Eric said. "But as it is, we are such attractive scapegoats . . . it's galling, when you think of how much stronger we are."

"Hey, guys, I'm not a Martian, I'm a human, and I can hear you just fine," I said. I was glaring at them, and they were looking perhaps one-fiftieth embarrassed, when Portia Bellefleur got out of her car and ran to her brother. "What have you done to Andy?" she said, her voice harsh and cracking. "You damn vampires." She pulled the collar of Andy's shirt this way and that, looking for puncture marks.

"They saved his life," I told her.

Eric looked at Portia for a long moment, evaluating her, and then he began to search the cars of the dead revelers. He'd gotten their car keys, which I didn't want to picture.

Bill went over to Andy and said, "Wake up," in the quietest voice, so quiet it could hardly be heard a few feet away.

Andy blinked. He looked over at me, confused that I wasn't still in his grasp, I guess. He saw Bill, so close to him, and he flinched, expecting retaliation. He registered that Portia was at his side. Then he looked past Bill at the cabin.

"It's on fire," he observed, slowly.

"Yes," Bill said. "They are all dead, except the two who've gone back into town. They knew nothing."

"Then . . . these people did kill Lafayette?"

"Yes," I said. "Mike, and the Hardaways, and I guess maybe Jan knew about it."

"But I haven't got any proof."

"Oh, I think so," Eric called. He was looking down into the trunk of Mike Spencer's Lincoln.

We all moved to the car to see. Bill's and Eric's superior vision made it easy for them to tell there was blood in the trunk, blood and some stained clothes and a wallet. Eric reached down and carefully flipped the wallet open.

"Can you read whose it is?" Andy asked.

"Lafayette Reynold," Eric said.

"So if we just leave the cars like this, and we leave, the police will find what's in the trunk and it'll all be over. I'll be clear."

"Oh, thank God!" Portia said, and gave a kind of sobbing gasp. Her plain face and thick chestnut hair caught a gleam of moonlight filtering through the trees. "Oh, Andy, let's go home."

"Portia," Bill said, "look at me."

She glanced up at him, then away. "I'm sorry I led you on like that," she said rapidly. She was ashamed to apologize to a vampire, you could tell. "I was just trying to get one of the people who came here to invite me, so I could find out for myself what was going on."

"Sookie did that for you," Bill said mildly.

Portia's gaze darted over to me. "I hope it wasn't too awful, Sookie," she said, surprising me.

"It was really horrible," I said. Portia cringed. "But it's over."

"Thank you for helping Andy," Portia said bravely.

"I wasn't helping Andy. I was helping Lafayette," I snapped.

She took a deep breath. "Of course," she said, with some dignity. "He was your coworker."

"He was my *friend*," I corrected.

Her back straightened. "Your friend," she said.

The fire was catching in the cabin now, and soon there would be police and firefighters. It was definitely time to leave.

I noticed neither Eric nor Bill offered to remove any memories from Andy.

"You better get out of here," I said to him. "You better go back to your house, with Portia, and tell your grand-mama to swear you were there all night."

Without a word, brother and sister piled into Portia's Audi and left. Eric folded himself into the Corvette for the drive back to Shreveport, and Bill and I went through the woods to Bill's car, concealed in the trees across the road. He carried me, as he enjoyed doing. I have to say, I enjoyed it, too, on occasion. This was definitely one of the occasions.

It wasn't far from dawn. One of the longest nights of my life was about to come to a close. I lay back against the seat of the car, tired beyond reckoning.

"Where did Callisto go?" I asked Bill.

"I have no idea. She moves from place to place. Not too many maenads survived the loss of the god, and the ones that did find woods, and roam them. They move be-fore their presence is discovered. They're crafty like that. They love war and its madness. You'll never find them far from a battlefield. I think they'd all move to the Middle East if there were more woods."

"Callisto was here because . . . ?"

"Just passing through. She stayed maybe two months, now she'll work her way . . . who knows? To the Ever-glades, or up the river to the Ozarks."

"I can't understand Sam, ah, palling around with her."

"That's what you call it? Is that what we do, pal around?"

I reached over and poked him in the arm, which was like pressing on wood. "You," I said.

"Maybe he just wanted to walk on the wild side," Bill said. "After all, it's hard for Sam to find someone who can accept his true nature." Bill paused significantly.

"Well, that can be hard to do," I said. I recalled Bill coming back in the mansion in Dallas, all rosy, and I gulped. "But people in love are hard to pry apart." I thought of how I'd felt when I'd heard he'd been seeing Portia, and I thought of how I'd reacted when I'd seen him at the football game. I stretched my hand over to rest on his thigh and I gave it a gentle squeeze.

With his eyes on the road, he smiled. His fangs ran out a little.

"Did you get everything settled with the shapeshifters in Dallas?" I asked after a moment.

"I settled it in an hour, or rather Stan did. He offered them his ranch for the nights of the full moon, for the next four months."

"Oh, that was nice of him."

"Well, it doesn't cost him anything exactly. And he doesn't hunt, so the deer need culling anyway, as he pointed out."

"Oh," I said in acknowledgment, and then after a second, "ooooh."

"They hunt."

"Right. Gotcha."

When we got back to my house, it didn't lack much till dawn. Eric would just make it to Shreveport, I figured.

While Bill showered, I ate some peanut butter and jelly, since I hadn't had anything for more hours than I could add up. Then I went and brushed my teeth.

At least he didn't have to rush off. Bill had spent several nights the month before creating a place for himself at my house. He'd cut out the bottom of the closet in my old bedroom, the one I'd used for years before my grandmother died and I'd started using hers. He'd made the whole closet floor into a trapdoor, so he could open it, climb in, and pull it shut after him, and no one would be the wiser but me. If I was still up when he went to earth, I put an old suitcase in the closet and a couple of pairs of shoes to make it look more natural. Bill kept a box in the crawl space to sleep in, because it was mighty nasty down there. He didn't often stay there, but it had come in handy from time to time.

"Sookie," Bill called from my bathroom. "Come, I have time to scrub you."

"But if you scrub me, I'll have a hard time getting to sleep."

"Why?"

"Because I'll be frustrated."

"Frustrated?"

"Because I'll be clean but . . . unloved."

"It is close to dawn," Bill admitted, his head poking around the shower curtain. "But we'll have our time tomorrow night."

"If Eric doesn't make us go somewhere else," I muttered, when his head was safely under the cascade of water. As usual, he was using up most of my hot. I wriggled out of the damn shorts and resolved to throw them away tomorrow. I pulled the tee shirt over my head and stretched

out on my bed to wait for Bill. At least my new bra was intact. I turned on one side, and closed my eyes against the
light coming from the half-closed bathroom door.

"Darling?"

"You out of the shower?" I asked drowsily.

"Yes, twelve hours ago."

"What?" My eyes flew open. I looked at the windows.
They were not pitch-black, but very dark.

"You fell asleep."

I had a blanket over me, and I was still wearing the
steel blue bra and panty set. I felt like moldy bread. I
looked at Bill. He was wearing nothing at all.

"Hold that thought," I said and paid a visit to the bathroom. When I came back, Bill was waiting for me on the
bed, propped on one elbow.

"Did you notice the outfit you got me?" I rotated to
give him the full benefit of his generosity.

"It's lovely, but you may be slightly overdressed for
the occasion."

"What occasion would that be?"

"The best sex of your life."

I felt a lurch of sheer lust down low. But I kept my face
still. "And can you be sure it will be the best?"

"Oh, yes," he said, his voice becoming so smooth and
cold it was like running water over stones. "I can be sure,
and so can you."

"Prove it," I said, smiling very slightly.

His eyes were in the shadows, but I could see the curve
of his lips as he smiled back. "Gladly," he said.

Some time later, I was trying to recover my strength,
and he was draped over me, an arm across my stomach, a
leg across mine. My mouth was so tired it could barely

pucker to kiss his shoulder. Bill's tongue was gently licking the tiny puncture marks on my shoulder.

"You know what we need to do?" I said, feeling too lazy to move ever again.

"Um?"

"We need to get the newspaper."

After a long pause, Bill slowly unwrapped himself from me and strolled to the front door. My paperwoman pulls up my driveway and tosses it in the general direction of the porch because I pay her a great big tip on that understanding.

"Look," said Bill, and I opened my eyes. He was holding a foil-wrapped plate. The paper was tucked under his arm.

I rolled off the bed and we went automatically to the kitchen. I pulled on my pink robe as I padded after Bill. He was still natural, and I admired the effect.

"There's a message on the answering machine," I said, as I put on some coffee. The most important thing done, I rolled back the aluminum foil and saw a two-layer cake with chocolate icing, studded with pecans in a star pattern on the top.

"That's old Mrs. Bellefleur's chocolate cake," I said, awe in my voice.

"You can tell whose it is by looking?"

"Oh, this is a famous cake. It's a legend. Nothing is as good as Mrs. Bellefleur's cake. If she enters it in the county fair, the ribbon's as good as won. And she brings it when someone dies. Jason said it was worth someone dying, just to get a piece of Mrs. Bellefleur's cake."

"What a wonderful smell," Bill said, to my amazement. He bent down and sniffed. Bill doesn't breathe, so I haven't exactly figured out how he smells, but he does. "If you could wear that as a perfume, I would eat you up."

"You already did."

"I would do it a second time."

"I don't think I could stand it." I poured myself a cup of coffee. I stared at the cake, full of wonderment. "I didn't even know she knew where I live."

Bill pressed the message button on my answering machine. "Miss Stackhouse," said the voice of a very old, very Southern, aristocrat. "I knocked on your door, but you must have been busy. I left a chocolate cake for you, since I didn't know what else to do to thank you for what Portia tells me you've done for my grandson, Andrew. Some people have been kind enough to tell me that the cake is good. I hope you enjoy it. If I can ever be of service to you, just give me a call."

"Didn't say her name."

"Caroline Holliday Bellefleur expects everyone to know who she is."

"Who?"

I looked up at Bill, who was standing by the window. I was sitting at the kitchen table, drinking coffee from one of my grandmother's flowered cups.

"Caroline Holliday Bellefleur."

Bill could not get any paler, but he was undoubtedly stunned. He sat down very abruptly into the chair across from me. "Sookie, do me a favor."

"Sure, baby. What is it?"

"Go over to my house and get the Bible that is in the glass-fronted bookshelf in the hallway."

He seemed so upset, I grabbed my keys and drove over in my bathrobe, hoping I wouldn't meet anyone along the way. Not too many people live out on our parish road, and none of them were out at four in the morning.

I let myself into Bill's house and found the Bible exactly where he'd said. I eased it out of the bookcase very carefully. It was obviously quite old. I was so nervous carrying it up the steps to my house that I almost tripped. Bill was sitting where I'd left him. When I'd set the Bible in front of him, he stared at it for a long minute. I began to wonder if he could touch it. But he didn't ask for help, so I waited. His hand reached out and the white fingers caressed the worn leather cover. The book was massive, and the gold lettering on the cover was ornate.

Bill opened the book with gentle fingers and turned a page. He was looking at a family page, with entries in faded ink, made in several different handwritings.

"I made these," he said in a whisper. "These here." He pointed at a few lines of writing.

My heart was in my throat as I came around the table to look over his shoulder. I put my own hand on his shoulder, to link him to the here and now.

I could barely make out the writing.

William Thomas Compton, his mother had written, or perhaps his father. *Born April 9, 1840.* Another hand had written, *Died November 25, 1870.*

"You have a birthday," I said, of all the stupid things to say. I'd never thought of Bill having a birthday.

"I was the second son," Bill said. "The only son who grew up."

I remembered that Robert, Bill's older brother, had died when he was twelve or so, and two other babies had died in infancy. There all these births and deaths were recorded, on the page under Bill's fingers.

"Sarah, my sister, died childless." I remembered that. "Her young man died in the war. All the young men died in the war. But I survived, only to die later. This is the date of my death, as far as my family is concerned. It's in Sarah's handwriting."

I held my lips pressed tight, so I wouldn't make a sound. There was something about Bill's voice, the way he touched the Bible that was almost unbearable. I could feel my eyes fill with tears.

"Here is the name of my wife," he said, his voice quieter and quieter.

I bent over again to read, *Caroline Isabelle Holliday*. For one second, the room swung sideways, until I realized it just could not be.

"And we had children," he said. "We had three children."

Their names were there, too. *Thomas Charles Compton, b. 1859*. She'd gotten pregnant right after they'd married, then.

I would never have Bill's baby.

Sarah Isabelle Compton, b. 1861. Named after her aunt (Bill's sister) and her mother. She'd been born around the time Bill had left for the war. *Lee Davis Compton, b. 1866*. A homecoming baby. *Died 1867*, a different hand had added.

"Babies died like flies then," Bill whispered. "We were so poor after the war, and there wasn't any medicine."

I was about to take my sad weepy self out of the kitchen, but then I realized that if Bill could stand this, I pretty much had to.

"The other two children?" I asked.

"They lived," he said, the tension in his face easing a

little. "I had left then, of course. Tom was only eleven when I died, and Sarah was nine. She was towheaded, like her mother." Bill smiled a little, a smile that I'd never seen on his face before. He looked quite human. It was like seeing a different being sitting here in my kitchen, not the same person I'd made love with so thoroughly not an hour earlier. I pulled a Kleenex out of the box on the baker's rack and dabbed at my face. Bill was crying, too, and I handed him one. He looked at it in surprise, as if he'd expected to see something different—maybe a monogrammed cotton handkerchief. He patted his own cheeks. The Kleenex turned pink.

"I hadn't ever looked to see what became of them," he said wonderingly. "I cut myself off so thoroughly. I never came back, of course, while there was any chance any one of them would be alive. That would be too cruel." He read down the page.

"My descendant Jessie Compton, from whom I received my house, was the last of my direct line," Bill told me. "My mother's line, too, has thinned down, until the remaining Loudermilks are only distantly related to me. But Jessie did descend from my son Tom, and apparently, my daughter Sarah married in 1881. She had a baby in— Sarah had a baby! She had four babies! But one of them was born dead."

I could not even look at Bill. Instead, I looked at the window. It had begun raining. My grandmother had loved her tin roof, so when it had had to be replaced, we'd gotten tin again, and the drumming of the rain was normally the most relaxing sound I knew. But not tonight.

"Look, Sookie," Bill said, pointing. "Look! My Sarah's daughter, named Caroline for her grandmother, married a cousin of hers, Matthew Phillips Holliday. And her second child was Caroline Holliday." His face was glowing.

"So old Mrs. Bellefleur is your great-granddaughter."

"Yes," he said unbelievingly.

"So Andy," I continued, before I could think twice about it, "is your, ah, great-great-great-grandson. And Portia . . ."

"Yes," he said, less happily.

I had no idea what to say, so for once, I said nothing. After a minute, I got the feeling it might be better if I made myself scarce, so I tried to slip by him to get out of the small kitchen.

"What do they need?" he asked me, seizing my wrist.

Okay. "They need money," I said instantly. "You can't help them with their personality problems, but they are cash-poor in the worst possible way. Old Mrs. Bellefleur won't give up that house, and it's eating every dime."

"Is she proud?"

"I think you could tell from her phone message. If I hadn't known her middle name was Holliday, I would have thought it was 'Proud.'" I eyed Bill. "I guess she comes by it natural."

Somehow, now that Bill knew he could do something for his descendants, he seemed to feel much better. I knew he would be reminiscing for a few days, and I would not grudge him that. But if he decided to take up Portia and Andy as permanent causes, that might be a problem.

"You didn't like the name Bellefleur before this," I said, surprising myself. "Why?"

"When I spoke to your grandmother's club, you remember, the Descendants of the Glorious Dead?"

"Yes, sure."

"And I told the story, the story of the wounded soldier out in the field, the one who kept calling for help? And how my friend Tolliver Humphries tried to rescue him?"

I nodded.

"Tolliver died in the attempt," Bill said bleakly. "And the wounded soldier resumed calling for help after his death. We managed to retrieve him during the night. His name was Jebediah Bellefleur. He was seventeen years old."

"Oh my gosh. So that was all you knew of the Belle-fleurs until today."

Bill nodded.

I tried to think of something of significance to say. Something about cosmic plans. Something about throwing your bread upon the waters. What goes around, comes around?

I tried to leave again. But Bill caught my arm, pulled me to him. "Thank you, Sookie."

That was the last thing I had expected him to say. "Why?"

"You made me do the right thing with no idea of the eventual reward."

"Bill, I can't make you do anything."

"You made me think like a human, like I was still alive."

"The good you do is in you, not in me."

"I am a vampire, Sookie. I have been a vampire far longer than I was human. I have upset you many times. To tell the truth, sometimes I can't understand why you do what you do, because it's been so long since I was a person. It's not always comfortable to remember what it was like to be a man. Sometimes I don't want to be re-minded."

These were deep waters for me. "I don't know if I'm right or wrong, but I don't know how to be different," I said. "I'd be miserable if it wasn't for you."

"If anything happens to me," Bill said, "you should go to Eric."

"You've said that before," I told him. "If anything happens to you, I don't have to go to anyone. I'm my own person. I get to make up my mind what I want to do. You've got to make sure nothing happens to you."

"We'll be having more trouble from the Fellowship in the years to come," Bill said. "Actions will have to be taken that may be repugnant to you as a human. And there are the dangers attached to your job." He didn't mean waiting tables.

"We'll cross that bridge when we get to it." Sitting on Bill's lap was a real treat, especially since he was still naked. My life had not exactly been full of treats until I met Bill. Now every day held a treat, or two.

In the low-lit kitchen, with the coffee smelling as beautiful (in its own way) as the chocolate cake did, and the rain drumming on the roof, I was having a beautiful moment with my vampire, what you might call a warm human moment.

But maybe I shouldn't call it that, I reflected, rubbing my cheek against Bill's. This evening, Bill had looked quite human. And I—well, I had noticed while we made love on our clean sheets, that in the darkness Bill's skin had been glowing in its beautiful otherworldly way.

And mine had, too.

Bill was hunched over the computer when I let myself in his house. This was an all-too-familiar scenario in the past month or two. He'd torn himself away from his work when I came home, until the past couple of weeks. Now it was the keyboard that attracted him.

"Hello, sweetheart," he said absently, his gaze riveted to the screen. An empty bottle of type-O TrueBlood was on the desk beside the keyboard. At least he'd remembered to eat.

Bill, not a jeans-and-tee kind of guy, was wearing khakis and a plaid shirt in muted blue and green. His skin was glowing, and his thick dark hair smelled like Herbal Essences. He was enough to give any woman a hormonal surge. I kissed his neck, and he didn't react. I licked his ear. Nothing.

I'd been on my feet for six hours straight at Merlotte's Bar, and every time some customer had under-tipped, or some fool had patted my fanny, I'd reminded myself that in a short while I'd be with my boyfriend, having incredible sex and basking in his attention.

That didn't appear to be happening.

I inhaled slowly and steadily, and glared at Bill's back. It was a wonderful back, with broad shoulders, and I had planned on seeing it bare with my nails dug into it. I had counted on that very strongly. I exhaled, slowly and steadily.

"Be with you in a minute," Bill said. On the screen, there was a snapshot of a distinguished man with silver hair and a dark tan. He looked sort of Anthony Quinn–type sexy, and he looked powerful. Under the picture was a name, and under that was some text. "Born 1756 in Sicily," it began. Just as I opened my mouth to comment that vampires *did* appear in photographs despite the legend, Bill twisted around and realized I was reading.

He hit a button and the screen went blank.

I stared at him, not quite believing what had just happened.

"Sookie," he said, attempting a smile. His fangs were retracted, so he was totally not in the mood in which I'd hoped to find him; he wasn't thinking of me carnally. Like all vampires, his fangs are only fully extended when he's in the mood for the sexy kind of lust, or the feeding-and-killing kind of lust. (Sometimes, those lusts all get kind of snarled up, and you get your dead fangbangers. But that element of danger is what attracts most fangbangers, if you ask me.) Though I've been accused of being one of those pathetic creatures that hang around vampires in the hope of attracting their attention, there's only one vampire I'm involved with (at least voluntarily), and it was the one sitting right in front of me. The one who was keeping secrets from me. The one who wasn't nearly glad enough to see me.

"Bill," I said coldly. Something was Up, with a capital *U*. And it wasn't Bill's libido. (*Libido* had just been on my Word of the Day calendar.)

"You didn't see what you just saw," he said steadily. His dark brown eyes regarded me without blinking.

"Uh-huh," I said, maybe sounding just a little sarcastic. "What are you up to?"

"I have a secret assignment."

I didn't know whether to laugh or stalk away in a snit. So I just raised my eyebrows and waited for more. Bill was the investigator for Area 5, a vampire division of Louisiana. Eric, the head of Area 5, had never given Bill an "assignment" that was secret from me before. In fact, I was usually an integral part of the investigation team, however unwilling I might be.

"Eric must not know. None of the Area 5 vampires can know."

My heart sank. "So—if you're not doing a job for Eric, who are you working for?" I knelt because my feet were so tired, and I leaned against Bill's knees.

"The Queen of Louisiana," he said, almost in a whisper.

Because he looked so solemn, I tried to keep a straight face, but it was no use. I began to laugh, little giggles that I couldn't suppress.

"You're serious?" I asked, knowing he must be. Bill was almost always a serious kind of fellow. I buried my face on his thigh so he couldn't see my amusement. I rolled my eyes up for a quick look at his face. He was looking pretty pissed.

"I am as serious as the grave," Bill said, and he sounded so steely, I made a major effort to change my attitude.

"Okay, let me get this straight," I said in a reasonably level tone. I sat back on the floor, cross-legged, and rested my hands on my knees. "You work for Eric, who is the boss of Area 5, but there is also a queen? Of Louisiana?"

Bill nodded.

"So the state is divided up into areas? And she's Eric's superior, since he runs a business in Shreveport, which is in Area 5."

Again with the nod. I put my hand over my face and shook my head. "So, where does she live, Baton Rouge?" The state capital seemed the obvious place.

"No, no. New Orleans, of course."

Of *course*. Vampire central. You could hardly throw a rock in the Big Easy without hitting one of the undead, according to the papers (though only a real fool would do so). The tourist trade in New Orleans was booming, but it was not exactly the same crowd as before, the hard-drinking, rollicking crowd who'd filled the city to party hearty. The newer tourists were the ones who wanted to rub elbows with the undead; patronize a vampire bar, visit a vampire prostitute, watch a vampire sex show.

This was what I'd heard; I hadn't been to New Orleans since I was little. My mother and father had taken my brother, Jason, and me. That would have been before I was seven, because that's when they died.

Mama and Daddy died nearly twenty years before vampires had appeared on network television to announce the fact that they were actually present among us, an announcement that had followed on the Japanese development of synthetic blood that actually maintained a vampire's life without the necessity of drinking from humans.

The United States vampire community had let the Japanese vampire clans come forth first. Then, simultaneously, in most of the nations of the world that had television— and who doesn't these days?—the announcement had been made in hundreds of different languages, by hundreds of carefully picked, personable vampires.

That night, two and a half years ago, we regular old live people learned that we had always lived with monsters among us.

"But"—the burden of this announcement had been— "now we can come forward and join with you in harmony. You are in no danger from us anymore. We don't need to drink from you to live."

As you can imagine, this was a night of high ratings and tremendous uproar. Reaction varied sharply, depending on the nation.

The vampires in the predominantly Islamic nations had fared the worst. You don't even want to know what happened to the undead spokesman in Syria, though perhaps the female vamp in Afghanistan died an even more horrible—and final—death. (What were they thinking, selecting a female for that particular job? Vampires could be so smart, but they sometimes didn't seem quite in touch with the present world.)

Some nations—France, Italy, and Germany were the most notable—refused to accept vampires as equal citizens. Many—like Bosnia, Argentina, and most of the African nations—denied any status to the vampires, and declared them fair game for any bounty hunter. But America, England, Mexico, Canada, Japan, Switzerland, and the Scandinavian countries adopted a more tolerant attitude.

It was hard to determine if this reaction was what the vampires had expected or not. Since they were still struggling to maintain a foothold in the stream of the living, the vampires remained very secretive about their organization and government, and what Bill was telling me now was the most I'd ever heard on the subject.

"So, the Louisiana queen of the vampires has you working on a secret project," I said, trying to sound neutral. "And this is why you have lived at your computer every waking hour for the past few weeks."

"Yes," Bill said. He picked up the bottle of TrueBlood and tipped it up, but there were only a couple of drops left. He went down the hall into the small kitchen area (when he'd remodeled his old family home, he'd pretty much left out the kitchen, since he didn't need one) and extracted another bottle from the refrigerator. I was tracking him by sound as he opened the bottle and popped it into the microwave. The microwave went off, and he reentered, shaking the bottle with his thumb over the top so there wouldn't be any hot spots.

"So, how much more time do you have to spend on this project?" I asked—reasonably, I thought.

"As long as it takes," he said, less reasonably. Actually, Bill sounded downright irritable.

Hmmm. Could our honeymoon be over? Of course I mean figurative honeymoon, since Bill's a vampire and we can't be legally married, practically anywhere in the world.

Not that he's asked me.

"Well, if you're so absorbed in your project, I'll just stay away until it's over," I said slowly.

"That might be best," Bill said, after a perceptible pause, and I felt like he'd socked me in the stomach. In a flash, I was on my feet and pulling my coat back over my cold-weather waitress outfit—black slacks, white boatneck long-sleeved tee with "Merlotte's" embroidered over the left breast. I turned my back to Bill to hide my face.

I was trying not to cry, so I didn't look at him even after I felt Bill's hand touch my shoulder.

"I have to tell you something," Bill said in his cold, smooth voice. I stopped in the middle of pulling on my gloves, but I didn't think I could stand to see him. He could tell my backside.

"If anything happens to me," he continued (and here's where I should have begun worrying), "you must look in the hiding place I built at your house. My computer should be in it, and some disks. Don't tell anyone. If the computer isn't in the hiding place, come over to my house and see if it's here. Come in the daytime, and come armed. Get the computer and any disks you can find, and hide them in my hidey-hole, as you call it."

I nodded. He could see that from the back. I didn't trust my voice.

"If I'm not back, or if you don't get word from me, in say . . . eight weeks—yes, eight weeks—then tell Eric everything I said to you today. And place yourself under his protection."

I didn't speak. I was too miserable to be furious, but it wouldn't be long before I reached meltdown. I acknowledged his words with a jerk of my head. I could feel my ponytail switch against my neck.

"I am going to . . . Seattle soon," Bill said. I could feel his cool lips touch the place my ponytail had brushed.

He was lying.

"When I come back, we'll talk."

Somehow, that didn't sound like an entrancing prospect. Somehow, that sounded ominous.

Again, I inclined my head, not risking speech because I was actually crying now. I would rather have died than let him see the tears.

And that was how I left him, that cold December night.

The next day, on my way to work, I took an unwise detour. I was in that kind of mood where I was rolling in how awful everything was. Despite a nearly sleepless night, something inside me told me I could probably make my mood a little worse if I drove along Magnolia Creek Road: so sure enough, that's what I did.

The old Bellefleur mansion, Belle Rive, was a beehive of activity, even on a cold and ugly day. There were vans from the pest control company, a kitchen design firm, and a siding contractor parked at the kitchen entrance to the antebellum home. Life was just humming for Caroline Holliday Bellefleur, the ancient lady who had ruled Belle Rive and (at least in part) Bon Temps for the past eighty years. I wondered how Portia, a lawyer, and Andy, a detective, were enjoying all the changes at Belle Rive. They had lived with their grandmother (as I had lived with mine) for all their adult lives. At the very least, they had to be enjoying her pleasure in the mansion's renovation.

My own grandmother had been murdered a few months ago.

The Bellefleurs hadn't had anything to do with it, of course. And there was no reason Portia and Andy would share the pleasure of this new affluence with me. In fact, they both avoided me like the plague. They owed me, and they couldn't stand it. They just didn't know how *much* they owed me.

The Bellefleurs had received a legacy from a relative who had "died mysteriously over in Europe somewhere," I'd heard Andy tell a fellow cop while they were drinking at Merlotte's. When she dropped off some raffle tickets for Gethsemane Baptist Church's Ladies' Quilt, Maxine Fortenberry told me Miss Caroline had combed every family record she could unearth to identify their benefactor, and she was still mystified at the family's good fortune.

She didn't seem to have any qualms about spending the money, though.

Even Terry Bellefleur, Portia and Andy's cousin, had a new pickup sitting in the packed dirt yard of his double-wide. I liked Terry, a scarred Vietnam vet who didn't have a lot of friends, and I didn't grudge him a new set of wheels.

But I thought about the carburetor I'd just been forced to replace in my old car. I'd paid for the work in full, though I'd considered asking Jim Downey if I could just pay half and get the rest together over the next two months. But Jim had a wife and three kids. Just this morning I'd been thinking of asking my boss, Sam Merlotte, if he could add to my hours at the bar. Especially with Bill gone to "Seattle," I could just about live at Merlotte's, if Sam could use me. I sure needed the money.

I tried real hard not to be bitter as I drove away from

Belle Rive. I went south out of town and then turned left onto Hummingbird Road on my way to Merlotte's. I tried to pretend that all was well; that on his return from Seattle—or wherever—Bill would be a passionate lover again, and Bill would treasure me and make me feel valuable once more. I would again have that feeling of belonging with someone, instead of being alone.

Of course, I had my brother, Jason. Though as far as intimacy and companionship goes, I had to admit that he hardly counted.

But the pain in my middle was the unmistakable pain of rejection. I knew the feeling so well, it was like a second skin.

I sure hated to crawl back inside it.

I TESTED THE DOORKNOB TO MAKE SURE I'D LOCKED it, turned around, and out of the corner of my eye glimpsed a figure sitting in the swing on my front porch. I stifled a shriek as he rose. Then I recognized him.

I was wearing a heavy coat, but he was in a tank top; that didn't surprise me, really.

"El—" Uh-oh, close call. "Bubba, how are you?" I was trying to sound casual, carefree. I failed, but Bubba wasn't the sharpest tool in the shed. The vampires admitted that bringing him over, when he'd been so very close to death and so saturated with drugs, had been a big mistake. The night he'd been brought in, one of the morgue attendants happened to be one of the undead, and also happened to be a huge fan. With a hastily constructed and elaborate plot involving a murder or two, the attendant had "brought him over"—made Bubba a vampire. But the process doesn't always go right, you know. Since then, he's been passed around like idiot royalty. Louisiana had been hosting him for the past year.

"Miss Sookie, how you doin'?" His accent was still thick and his face still handsome, in a jowly kind of way. The dark hair tumbled over his forehead in a carefully careless style. The heavy sideburns were brushed. Some undead fan had groomed him for the evening.

"I'm just fine, thank you," I said politely, grinning from ear to ear. I do that when I'm nervous. "I was just fixing to go to work," I added, wondering if it was possible I would be able to simply get in my car and drive away. I thought not.

"Well, Miss Sookie, I been sent to guard you tonight."

"You have? By who?"

"By Eric," he said proudly. "I was the only one in the office when he got a phone call. He tole me to get my ass over here."

"What's the danger?" I peered around the clearing in the woods in which my old house stood. Bubba's news made me very nervous.

"I don't know, Miss Sookie. Eric, he tole me to watch you tonight till one of them from Fangtasia gets here— Eric, or Chow, or Miss Pam, or even Clancy. So if you go to work, I go with you. And I take care of anyone who bothers you."

There was no point in questioning Bubba further, putting strain on that fragile brain. He'd just get upset, and you didn't want to see that happen. That was why you had to remember not to call him by his former name . . .

though every now and then he would sing, and that was a moment to remember.

"You can't come in the bar," I said bluntly. That would be a disaster. The clientele of Merlotte's is used to the occasional vampire, sure, but I couldn't warn *everyone* not to say his name. Eric must have been desperate; the vampire community kept mistakes like Bubba out of sight, though from time to time he'd take it in his head to wander off on his own. Then you got a "sighting," and the tabloids went crazy.

"Maybe you could sit in my car while I work?" The cold wouldn't affect Bubba.

"I got to be closer than that," he said, and he sounded immovable.

"Okay, then, how about my boss's office? It's right off the bar, and you can hear me if I yell."

Bubba still didn't look satisfied, but finally he nodded. I let out a breath I hadn't realized I'd been holding. It would be easiest for me to stay home, call in sick. However, not only did Sam expect me to show up, but also I needed the paycheck.

The car felt a little small with Bubba in the front seat beside me. As we bumped off my property, through the woods and out to the parish road, I made a mental note to get the gravel company to come dump some more gravel on my long, meandering driveway. Then I canceled that order, also mentally. I couldn't afford that right now. It'd have to wait until spring. Or summer.

We turned right to drive the few miles to Merlotte's, the bar where I work as a waitress when I'm not doing Heap Big Secret Stuff for the vampires. It occurred to me when we were about halfway there that I hadn't seen a car

Bubba could've used to drive to my house. Maybe he'd flown? Some vamps could. Though Bubba was the least talented vampire I'd met, maybe he had a flair for it.

A year ago I would've asked him, but not now. I'm used to hanging around with the undead now. Not that I'm a vampire. I'm a telepath. My life was hell on wheels until I met a man whose mind I couldn't read. Unfortunately, I couldn't read his mind because he was dead. But Bill and I had been together for several months now, and until recently, our relationship had been real good. And the other vampires need me, so I'm safe—to a certain extent. Mostly. Sometimes.

Merlotte's didn't look too busy, judging from the half-empty parking lot. Sam had bought the bar about five years ago. It had been failing—maybe because it had been cut out of the forest, which loomed all around the parking lot. Or maybe the former owner just hadn't found the right combination of drinks, food, and service.

Somehow, after he renamed the place and renovated it, Sam had turned the balance sheets around. He made a nice living off it now. But tonight was a Monday night, not a big drinking night in our neck of the woods, which happened to be in northern Louisiana. I pulled around to the employee parking lot, which was right in front of Sam Merlotte's trailer, which itself is behind and at right angles to the employee entrance to the bar. I hopped out of the driver's seat, trotted through the storeroom, and peeked through the glass pane in the door to check the short hall with its doors to the restrooms and Sam's office. Empty. Good. And when I knocked on Sam's door, he was behind his desk, which was even better.

Sam is not a big man, but he's very strong. He's a

strawberry blond with blue eyes, and he's maybe three years older than my twenty-six. I've worked for him for about that many years. I'm fond of Sam, and he's starred in some of my favorite fantasies; but since he dated a beautiful but homicidal creature a couple of months before, my enthusiasm has somewhat faded. He's for sure my friend, though.

"'Scuse me, Sam," I said, smiling like an idiot.

"What's up?" He closed the catalog of bar supplies he'd been studying.

"I need to stash someone in here for a little while."

Sam didn't look altogether happy. "Who? Has Bill gotten back?"

"No, he's still traveling." My smile got even brighter. "But, um, they sent another vampire to sort of guard me? And I need to stow him in here while I work, if that's okay with you."

"Why do you need to be guarded? And why can't he just sit out in the bar? We have plenty of TrueBlood." True-Blood was definitely proving to be the front-runner among competing blood replacements. "Next best to the drink of life," its first ad had read, and vampires had responded to the ad campaign.

I heard the tiniest of sounds behind me, and I sighed. Bubba had gotten impatient.

"Now, I asked you—" I began, starting to turn, but never got further. A hand grasped my shoulder and whirled me around. I was facing a man I'd never seen before. He was cocking his fist to punch me in the head.

Though the vampire blood I had ingested a few months ago (to save my life, let me point out) had mostly worn off—I barely glowed in the dark at all now—I was still quicker than most people. I dropped and rolled into the man's legs, which made him stagger, which made it easier for Bubba to grab him and crush his throat.

I scrambled to my feet and Sam rushed out of his office. We stared at each other, Bubba, and the dead man.

Well, now we were really in a pickle.

"I've kilt him," Bubba said proudly. "I saved you, Miss Sookie."

Having the Man from Memphis appear in your bar, realizing he's become a vampire, and watching him kill a would-be assailant—well, that was a lot to absorb in a couple of minutes, even for Sam, though he himself was more than he appeared.

"Well, so you have," Sam said to Bubba in a soothing voice. "Do you know who he was?"

I had never seen a dead man—outside of visitation at the local funeral home—until I'd started dating Bill (who of course was technically dead, but I mean human dead people).

It seems I run across them now quite often. Lucky I'm not too squeamish.

This particular dead man had been in his forties, and every year of that had been hard. He had tattoos all over his arms, mostly of the poor quality you get in jail, and he was missing some crucial teeth. He was dressed in what I thought of as biker clothes: greasy blue jeans and a leather vest, with an obscene T-shirt underneath.

"What's on the back of the vest?" Sam asked, as if that would have significance for him.

Bubba obligingly squatted and rolled the man to his side. The way the man's hand flopped at the end of his arm made me feel pretty queasy. But I forced myself to look at the vest. The back was decorated with a wolf's head insignia. The wolf was in profile, and seemed to be howling. The head was silhouetted against a white circle, which I decided was supposed to be the moon. Sam looked even more worried when he saw the insignia. "Werewolf," he said tersely. That explained a lot.

The weather was too chilly for a man wearing only a vest, if he wasn't a vampire. Weres ran a little hotter than regular people, but mostly they were careful to wear coats in cold weather, since Were society was still secret from the human race (except for lucky, lucky me, and probably a few hundred others). I wondered if the dead man had left a coat out in the bar hanging on the hooks by the main entrance; in which case, he'd been back here hiding in the men's room, waiting for me to appear. Or maybe he'd come through the back door right after me. Maybe his coat was in his vehicle.

"You see him come in?" I asked Bubba. I was maybe just a little light-headed.

"Yes, ma'am. He must have been waiting in the big parking lot for you. He drove around the corner, got out of his car, and went in the back just a minute after you did. You hightailed it through the door, and then he went in. And I followed him. You mighty lucky you had me with you."

"Thank you, Bubba. You're right; I'm lucky to have you. I wonder what he planned to do with me." I felt cold all over as I thought about it. Had he just been looking for a lone woman to grab, or did he plan on grabbing me specifically? Then I realized that was dumb thinking. If Eric had been alarmed enough to send a bodyguard, he must have known there was a threat, which pretty much ruled out me being targeted at random. Without comment, Bubba strode out the back door. He returned in just a minute.

"He's got him some duct tape and gags on the front seat of his car," Bubba said. "That's where his coat is. I brought it to put under his head." He bent to arrange the heavily padded camouflage jacket around the dead man's face and neck. Wrapping the head was a real good idea, since the man was leaking a little bit. When he had finished his task, Bubba licked his fingers.

Sam put an arm around me because I had started shaking.